GW00864983

# Catiline

# Catiline

*A Novel*

*Brandon D. Winningham*

iUniverse, Inc.
New York  Lincoln  Shanghai

# Catiline

iUniverse books may be ordered through booksellers or by contacting:

iUniverse
2021 Pine Lake Road, Suite 100
Lincoln, NE 68512
www.iuniverse.com
1-800-Authors (1-800-288-4677)

Certain characters in this work are historical figures, and certain events portrayed did take place. However, this is a work of fiction. All of the other characters, names, and events as well as all places, incidents, organizations, and dialogue in this novel are either the products of the author's imagination or are used fictitiously.

ISBN-13: 978-0-595-42416-0 (pbk)
ISBN-13: 978-0-595-67996-6 (cloth)
ISBN-13: 978-0-595-86752-3 (ebk)
ISBN-10: 0-595-42416-3 (pbk)
ISBN-10: 0-595-67996-X (cloth)
ISBN-10: 0-595-86752-9 (ebk)

Printed in the United States of America

For Krystina and Madalyn
"Ego amo te"

# *Acknowledgments*

Phillip Francis—For your valuable advice from years of publishing experience; you helped to make my dream come true. I will never forget your kindness and friendship.

Krystina, my wife—We just had our first baby when I began this project, yet you patiently allowed me to work on my dream and encouraged me with your love and understanding; this is for you, my love; thanks for making me a success.

Rhonda (Hitchcock) Riffel, my high school English teacher—To you I owe my love for the classics. You first introduced me to them in your classroom. I still love Shakespeare and *Sir Gawain and the Green Knight* thanks to you; you are one of my heroes and always will be.

Dad, Mom, and Brother—Thanks for the great family life that you helped me to carry into my own home; because of you I am a successful father, husband, and provider. I love you all.

Those who contributed to my dream:
Rhonda Riffel; Duane, Barb, Jeremy, and April Winningham; Ledena Suvant; Louise Calcut; Gary Starchman; Shyrle Hall; Shane and Terris Rhoads; Wes and Michelle Bridges; Jim and Pam Dunn; Terry and Sarah Tarr; Ron and Paula Richardson; Rev. Telford and Jonnie Tharp; and Chris Prosser.

# Introduction

Lucius Sergius Catiline was born in the year 108 BC to the patrician clan known as the Sergii. Virtually nothing is known of his early life and boyhood. The clan from which Lucius Catiline descended had over time become poor, and, while still noble, in Rome money was everything. Catiline was just the man to revive them. What is known is that he served in the Social War along with Gnaeus Pompey and Marcus Tullius Cicero with Pompey's father, Gnaeus Pompeius Strabo, in command. From here he became a supporter of Sulla, particularly during the times of the proscriptions, and he sought to enter the political realm by then joining the Populare party, the party of revolutionaries and contrary to the policies of Sulla.

The Populare party was often the party that those who lacked discretion or needed money tended to join. Step-by-step, the Populare party sought to destroy the reforms that Sulla had instituted as dictator, and once he died the onslaught to see how much could be done away with began. Slowly the Populare party began to rise—more powerful and more influential than ever before—and now it had a new face in Lucius Catiline, as well as Gaius Julius Caesar, the future dictator himself.

Students and teachers alike have made it their life's work to discover the person of Lucius Catiline, but to no avail. Opinions about his life abound, but history has chosen to keep the true nature of Catiline a secret only known by himself. Often classified as a monster, Catiline has become the poster child of deceit and treachery in classical literature, and, after reading Cicero's speeches denouncing him, one would wonder how he ever managed to show his face in public. Surrounding himself with bodyguards and making company with the lowest of citizens, Catiline made it his goal to champion the down and out, who the privileged class determined was not worth their time.

Hopefully new research and a missing manuscript will uncover the true nature of Catiline and give us incite to his mind as Cicero's letters to his friend Atticus do for him. Until that day arrives, the debate as to whether Catiline was a man or a monster will continue to rage. Whatever the case may be, one man in the year 63 BC nearly brought one the world's greatest powers to its knees through conspiracy and random acts of treason; this man was Lucius Sergius Catiline.

# 1

## *Sulla Returns*

### 82 BC

A cool breeze blows across the Adriatic Sea as Roman warships glide with careful ease, carrying their precious cargo of victorious soldiers and their great general, Lucius Cornelius Sulla Felix, back to the fatherland, the great land of Italy. One centurion in a gruff voice shouts an order to adjust the sails to some, and another centurion shouts for the crew to come to order as the general makes his way from his quarters to admire the view of the home he has been so far away from. As Italy grows nearer, each man slowly forgets the years of war and only one thing becomes important: a small portion of land with their homes and families in the land of their birth. Sulla has promised each of them who make it back to Roman lands a new government—and long proscriptions to help fill the pockets that have long been emptied by the privileged few.

However, a fearful sense of awe takes hold of the men as they see their general, the great warrior of Rome, step out of his quarters and into the crisp sea air, clad in the regalia of a high-ranking Roman. At the age of fifty-five, the battle-hardened general shows the telltale signs of years of fatigue and bloodshed. Hate has taken its toll in the lines of his face, and all who have dared to look directly at him could see the glare of anger and a thirst for vengeance in his eyes. Rough and pockmarked, his face is unsympathetic. One hand rests firmly on his gladius while the other blocks the unforgiving rays of a hot sun as he makes his way across the deck to his group officers as they quickly snap to attention.

"Do you know how long exactly, Commander, it has been since I have seen my wife?" Sulla comments dryly to his attending officer.

"No, General," the centurion replies cautiously, "I do not."

Noticing his officers' carefulness to answer, Sulla lets out a laugh that startles all around him. They are aware of the mad fits that the general is prone to, often leading to the deaths of those who are not mindful of his demeanor. "Well, that's good then, isn't it?" Sulla replies. "Because I don't either!" He turns to lean on the rails of the ship, looking out at the shores of Italy, Brundisium to be exact. Lowering his head and clasping his hands, he begins to go over in his mind what his plans will be once he lands.

Hastily drawing his war with King Mithradates to an uneasy peace, Sulla had given orders to load all men on the ships and head directly for Italy, as his worst nightmare had come true. The year is 82 BC,. and civil war between his political party—the Optimates, and Gaius Marius's party—the Populares, has been raging with more bloodshed than any decent human being should be able to tolerate. After Sulla had gained control of Rome and pushed the Senate to exile Marius, another vote had been taken to pursue war with King Mithradates of Pontus. Sulla was to lead the charge.

Before leaving, however, he had held Gaius Marius and Gaius Julius Caesar's father-in-law, Lucius Cinna, to an oath that no action would be taken against him or his party in his absence. But upon Sulla's exit, this charge had quickly been broken, and Gaius Marius had made his way back to Rome. Looking up at the city gates, Marius had shouted, "I shall not enter this city and cross the pomerium until another vote is taken and my exile is not only revoked but I am welcomed back!" Senator after senator quickly made their way back to the curia to take a vote so as not to be among those who Marius would surely target when he re-entered the city.

However, the anger and hatred burned so deeply inside the breast of Marius that he had broken his own word and paraded himself triumphantly through the streets of Rome, passing the throngs of people who came to greet him, either in fear or genuine respect. Turning neither to the right nor the left, Marius had held his head high and had refused to acknowledge even friends as he passed. Those who thought they had been fortunate to catch his attention were soon proven wrong as he gave the command for his officers to kill the offending citizens.

The rest of the night, the story had been much the same, as proscription lists were posted and people were given the opportunity to beg for their lives before Marius, even while he ate. Those who were allowed in the presence of Marius found that compassion and feeling were gone from the bitter, old man, as he once again refused to acknowledge those who cried and begged before him, but merely stopped chewing long enough to utter the dreaded phrase "Kill him," while the offender was mercilessly cut down before him. For the next few months, Rome had been filled with the sound of mothers, fathers, sons, daughters, brothers, and sisters crying as loved ones and friends had been butchered like animals to satisfy the lust of a madman.

All of this is weighing on the mind of Sulla as he watches the ocean beat upon the sides of the ship, and it occasionally splashes his face, bringing him back to the reality that Marius is dead and the new threat of his son, known as Gaius Marius the Younger, who is leading an army as well as his father's Populare party. Pulling a letter from his pocket, Sulla silently reads the details of his loved ones being dragged into the streets, beaten, and left to die—all because they were acquainted with him. He slowly crumples the letter in his hand and drops the letter into the sea, hanging his head once again.

The commanders on deck give the call that the ship is approaching Brundisium, but it seems that the great commander has thoughts only of revenge and plans for battle. Soldiers dash around him as if he is invisible as he stares into the sea depths and ponders his next move. "Sulla!" a high-pitched male voice calls out from the general's quarters. "Sulla, I have prepared your lunch. Won't you join me? Allow me to take your mind off these dreadful thoughts you are having."

New recruits turn to see who the unusual voice belongs to, while veterans are aware that the general has always kept strange company and merely ignore it. Clad in a flowing scarlet robe, Metrobius, a feminine-looking figure wearing makeup and rings on his fingers, lightly makes his way to the general's side and intertwines their arms. A Greek stage actor of Roman birth, Metrobius has not only made a name for himself in the acting world but also in the ranks of the Roman army as the companion of the fearless Sulla. Everywhere Sulla travels, Metrobius is faithfully by his side. Under normal circumstances, that such a man should be wrapped up in a homosexual affair would be a cause for derision, but Roman custom has always dictated that the problem is found with the passive partner in the relationship and not the stronger, which is the general.

As Sulla stands looking over the sea, Metrobius gently massages his shoulders and tugs slightly on his arm, coaxing him to return to his cabin. Within a few moments, a knock is heard at the door, followed by a call from the general to enter. Quickly entering and standing at attention, an officer enters holding a stack of reports and finds Sulla and his companion reclining on a bed across the room and eating.

"General, a ship has just returned from a reconnaissance mission and found that Gaius Marius the Younger has his army stationed about three hundred miles from Brundisium with foraging parties all around the area." Walking forward, the officer hands Sulla the reports and awaits an answer as the general rises.

Sully dryly asks, "It seems that this Marius has about as much craftiness as the dead one, did don't you think, Metrobius?"

"Personally, I think they are both terrible bores, and I can't wait until you stop talking about them." Metrobius smiles and brings a cup to his lips.

"Yes, I figured as much." Turning to the officer, the general replies, "Tell Pompey and Crassus to arm their men for battle. We *will* be ready to engage the enemy from the moment that we disembark from the ship, no matter how far we have to march to engage them. Understood?"

"Yes, General Sulla," the officer replies, taking the reports and leaving the room.

"This Marius has become as much a pain as his stupid father," Sulla mumbles. Slowly turning, he ruthlessly utters, "It will be all too comforting to look him in the eyes as I hold his severed head in my hands," much to Metrobius's disgust.

Meanwhile, outside of the general's quarters, the young officer dictates the general's orders to a scribe who pens them on two separate letters, seals them, and hands them back to the officer, who then turns to board a small ship to take him to Pompey and Crassus, generals under Sulla who are awaiting orders for the other ships in the fleet.

"Marcus Petreius!" a soldier cries out after the young man stepping over the side of the ship, "Tell that shrewd scoundrel Crassus that I am still waiting for the five thousand sesterces he owes me!" much to the amusement of the other soldiers, who know Crassus to be crafty on matters of money and personal finance.

"I'll tell him," the young Marcus replies, "but I doubt it will do any good. This King Midas tends to keep his golden touch to himself!" He laughs and gives the signal to release the line for his ship.

Slowly he makes his way past the other ships in the fleet, looking for the standards of Pompey's and Crassus's ships. Sighting Pompey's first, he rows toward the ship, waving the standard of Sulla as the men aboard drop ropes to hoist him aboard.

"I have orders for Generals Pompey and Crassus from General Sulla, if you please. Where is General Pompey?" he quickly utters, out of breath from rowing and climbing onto this one.

"Well, fortune has blessed you with one less trip to make," the centurion on board states, smiling at the nervous Marcus, "both Pompey and Crassus are in Pompey's quarters. I'll take you to them." He offers his hand, noticeably scarred from years of battle, to Marcus, who is still climbing aboard. Reaching down, the sleeve of his tunic shifts, revealing a tattoo that captures the eye of the young Marcus.

"Where did you get that?" he asks, staring at the soldier's muscular arm.

Seeing a chance to show his pride, the centurion reveals the eagle of Rome above the acronym SPQR. "The Senate and the people of Rome—that's who pays my wages, along with some hearty contributions by General Sulla when we capture a city, of course." The centurion turns to lead Marcus to the general's quarters. "I got this tattoo while serving in the Social War under Pompey's father and a fine young man named Marcus Tullius Cicero, who we always called Tully. He seemed to enjoy it, so we just kept it up. When you get back to Rome, you should look him up and tell him Andronicus said hello. He should remember me. He has a mind like a steel trap, just don't talk to him about it or you'll never get him to stop! He tends to be his favorite subject, if you get my drift."

"Yes," Marcus replies with a smile, "I've met a few men like that already." Andronicus knocks on the door to the general's quarters.

"Who is it?" a voice inquires as the two men enter.

"Generals, this young man, Marcus Petreius by name, comes from Sulla's ship with orders in hand," Andronicus replies as he stands at attention.

"Well, what does the old man want?" Pompey replies, tilting his cup with a slight grimace.

"What do you mean by that?" Crassus dryly replies. "He's not much older than me!"

"I meant exactly what I said." Pompey laughs at Crassus's easily wounded spirit.

With more than ten years and different political backgrounds between the two, it is readily agreed that fate brought the two warriors together under Sulla. Originally a member of Lucius Cinna's army, Gnaeus Pompey had retreated to his estate in Picenum shortly before Cinna's death two years prior. Marcus Licinius Crassus, on the other hand, had fled from Marius and Cinna to Spain upon the former's orders to kill his father. Pompey, now twenty-four with a muscular build and firm facial features, is a stark contrast to Crassus, now in his mid-thirties with a thin frame, who is known more for his shrewdness and cruelty than his strength. Seeing that the future of Rome was in the hands of Sulla, the two had agreed to join the general when he had invaded Italy and sent Marius into exile.

"What do you have, Soldier?" Pompey continues.

"General Sulla wants you to have your men battle-ready from the moment that the ships land at Brundisium," Marcus nervously states as he paraphrases the letter he is reading. "The general sent a reconnaissance and found that Gaius Marius has his army stationed about three hundred miles from Brundisium at a place called Signia."

"Well, isn't that interesting?" Crassus replies. "I've been made an equal to the great Pompey." He reclines once more, allowing a slave to refill his cup.

"Perhaps if you weren't so cruel and tightfisted you would have a long time ago, Crassus," Pompey says while a smile makes its way across his face.

"Does Sulla really think that Marius would be stupid enough to attack us as soon as we leave our ships?" Crassus ignores Pompey's rebuke by quickly getting back to the business at hand.

"It sounds like an attempt to discourage the men, general. If he can make it look like he is ready before we are, Marius could gain a great advantage over us," Andronicus offers, still standing at attention in the doorway.

"I agree, Andronicus, and very seldom have you been wrong. My father always made mention of that," Pompey replies as he stands and offers a cup to Andronicus and Marcus.

"Once you have eaten, take word to General Sulla that we will have our men ready. We will end this business with the Marii family once and for all," Pompey confidently says, motioning for a slave to make a plate for the two men. "Well then, let us drink to the health—and not to mention wealth—of the Roman Republic, and of course to all of the gods. Let's not forget them." Crassus lifts his cup to a statuette of Jupiter Optimus Maximus.

"Yes," Andronicus replies, "by the time this next battle is over, the Roman Republic will never be the same." Silence overcomes them when a deeper meaning sinks in.

"To the republic, long may it thrive!" Marcus shouts, lifting his cup, and the battle-hardened men all smile.

On shore, however, it is quite a different story. Gaius Marius assembles his generals and lays plans to wipe out Sulla and remove that plague from Rome and its people. Signia, now home to the armies of Marius, is situated high in the Volscian mountains, overlooking the valley of the river Sacco. Founded by the last Roman king, Lucius Tarquinius Superbus, in 510 BC, the city is seen as a major strategic military post that allows the Romans to keep an eye on the cities of Latinum and guard the road to southern Italy. Known for its high walls, which the Romans have strengthened and added a double city gate, and splendid views, Signia's only rival for military position is the nearby city of Praeneste.

It is from this position that Marius looks over the road to southern Italy that Sulla is sure to march along and plans his next move: to wait on his adversary to move in closer and then surround and crush his army. Marius feels it is the need for revenge that will be the final blow to Sulla, as he will be too blinded by his own hate to make an intelligent military decision and see the trap that has been laid for his men. With officers and aides rushing to and fro, continuous updates come into the camp on Sulla's position, the latest being that his fleet has been spotted not far off of the coast of Brundisium. With a battle soon to come, Marius sends soldiers to dig trenches around the city and to prepare for a quick and merciless assault. If Marius has his way, his enemy will be wiped out without his even having to lift a finger.

The product of years of hearing the tales of his father's victories at war, young Marius is hungry for victories of his own. Over and over, he has heard the story of how his father earned the respect of Scipio Africanus, one of Rome's greatest generals, during the war with Jugurtha. He heard about how his father, a young politician with little experience, successfully challenged Consul Lucius Aurelius Cotta before the Senate and left in victory. Now in his twenties, Marius's mind is overwhelmed with the great things that his father accomplished. However, now it is time for a new Marius to make a name for himself in Rome; there will no longer be tales of his dead father but of his victorious son. A last act before his death, Gaius Marius had instituted the *capite censi,* which placed soldiers directly under the care of the general in command, his son, following his every order—even if that meant marching on Rome itself.

The *capite censi* was a weapon forged out of a lust for power that Marius Sr. had never been able to use. A weapon that cut so deeply only a cruel madman such as Marius could contrive it. His father had not used it, but that did not mean he would not. Soon Sulla would come marching into the trap set for him, and his army would be mercilessly slaughtered; then the victorious army of Gaius Marius the Younger would turn to Rome and march through the gates, instituting order and revenge—whichever came first. As an added bonus, he carries his father's gladius. When the time is right, he will pull it out of Sulla's back, remove his head, and carry it triumphantly through the streets of Rome, sanctifying them with the blood of his enemy. However, the young Marius does not realize that while Sulla is blinded by hate he is blinded by ambition and thirst for power—the two things that brought the downfall of his father.

Sulla is a seasoned enough soldier to know the trickery of the Marii and that to deal with one is to deal with the other. As ships anchor on the beach of Brundisium, Sulla's mind is already past the upcoming battle with Marius and concentrates on his actions once he returns to Rome. The bait has been laid for Sulla, but Sulla has seen the plans. Along with Pompey and Crassus, they begin to lay plans of their own to rid Italy of the family of Marius. The Populares have ruled, corrupted, and raped Rome long enough; it is time for someone to set the city back on the right path, and Sulla is just the man to do it.

"Marius is at Signia," Sulla proclaims confidently to those gathered nearby. "It is the only logical place he could set up his base camp besides Praeneste, and, with his need to be seen, he would naturally take the city with the higher elevation." All the men present are taking notes, waiting for further orders, when Crassus stands to speak.

"If Marius is at Signia, how do you propose, General Sulla, we get him out to fight? As you have stated, Signia is high above the valley. The one who controls the city has virtually no need to leave its walls. Or am I not correct?" Crassus speaks in his usual challenging tone.

"You are totally correct, my dear Crassus, but only on one count. You seem to have forgotten that the Marii are bent on victory; therefore we will wait him out at the far end of the valley. He wants us to come to him and be crushed, but he will come to me and I will send him screaming in retreat like a frightened child," he utters, clutching the hilt of his sword. Suddenly he pulls a small dagger from his armor, bloody and scratched from years of use, and hands it to Pompey. "This dagger was a gift to me from the soldier who slit the throat of Lucius Cinna and left his blood on the blade. Pompey, I give it to you with the provision that it be returned to me by the man who does the same favor to Gaius Marius."

Reluctantly, Pompey takes the blade. "I will make that announcement to my men," he replies, seeing the hate in Sulla's eyes. "I'm sure that one of them will bravely take up this challenge."

"Good. I have had my own victories, and nothing would make me happier than rewarding a common soldier for helping me enjoy another." With Metrobius now at his side, he takes a swig of the drink he is offered before uttering his final orders. "We will make our way across the fatherland toward Signia. We will march until we arrive, and when we do we will proceed to destroy Marius and his men until we offer up his worthless body to Pythian Apollo."

With each knowing what is expected of him, the gathering disperses. The armies are gathered to their cohorts and legions, and they begin the arduous march to Signia and the bloodshed that awaits them there. The Italian sun shines on the troops as they march in the garb of a victorious army. With banners waving and Roman eagles over head, young and old march with pride and respect for the great general they are sure will lead them to victory once again.

As mile after mile of the three hundred-mile journey passes, Sulla's suspicions are confirmed as foraging parties are seen at a distance turning in the direction of Signia.

"Look!" Sulla confidently shouts to his officers. "Just as I suspected. Marius has sent his spies to alert him of our every move. So long as we continue, we are on the right path."

"Yes, but what if he is not at Signia but is nearby with an ambush? Rome was disgraced once before in this manner, and we could not afford for that to happen again," an aide quickly replies.

In a sharp movement, more quickly than the aide can react, Sulla pulls his gladius and strikes him to the ground, severing the artery in his neck as he turns away. Falling to the ground, he is followed by the general, who leaps from his horse with the vitality of a man thirty years younger, sword drawn.

"General I ... I didn't mean anything by that," the aide mumbles, grasping his neck as blood flows through his fingers like water through a busted dam.

"You have spoken a word of ill omen to Sulla the Fortunate and Pythian Apollo, the patron of the Cornelii. For that you will die," Sulla calmly utters, wearing the man's blood on his face. "Hold him," Sulla orders to the men at his side. Reaching down, he cuts the hamstrings of the offending man as he screams in pain. Pointing to one of the men holding him, he callously orders, "You are to stay near him and see that no one helps him. He is to lie here and bleed to death as he has endeavored to bleed us of our victory." Amid the cries of the wounded man, Sulla mounts his horse and states, "Thus be it to those who challenge Lucius Sulla. If he lives, then you will die in his place." Then, spurring his horse, he leaves the man writhing in pain and bathed in his own blood and leads the army forward once again.

Soldiers pass by the man as the story of what occurred makes its way through the ranks, becoming embellished as it is retold. With the lone foot soldier standing at his side, the mortally wounded aide claws the ground, trying to capture the pity of a soldier willing to disobey Sulla's order and save him; however, no man in the ranks is that foolish. Time after time, he reaches out, occasionally gripping a man's leg, which is quickly pulled back, followed by a sneer or being spit on. Giving up, he rolls onto his back and stares into the sky as the life passes from his body, and his labored breathing is replaced by a blank stare as he passes into eternity.

At the head of the enormous line, General Sulla has put the events of the last few minutes behind him and begins a conversation with his subordinate generals and aides. "I want you at my side, Pompey, when I return to Rome," he casually remarks, leaning heavily on an unseen victory. "I have great plans for the people, the Senate, and the republic. I want you there. Goodness knows you need the experience, as a young man like you will surely be in politics one day." Unsure of what to say, Pompey remains quiet for a moment until the general glances in his direction, drawing an uneasy but thankful reply to his generosity.

"I am a soldier, General, as my father was, and nothing more. I'm actually not so sure I am cut out for politics," Pompey utters as Crassus smirks.

"Two things, Pompey," Sulla replies with a slight sigh, "number one, your father was a soldier and it got him killed. Number two, if a rich fool like Crassus can make it in politics, then surely you can. You have a personality that the people will love."

"I may be a rich fool, but I am a powerful rich fool," Crassus replies sharply, drawing a smile from Sulla and a look of disbelief from Pompey.

"You've been around me too long, Crassus." Sulla laughed loudly. "You've discovered that you can get away with much more than anyone else."

"Exactly what do you have in mind when you get to Rome, General?" Pompey asks, moving his horse closer to Sulla. This draws a smile from Sulla, as he knows his bait has worked on his young prodigy.

"We all know that Rome is full of corruption," he states, speaking as though he is reading a scripted response to crowd of curious people. "I have a series of reforms in mind that will drastically change the way things are done in the Roman government that will make it more efficient for the people and do away with the useless bureaucracy that bogs the system down. On my return to Rome, my army will march to the Senate, and I will assume the title of dictator and introduce a constitution that will outline my plans, one being the removal of the plebeian tribunes, useless as they are," Sulla replies confidently, drawing Pompey's interest all the more.

"What about the consuls?"

"What about them?" Sulla looks sharply at him. "The current consuls will stay in place, and, when the time comes, I will assume one position and nominate another as my partner."

"Tell that to Lucretius Ofella, General Sulla. He seems to be under the impression that once he returns to Rome he will run for the consulship," Crassus remarks, injecting himself into the conversation once again.

"Lucretius is a fool," Sulla responds bluntly. "His only qualification is that he has reached the age limit. He is inept when it comes to politics, and if need be I already have something in store for him, should he carry out his plan. Pompey, we have not returned yet, but you have a lot of things to consider. I suggest you do so wisely. I am going back to do something that no Roman has ever done before, and, while I do it, I will make a path for you to follow me. I do hope that you will." Sulla turns the conversation back to its original course.

As the mighty army continues to make its way across the Italian plain, night begins to fall, and, with it, a distant thunder rolls through the sky. No one knows what is waiting for them at Signia, only a few miles away, but each soldier is sure that it is where destiny resides, along with shame and or victory. Sulla knows that Marius waits for him, and, like two mortal enemies, each of them plan and plot how to destroy the other and win the glory for themselves. The moon begins to rise as the armies of Sulla make their way to Marius's stronghold, and only the gods know what awaits them after that.

# 2

## *Italy in the Hands of the Fortunate*

### 82 BC

A cool mist slowly begins to cover the Italian plain as Marius strides along, slowly cutting through the wet blanket of grass, leaving the marks of his footprints. Pausing for a moment, he looks over the field and sees the night sky lit by the fires of Sulla's camp. As he looks back toward the city of Signia, he can see his army stationed on the walls, ready to repel the invading force. Thunder peals, and clouds roll slowly in and hide the light of the moon from the earth below. The thunder calms Marius's troubled mind, as it reflects his tortured feelings. At the same time, the thunder brings to his men back in the city the threat of an approaching storm. His soldiers are faithful to their leader, but, like all god-fearing Romans, they can't help but think that the thunder is Jupiter's sign of disapproval at what is about to take place.

The calm night has drawn young Marius out of his safe haven to survey his prey, like a vulture casually watching the deer die slowly before consuming it. A quick chill runs over the young man, as if an eerie presence has wrapped itself around him.

"Marius," a weak, old voice whispers in the dark, frightening him, as he thought he was alone. Quickly drawing his sword and turning to meet the offending person, he sees to his surprise the figure bearing the pallor of death. Standing amazed and yet confused, the young general is unsure what to do for the first time in his military career.

"The gods have sent you to confirm my victory, Father?" he confidently asks after regaining his composure, deciding to treat the apparition as a figure of good omen as opposed to ill.

"My son, tomorrow you will die. The gods have decreed it," the pale figure utters, as if drawing his last breath. "I have warned you, have I not, that the very thing that brought my downfall would plague you as well? You have circumvented the will of the gods, and Jupiter Greatest and Best has deemed you worthy to die on this field." A look of disgust comes over the face of the young Marius as he throws his dagger at the apparition, drawing a hateful scowl from his father. "The gods have willed it, my son," the dead man mumbles, as his pallor is now gone and he is visibly younger in appearance.

"Then I defy the gods this day. The Marii make their own destiny, and my destiny is to kill Sulla—even if I must rob Jupiter of his thunderbolt to do it!"

The look of anger on the specter's face turns to a soft fatherly smile as he slowly walks toward his wary son with open arms. "Give me time then, my son, and allow me to return to the court of the gods and appeal your cause. One day is all I ask of you. Sulla has waited all this time for a final battle. Surely you can give your father one more day," the soft-spoken shade utters, embracing his son with transparent arms.

Slowly Marius the Younger puts his arms around the shade, trying to ignore the lack of substance. He sorrowfully says, "For you, my father, I will do anything, even in death."

With a sullen look, the spirit comforts his son, quickly contorts his face into an evil smile, and makes one last request as he continues to embrace his son. "May I then ask one last favor from my brave son?"

"Anything, my father," the son, with his guard down, answers as though it is truly the bodily form of his revered father embracing him.

"Good. I have loved you, my son, and always will. All that I ask is that you die well," the spirit whispers with a devilish look as his son sinks to his knees, grasping his chest. He pulls his hands away from his chest and notices them covered in blood. A small white dagger bearing the inscription: "Property of L. Cinna" on the hilt sticks out of his chest. In a desperate attempt to save his own life, he pulls out the knife as he gazes at the ghost in horror; the face of his departed father is no more than a sunken and decomposed face laughing at him. Falling to the ground, the young warrior coughs up his own blood, as the wet mist becomes his death shroud. He sees the image of Sulla standing only a few feet away.

"Lucius Sulla the Fortunate!" the decomposing spirit cries out with an unworldly shriek. "You have won, Sulla! Pythian Apollo has secured your victory. The Marii are vanquished!" At that moment, a flash of lightning streaks across the sky, illuminating the face of Sulla, as the crash of thunder wakes Sulla from a deep sleep.

A cold sweat breaks out across the general's face as he realizes it was merely a dream. The gods have declared his victory even while he has slept. Rising from his bed, he looks to the corner of his tent to see the eagle standards of Rome seemingly bowed before him. With a smile, the general once again lies down, careful not to awaken the sleeping Metrobius by his side.

As morning dawns, a distant thunder is heard over the plains of Italy, as dark clouds cover the sun and bring comfort to the eyes of Sulla. A storm foretold his victory in a dream the previous night, and now, as he opens the door to his tent, he also sees the storm that will bring the death of the young Marius.

"Good morning, General Sulla," a lighthearted Pompey utters, noting the smile on Sulla's face—a sight that is most uncommon.

"And a good morning to you, Pompey. It's a fine day for Marius to die, isn't it?"

"Well, yes, I suppose it is," Pompey cautiously answers, unsure of the general's intentions.

"Walk with me, Pompey, and allow me to share my thoughts with you." Sulla places his hand on Pompey's shoulder, catching the surprised young general off guard. Slowly they make their way from the assembled army, and, as they reach the top of a hill overlooking their route, Sulla begins to share his thoughts with Pompey. "Last night I had a dream," Sulla states, looking over the plain in every direction. "Do you still have that dagger I gave you?"

Pompey pulls the small bloodstained knife out of his breastplate and hands it to Sulla. "Property of L. Cinna" he calmly reads taking a glance at the handle allowing his now blurred vision to come into focus. "I had a strange yet comforting dream last night—that in this plain Gaius Marius, in a dead, decrepit form, stabbed his son to death with this knife and pronounced me the victor," the general calmly states, once again looking over the plain toward Signia.

"General, the soldiers talk of victory as if it has already taken place. It must be a message from the gods that you will rule in Rome, and they have used your enemy to proclaim it," Pompey confidently utters, placing his hand upon Sulla's shoulder.

"That is very kind of you to say, Pompey. I have valued your opinion ever since you came to my cause. When I am gone, I want you to take my place in Rome and see to it that another Marius does not arise." The battle-worn general hands the dagger back to Pompey as an orderly of Pompey's hesitantly walks up.

"Pardon me for intruding, General Sulla and General Pompey, but Crassus wishes me to inform General Pompey that the legions are ready to march at your leisure" a strapping young soldier remarks as he carefully approaches the generals from behind. His dark black hair shines in the Italian sun as his handsome features strike a note in the old general Sulla. With a pleasant smile the young man courteously bows to his superiors though not taking his eyes off of them.

"Thank you, Lucius. Let Crassus know that I will be right there as soon as the general and I finish." Pompey waves his hand in a thankful gesture.

Sulla frowns. "Who is that young man, Pompey? I don't recall ever seeing him before."

"His name is Lucius Catiline of the Sergii clan. He fought with Andronicus and me in the Social War under my father. He is a very interesting character, to say the least."

"Yes, he appears to have desire in his eyes," Sulla guardedly states, looking again over the plain and then turning to go. "Watch him. That fire in his eyes is dangerous, and if it goes unchecked that fire will burn out of control."

As they make their way down the hill, Pompey catches site of the assembled Roman forces and pauses for a moment, much to Sulla's surprise. "You seem as if you have never seen an assembled army before, Pompey," Sulla declares with a faint smile on his face.

"The majesty of Rome, General Sulla, lies in the plain below us. There is nothing more beautiful than a victorious army on its way to another victory." Pompey once again moves toward his men down the hill. As they approach, the troops snap to attention, drawing their arms up and lifting standards high in the air, confirming to Sulla that this army—with the help of the gods—will bring him the victory he so richly desires.

Column after column, the legions under the command of Sulla, Crassus, and Pompey begin their grand parade into the countryside of Italy, crossing rivers and plains and drawing crowds of villagers on their procession. Young and old are drawn by the spectacle that very few Romans ever see. Through the Italian countryside, three of Rome's most powerful men march in all of their glory as a testament to the might and power of the ideals they represent. As each make their way with their respective legions, thoughts of power and grandeur fill their minds, until it is as if they are marching in triumph up the Via Sacra instead of through the dusty plains.

The cloud of dust the soldiers produce ascends into the air as, with each footstep, the sky darkens with the approaching storm. As the group of battle-hungry troops near the plain surrounding Signia, reconnaissance missions return with the same report: Marius is within the walls of Signia, with a few troops outside waiting for Sulla to arrive. The reports whet the appetite of Sulla, as he knows his enemy is only a mile or so away. However, it is early in the evening, and the long day's march has now worn his men down and taken some of the battle lust from their minds. As a cool, misty rain begins to fall, the soldier's petition their generals for an evening rest, as they can see Signia from where they are.

Seemingly disgusted by the lack of determination, Sulla wheels his horse around and rides through the ranks, looking at the men one by one, piercing deep into their eyes with his hateful glance. Each man knows what is expected of him, but fatigue has begun to cloud their minds. "We will march to Signia!" Sulla shouts. "And you will give your all to the glory of Rome and your generals, unless you wish to die as a traitor!" Under normal circumstances, the noise produced by rattling armor and clanging shields would have drown out a normal man's voice, but to these men Sulla is not a normal man.

Throughout the ranks, men can be seen mustering what little strength they have for their general and once again take on the likeness of an army that could conquer the whole world. Sulla sits tall and proud in his saddle as he sees his men react in fear. At that moment, Pompey rides to his side, also admiring the trained and disciplined group that marches before them. "General, may I have a word?" Pompey courteously asks, drawing a glance and a mere nod from Sulla.

"General, the men are requesting a night of rest and to march on Signia first thing in the morning." Pompey again draws a nod, but now accompanied by a hateful sneer.

"I did not bow to the Marii Pompey. What makes you think that I will do it for these men?"

"Because you know that it is wise, General Sulla. I must also say that I believe it would be in their best interest to rest and allow the gods to replenish their strength. You and I and Crassus cannot win this battle on our own. We need them at full strength," Pompey states, drawing the general's complete attention.

"Do you remember your history? Hannibal missed his opportunity to conquer Rome because he waited," the general tells his young adviser. "We march on Signia, and we will take it." Sulla fixes his eyes on Signia as the sky fills with thunder and an occasional lightning flash.

"General, if you please, I am also reminded of the famed Consul Quintus Fabius Maximus, of who it is said by his patience saved an army. You are a great man of war, and you know in your heart that these men need to rest tonight. Allow Apollo, to whom you have prayed, to equip them in sleep." Pompey finishes his argument, much to the delight of Sulla, who, though hungry for battle, knows that his men need rest.

"You drive a hard bargain," Sulla states, motioning to a group of young aides. "Signal the men to halt and set up camp for the night. Pompey, circulate word that we will march on Signia at first light. Every man is to be ready."

Within the walls of Signia, however, the tone is much different, as spies recount the position of Sulla's army to Marius, who anxiously awaits the opportunity to strike his blow. For almost an hour, Marius watches the fires from Sulla's camp while priests within Signia tend to the fires of sacrifice at the nearby temples, continually returning with words of good omen for the young general.

The wait for action finally ends when a lone scout runs toward Marius, breathing hard and covered in dust and sweat after a visibly strenuous ride. After making his way past the guards, he continues to pant and gather his wits to give his report. "General Marius, Sulla has given the order to set up camp in the plain. I have ridden around the army and observed that he has positioned himself so dangerously that if we move quickly he can be cut off from the main roads and any reinforcements before the sun even sets."

Marius holds the map and turns his back to the scout to look at the plain as a slow rain begins to fall. "This map you have drawn, is it as accurate as you claim it to be, or is Sulla really this stupid as to allow us to trap him in the plain?"

"Sulla has positioned himself as I have indicated, General Marius."

Another aide steps up and draws Marius's glance. "General, the gods have given Sulla into your hands—even the sacrifices have said this. We must attack him while his men are weak from marching."

Another aide eagerly steps close to Marius and grabs his arm. "Your father was able to kill the elder Crassus but not his son, and now we have our chance, as he commands legions in Sulla's force! If we leave the city walls, Sulla will never expect it, and he will not be ready for a full attack."

"Yes, and yet you both forget a vitally important detail: if we leave the city, we give up the entire reason we came here, which is safety and position. As I recall, the plan was to make Sulla come to us, or am I mistaken?" Marius asks those surrounding him. Silence falls over the soldiers, each one hungry for battle and each one with a plan of their own on how to execute it. "We will settle this then as true Romans would. Call me a priest of Apollo and let us inquire what he would have us to do." Marius draws approving looks from some and disbelief from others.

Through the crowd walks a middle-aged man clad in the robes of a holy office, bearing the remnants of a fresh sacrifice on his hands and holding the entrails as further evidence.

"You are a priest of Apollo in this city, are you not?" Marius inquires as he takes a cup from a nearby servant girl.

"I am, General. How might I be of service to you?"

"These men who stand around you suggest that we leave the safety of Signia's walls and attack Sulla. I feel that we should wait for my enemy to come to me. I respect the will of the gods and wish to hear the advice of Pythian Apollo in this matter. I will do as he bids," the young general replies, placing his hand over his heart and bowing his head as he awaits his answer.

The priest moves his hands over the bloody animal intestines, looking intently at certain areas that capture his attention. He pulls a small white dagger from his robes and stabs it fiercely into the entrails. He raises his head as if in a trance. "The words of Apollo for Gaius Marius the Younger," he utters. "Death. This night, if you attack the army of Lucius Cornelius Sulla, I will bring death to the enemy of Rome and wipe out his name from the families of Rome forever," he states as he closes his eyes, drops the entrails, and then whispers, "Attack," in the ear of Marius the Younger.

Drawing his sword, Marius thrusts it through the priest's chest as he slowly sinks to the ground, uttering a groan. "Mount your horses, men. I have sealed the prophecy in blood, and this night we will rain vengeance upon the armies of Sulla, even as the coming storm brings thunder and lightning. It has been promised that Pythian Apollo will fight for us and wipe out the name of Cornelius forever!" Marius shouts, waving his blood-soaked sword in the air, urging his men to the action he once opposed. Now man after man straps on his armor and mount his horse, while the infantry arm themselves and prepare for the promised victory.

In the nearby camp of Sulla, men worn from the day's continuous journey begin to find quick shelter from the storm that is rolling in; some beneath large trees while others lie on the ground protected by their shields. Sighs of relief are heard in the camp as no signs of movement are seen from Signia, and the soldiers begin to remove pieces of the heavy armor strapped to their bodies. Higher-ranking men have begun to make their way to Sulla's tent in the center of the camp, where the general is meeting with Crassus and Pompey to plan the next day's attack.

With the wind increasing, each man entering the tent tries to hold maps in place as Sulla rehearses his plans to lay siege to Signia and force Marius from his hiding place. "Not only do we have Pythian Apollo on our side, but Jupiter the Thunderer will bring us victory tomorrow as well," Sulla confidently utters as a barrage of thunder shakes the ground. "Signia is set high on a precipice, and it will be virtually impossible to storm the city. Our best course of action is to stand close enough to launch an assault but to also stay clear of any they launch," Sulla states as he resumes his discourse.

Pompey interjects, "Sulla, might I suggest that we wrap our legions around the city walls to keep from any sallies either during the battle or during the night?" Pompey draws a snide glance from Crassus.

Sulla grasps the hilt of his gladius. "That is precisely my point, Pompey. We must use the terrain to our advantage, just as Marius has tried to use it against us. He has protected himself from our direct attack, but he cannot protect himself from our forcing him out," Sulla arrogantly states.

At that moment, the sound of chaos begins to fill camp, and several wayward spears make their way through the canvas, striking one of the officers in the leg. "Sulla!" a collapsing Andronicus covered in blood shouts as he runs into the tent. "Marius is storming the camp, and men are dying by the handfuls!" At that moment, a soldier from the small but effective invading force enters the tent and rams his sword through Andronicus and is in turn cut down by Pompey.

"This is no attack," Crassus dryly exclaims, as the officers stare in disbelief at the general's comment.

"You're right, Crassus," Sulla replies. "There's no way that an army large enough to fill Signia made it that quickly to the center of this camp. This is a raiding party sent to throw us into an unguarded panic, a virtual suicide mission for all who volunteered." Sulla opens the tent flaps. "Here comes the attack," the general calmly utters, as he tightens his helmet and sword belt, noticing the cloud of dust rising over the hill as Gaius Marius the Younger leads his men to storm the camp of Sulla.

"What on earth is that fool doing? Does he honestly think he is going to storm our defenses?" Crassus again comments in disbelief.

"Yes, I think he does, and I believe he is," Pompey exclaims, running from the tent and rallying various ones he passes. All across the camp, men are throwing on their arms and taking shield and sword in hand, proving to the oncoming forces that their tactic has failed against an army of well-seasoned troops. Within minutes, Marius himself storms the camp amid the shouts of battle as swords meet metal and flesh. Blood begins to cover the ground as the Marians are struck from their horses and the soldiers of Sulla are trampled beneath their hooves. The skies begin to open up as lightning streaks the sky and thunder shakes the battleground, unnerving soldiers and generals alike.

In a matter of moments, the whole camp is flooded by Marius and his men as he shouts his orders to kill all who oppose them and to push them on toward victory. Among their own legions, Pompey and Crassus push the enemy invaders and urge their men to do great acts of valor for Rome. Some begin to count how many they have killed, and others stake claims to the booty of each fallen soldier before another can. Romans are destroying Romans left and right, and the blood of the children of Romulus covers swords and faces, only to be washed away by the increasing rain.

At times it seems that one side has the upper hand, and then a moment later the tide has turned. Sulla withdraws a safe distance to survey the action, oblivious that Marius is nearby without his standard, watching and waiting for his time to strike the elder general down. Noticing a particularly heated area, the general mounts his horse with sword in hand, while closely followed by Marius, still on his own horse. Plunging into the thick of the battle, the general begins to cut down two and three men at a time; something that only the most skilled of soldiers could do.

Constantly wheeling around in every direction, Sulla unknowingly opens his rear to attack, which happens to be in plain sight of the young Marius. "Now we end the years of disgrace to my father's name," the young Marius mumbles, drawing his blood-soaked spear, which goes unnoticed by all except Lucius Catiline. Knocking a Marian from his horse, Catiline jumps on the horse and with his left hand grabs the reins of Sulla's horse, pulling him out of the way of Marius's spear, which merely nicks the rear of his horse.

"What are you doing, you idiot?" Sulla shouts as he sees Catiline release the reigns and ride after Marius, only then noticing the spear in the ground behind him and the wound on his horse.

Trampling those in his way, Catiline approaches the young general from his side, who is disgusted that his opportunity was robbed from him by an unknown. After dropping his head in disappointment, Marius rises, only to be met by Catiline, who shoves his dagger into Marius's jaw. "Sulla sends his regards!" he shouts, as Marius pulls the dagger from his bleeding mouth and spurs his horse, knocking Catiline to the ground. Marius rides over the hill with a handful of followers, holding his jaw and screaming in pain.

With their general gone, many of the soldiers of Marius quickly drop their weapons and beg for their lives, while others run after their retreating general amid the cheers of Sulla's soldiers. The sun now sets, and the rain begins to abate as Pompey and Crassus issue orders to their men. In spite of the blood that was spilled and the hatred spewed by Marius, the conquerors and conquered embrace each other with respect among the blood and mud, each knowing that the other had an obligation to fulfill. Lines of procession filter through the muddy plain to hastily constructed prisons for the defeated men, while another small force commanded by Crassus rides to subdue the forces in Signia.

"Separate those who wish to make amends from those who still side with Marius," Sulla proudly states as he surveys the number of prisoners by firelight. Systematically, the centurions of Sulla's legions move through the defeated and begin separating them by the general's qualifications. "I want to know where

Marius is, and I want to know now!" the general demands. "Someone here knows where he is, and I want him to step forward now!" he reiterates, with a cold mist beginning to fall. His own breath, as well as his horses', is visible in the night air, like smoke from the underworld.

Wheeling about several times, the general confronts many of the soldiers and then moves on to another, evoking fear in some and visible disgust in others. "My patience is wearing thin," he mumbles, snatching a soldier of Marius by the hair and motioning a centurion to his side. "Where has Marius gone? He had to have a meeting place in case of defeat, so tell me where it is!" Sulla shouts, twisting and turning the soldiers' head. Noticing no effort at response, the general calls the centurion closer and gives the command to kill the soldier.

"I have told you that my patience is thin. I have traveled long and hard to meet Marius, and he has retreated like a coward. Someone here *will* tell me where he went, or I will kill each and every one of you with my own hand!" the aged general coldly shouts to the worn mass of men. "So no one will step forward?" he calmly states, surveying the crowd of soldiers. "Very well, Centurion, bring me another man. It appears as though we will be here a while." He leaps from his horse and draws his sword.

"General Sulla," a broken, stuttering voice calls out from behind him. Turning to see who has called his name, he sees a man covered in bloody bandages, leaning on his spear. "General, I know where Marius is, if you will grant me immunity from my crimes against you and your army," the soldier utters through grasps for breath.

"Granted. Tell me where he is and what your name is, Soldier."

"Marius has gone to Praeneste. It was designated as our place to regroup should he lose," the soldier mumbles, leaning even more heavily upon his spear.

"Now tell me what your name so that we might honor you once we return to Rome."

"My name is Publius Cornelius Lentullus, General." He grasps a cup with shaking hands, spilling some and ingesting some. Sulla slowly looks the man over seeing the strength in his large hands and body which are capable of doing great feats but that Marius has weakened through his thirst for blood. Nearly collapsing before Sulla, he pours what is left of the cup on his head washing the blood and dirt from his matted brown hair.

"A Cornelii? A kinsman of Sulla does not drink from a common cup. Not only will you be pardoned, but you will join me in my tent tonight." The general smiles and throws his arm around the soldier, motioning servants to attend to his wounds.

"Pompey!" Sulla shouts, "Go to Praeneste with some of your men and check out his story. If it's true, take the city. I am headed back to Rome to take care of some unfinished business and will look for word from you." The old man turns and walks toward his tent, where he is approached by the centurion who stood by his horse earlier.

"General," the man interrupts, drawing a hateful glance from Sulla, "what do you want us to do with all of these men we captured? We don't have enough food, and Rome is too far to try taking them with us." Stopping in his tracks, Sulla looks at the centurion and calmly asks for his name. "Gaius Manlius, General Sulla, do you not remember my name?" the tall harsh looking man replies now with a note of curiosity on his face.

"Of course I do, Manlius. I just wanted to make sure that you remembered who you were. You are a centurion in the army of Rome, and what does a good commander do when his prisoners cannot be properly cared for except at the risk to his own men?" Sulla asks, gripping the handle of his sword.

"Kill them, General?" he replies standing at attention once more looking straight ahead and tightening his already firm facial features.

"All of them, Manlius. We do not have enough food, and no time to try them all," Sulla replies, pulling back the curtain to his tent. "Now."

Within a matter of moments, the shouts of murder and of men pleading for their lives are heard in the camp of Sulla, even as the general begins to dine. Young and old alike are systematically slaughtered after receiving a hasty trial from Sulla's centurions and being found guilty of treason against Rome, and a sentence of death is passed upon all. In a matter of a day or so, Rome will resemble the camp of Sulla. Slaughter and vengeance will prevail in its streets as a hard-hearted general, sick from years of war, will exact his justice. But now, reclining at the table, Sulla stares intently across the table at his newfound friend.

"So tell me, Publius Cornelius Lentullus, what made you change your mind tonight and go against your fellow soldiers and betray Marius to me?"

"Marius is a monster general. Within the last few days, he has totally lost his mind. He is no longer about Rome or its people but about carrying your head through the Colline Gate to Jupiter Optimus Maximus on the Capitoline Hill," Publius replies while stuffing his half-starved face.

"Do the screams of your fellow soldiers outside bother you? Is that why you joined me?"

"General, the Sibylline Books tell of a prophecy that three Cornelii will rule in Rome."

"I'm aware of this prophecy, and if it is true then my enemy Lucius Cinna was first, I will be the second, and I suppose you see yourself as the third?" Sulla asks with a smile. "There still remains the question of what shall be done for your punishment for joining Marius. You took up arms against me, a kinsman, and there should be punishment. Don't you agree?"

Frightened, Publius instantly stops eating and glancing at Metrobius he sees the same look as he is now wearing on his own face. With a look of fear and uncertainty. He merely nods in agreement to the general.

"Stick out your leg, Publius," Sulla demands as he rises from his seat. Publius hurriedly reveals his leg to the general for fear of what might happen if he doesn't. Sulla pulls a leather strap from behind his back and smacks Publius's shin, causing him to jump from his seat, at which Sulla laughs madly. "It was a childish mistake you made, Publius. That was something we used to do when I was a boy if one of us made a mistake in a game. It's called a sura, for where I hit you"

A look of relief comes over Publius's face as he turns back to the table, rubbing his leg, and Sulla sits as well. "From this day forward, you will be known as my sura. Serve me and my cause well, and you will be the third Cornelii."

# 3

## *Proscribed*

### 82 BC

The day that Sulla's enemies have feared has finally come: the aged general has returned to the city of Rome, only to be engaged in battle at the Colline Gate and to once more be deemed the victor. Most of his enemies had fled Rome upon his victory at Signia; a few more had fled at word of Marius's end at Praeneste. Most of the remnant have gathered to oppose him at the Colline Gate, and the rest have waited like true Romans for the fate that waits them in the city. Like Marius of old, the great Sulla triumphantly rides into the city down the Via Sacra, stopping momentarily at the Senate to inform them that he has assumed the title of dictator and declared immunity for his acts in the past. After a few choice words to a select few, he leaves the elders feeling uneasy when the young senator, Gaius Caecilius Metellus, asks him who he plans to kill, and Sulla merely replies that he has not yet decided.

That reply begins one of Rome's bloodiest days, as the general hands a list of hundreds of names to Publius Cornelius Lentullus, now nicknamed Sura, to post in the Forum. Flocks of people gather around, some crying for joy that they are not named, others weeping for the names found, which meant death on sight. Within an hour, cries are heard throughout the city as those greedy for the reward of killing a proscribed person begin their hunt, while the triumphant general watches from the steps of the Temple of Castor and Pollux. Fear is taken to new heights when citizens bring to him a centurion guilty of killing another soldier, intending to aim for the consulship. His reply is that he had given the order and the soldier had merely followed it.

Blood steadily begins to flow as citizens young and old bolt their doors to drown out the screams of men, women, and even children that are at the mercy of the unrelenting murderers. Supporters of Sulla who had kept their peace during the reign of Gaius Marius now begin to rise up and exact their own brand of justice, all the while earning a reward for doing it. Sulla and his supporters intend to eradicate all who ever supported his enemy and usher in a new government with a new constitution in Rome. However, even those who swore no political allegiance begin to find themselves at the end of a sword, simply because of a possession that some poor disenfranchised citizen desired. Havoc begins to rule in the streets of Sulla's Rome, and the proud battle-hardened dictator is pleased even while the aged citizens and Senators themselves look on in sadness at the decay that has become Rome.

All across the city, wealthy citizens watch the events in the Forum and wonder if they too will be next. From one window, a beautiful lady adorned in flowing robes for her soldier's homecoming gazes out the window and, when she spots him, waves. He returns the gesture, calling a young soldier to his side, handing him a letter, and sending him off. Within moments, a slave comes to her door, entering upon her summons.

"Lady Orestilla, there is a soldier here with a letter for you. Shall I send him in?"

"Yes, I noticed him in the Forum. Please send him in," she states, still staring at her soldier, accompanying the just-returned Pompey and Sulla.

Leaving for a moment, the slave returns with the soldier, who has letters in hand. "Gaius Cornelius Cethegus, my lady," the slave utters, keeping his head bowed and backing out of the room, motioning other slaves to leave with him. "Aurelia Orestilla?" Cethegus asks, holding the letters close, drawing a puzzled look from the lady.

"Yes, what do you have for me?" she asks, looking puzzled at the dirty and rough-looking soldier.

"Lucius Catiline has returned from Praeneste and sends you greetings, as he saw you from the Forum and wanted to get this to you immediately. He says he will contact you later," the soldier replies, removing his helmet and taking a seat at her invitation.

The lady claps her hands, and a young female slave enters the room with two cups, handing them each. Aurelia sits to read her letter.

---

My dear Aurelia,

I don't know what makes me happier, the fact that I will finally get to see Rome and you again after so long or the fact that I can tell you the news that I have.

Fortune has granted me the opportunity to not only save the life of General Sulla but I was also there with Pompey when we took Praeneste and all of Marius's army. Can you believe that when we found the coward he had already begun to take his own life? Some think that this is the way a Roman should die. Personally, I think a true Roman should fight his enemy until he is dead.

When we found him he had already cut his veins and was near death, so I took a knife that Sulla gave to Pompey and cut his head off as he watched, too weak to fight back. This was a prize for the great Sulla and brought him much joy when I returned. Not only did I save his life from Marius's spear, but I brought him the head of his enemy. I am certain to gain his favor for what I hope to accomplish, and that is marrying you.

Tomorrow, after the auctions for the goods of the proscribed have ended, I will trade in my favors for adding my wife, Gratidia, and my son, Lucius, to his list, thus freeing us and accomplishing your wish of having our home free of any children. I will personally take care of my daughter, and then we can spend the reward for killing my proscribed family. Sulla will go for this. I know, as Gratidia is sister to his enemy, Marcus Marius Gratidianus, whom I will also kill for him. I love you and am willing to seal it in blood.

—L. Sergius Catiline

Destroy this letter.

Closing the letter, Aurelia runs back to the window to see Catiline standing next to Sulla with a spear drove into the ground between them—the symbol of an auction for proscribed goods. Noticing her at the window, Catiline waves and taps Sulla. He too nods his head to her and pats Catiline on the back before returning to his auction.

"Would you like me to tell him anything when I return to him?" Cethegus asks, rising from his seat.

"Just let him know he has made me happy with his letter, and I look forward to seeing him," she states, smiling and taking a drink as Cethegus turns to leave.

For the next few days, blood runs through the streets of Rome as Sulla takes his revenge through proscriptions on those who turned on him. Wealthy land-holders answer their doors, only to be told that their estates had been sold at auction and then to be stabbed to death with a dagger. Slaves and relatives alike across the city begin to hide the proscribed, risking their own lives, as the soldiers of Sulla, as well as ordinary citizens, hunt for land and riches with swords in hand. No one is immune to the reign of terror that Sulla has begun to bring on Rome and its people.

Seeming immune to it all Catiline makes his way through the streets of Rome, greeted by some of his fellow soldiers, who are partaking in the massacres, as well as by the dregs of society that he had grown up with before his army service. Prostitutes wave to him, beckoning him by name, to which he merely replies with a smile and a casual offer to meet them later, and, upon hearing his name, men leave the bars desiring to have a drink with him. He stops for a moment and realizes that he is once again home, with no military tribunes to keep his vices in check, and at his fingers is every opportunity to become powerful—by showing his favor to the lowest citizens.

As he makes his way home, he begins to connive and scheme. The best investment of his reward will be to get the dregs of Rome indebted to him. However, all of that will come later. For now, he must deal with disposing of Gratidia and Lucius, as well as his daughter, Sergia, and her uncle. Gratidia would never grant him a divorce, and now he has found a way around it. Aurelia doesn't want any other male competition in the home, and that will be taken care of. And Marcus Gratidianus is a relative of Marius, so he must also die. The real problem, however, lies with his daughter, Sergia—so innocent, yet again a problem that must be solved.

From a short distance, he notices his home, which is situated near the city wall on the Palatine Hill, a privilege granted only to those of patrician birth, though the Sergii have not produced a consul in years. As he gets closer, his palms begin to sweat, and he grips the handle of his gladius nervously then wipes his hands on his tunic, endeavoring to keep the element of surprise if at all possible. From around the side of the ornate home plush with gardens and fountains, a young boy about the age of nine runs, calling his name, the evil that lurks in the mind of his father unbeknownst to him. Catiline smiles, concentrating more on the end of the matter that what is about to transpire. Picking young Lucius up, he twirls him a few times and sets him back down. The young boy laughs loudly, clearly excited about the return of his beloved father.

"Did you really get to see Marius up close, Father?" young Lucius asks, ignorant that Catiline's hand grips his sword.

"Yes, yes, I did. I even cut his head right off!" Catiline replies, grabbing the young boy's attention by whipping his sword from his side. "Do you want to know what else I did to him?"

"Yes, Father, but everyone at school has been telling stories of how you fought with Pompey, too!" Lucius shouts enthusiastically, grabbing his father's hand and pulling him toward the house.

"Let's go over here so that your mother doesn't see, all right? After all, we don't want to ruin the story for her, do we?" Catiline asks, guiding the young boy off to the side.

As soon as they are out of plain sight, he stops. His son continues walking. Catiline says in a cold tone, "Lucius, do you love your father?"

Hearing this, the young boy also stops, and, detecting the cruelty in his father's voice, he replies, "Of course, Father."

Catiline grips the boy's throat and breaks his neck. Lifting the limp body, Catiline lays it in the bed of a nearby wagon. "I love you, too, but this is how it has to be." He turns toward the house where his wife and daughter await, unaware that they are merely obstacles in his path. Pulling his dagger, he makes a small incision on his face and on each arm, drawing enough blood to serve as evidence for the story he is about to concoct.

Drawing a deep breath, he sprints to the house, endeavoring to appear out of breath as he rushes into the atrium where his wife is seated. He is in such a hurry that he stumbles over a chair, sending him tumbling and scratching him further—something he hadn't planned but that worked to his advantage.

"Lucius, what in the name of the gods are you doing?" his wife asks, jumping from her seat, unaware that he was even home. Walking toward him, she stoops down to help him up, motioning a slave to come to his aid, only to be pushed away.

"We have to go, and now! There are riots in the Forum, and people are being killed in the proscriptions!" he shouts, jumping to his feet and pulling her toward the door.

"What are you talking about? You've been here a moment, and all you've done is rave like a madman! Now what is going on?" Gratidia pulls her arm away from him and motions the servant away. Stopping for a moment and feigning fatigue, Catiline attempts to catch his breath while sitting in the same chair he had tripped over.

"We just marched back into town a couple hours ago, and I accompanied Sulla to the Senate house. While he was there, he said that he was making himself dictator and that he was going to settle his scores within the next few days," Catiline says, taking a cup from a slave boy. Sitting in front of her husband, a look of concern forms on Gratidia's face as Catiline begins to rehearse all that has happened in the Forum, tales of murder and auctions. She tries to comfort her husband by rubbing his hand. "Everywhere I passed on the way here I saw someone dead or being killed. There is nothing but death in the streets, and that's why we've got to get out of here now!" he shouts again, grabbing her arm.

Once again, she draws back, noticing the imprints of Catiline's hand on her arm. "You still haven't told me what's going on. Why are so many people permitted to murder while Sulla and the Senate sit by and watch?"

"You don't understand, do you?" He sticks his finger in her face. "Sulla has marked people for death who are either his enemies or who are friends and relatives of Marius and Cinna. You and your brother are on that list." Unsure of how to react, Gratidia falls to the floor, seemingly lifeless, with a blank stare on her face. "That's why I have been trying to get you to leave," he says calmly, lifting her up. "We have to get to your brother before the dregs roaming the streets do."

"Daddy!" a small voice calls out as six-year-old Sergia runs toward him. He motions a slave to stop her.

"Sergia, I have to get your mother out of the house for a while," he says amid the little girl's cries. "I'll be back to see you later though, I promise," he says, feigning a concerned look. "Put her in her room until I return," he instructs the slave. "Get her whatever she needs. I should only be gone a little while."

As they walk outside, the reality of what is taking place hits Gratidia, and she hears the cries from those being slaughtered. Men walk past their home, some carrying severed heads by the hair, others carrying bags with various treasures bulging from them.

"Lucius, where is our son? I haven't seen him since you arrived—have you?" she asks as they make their way to the wagon in the stable.

"Yes, he's in the wagon waiting for us. That's why I was trying to get you to hurry," he says, pulling her faster than she can walk. Catiline begins to usher her around the back of the wagon. "Gratidia, do you remember how I once wanted to divorce you?" he asks as he helps her into the wagon, bringing a concerned smile to her face.

"Yes, and I never would," she says, turning to get in the wagon, and then pausing when she sees the body of her son.

"Well, I found this to be much easier!" Catiline shouts as he pulls her back to him, driving his gladius through her body and throwing her to the ground. "Just who do think put your name on that list?" he whispers as she writhes in pain, unable to cry out. "Sulla doesn't care about you. You are only my pawn." Leaning over her, he wipes his blade clean on her dress and kisses her forehead. "Perhaps you should have given me what I wanted? But then again, proscribed you are worth more to me dead, so thank you for refusing. I almost forgot." He rises but kneels once again, holding his blade to her throat. "Sulla doesn't want all of you, so let's get rid of all this excess baggage."

Knowing that her head is about to be removed, she closes her eyes, and a single teardrop runs down her cheek. She utters a last gasp, and then her body is carelessly thrown into the wagon and covered.

Splattered with blood, Catiline wipes off what he can on Gratidia's dress and walks to the front of the wagon, climbing aboard and urging the horse onward. Once again, he draws recognition from the basest people flooding the streets, some gathering to congratulate him, as he too has won a prize for killing a proscribed person. With the feet of his loved ones hanging from the wagon, he leaves the city, heading for his brother-in-law's home and to finish his task and earn his reward. He knows that Marcus is far smarter than his sister was, and, should there be any suspicion in his eyes, his plan could fail. With the reins in one hand and his chin resting on his fist, he contemplates how Rome might be rid of another member of Marius's family.

Lost in thought, he glances up and realizes he is coming to his brother-in-law's home. With a quick pull of the reigns, he avoids missing it. He knows Marcus is too smart to leave Rome quickly; he is most likely in hiding until the proscriptions die down, and then he will make his escape. Slowly driving the wagon up to the house, two slaves make their way out to meet Catiline, recognizing him from a distance but still wanting to know what his business is with their master.

"Lucius Catiline to see his brother-in-law, Marcus Gratidianus, if you please."

"Master Marcus is not here at the moment, but we will let him know you called on him when he returns," one slave says, walking closer to Catiline.

"I have come to warn him of his name being on the proscription list. I have taken care of my wife, and I was coming for him also."

"As we stated, Master Marcus is not here." The other slave steps forward, brandishing a rod from behind his back. "It is time that you leave." He continues tapping the rod against the wagon's bench.

Catiline scowls at the slave, grabs the rod, and kicks the slave in the face, sending him to the ground. "Just who do think you are?" he shouts, jumping from the wagon. "I have forgotten more than you will ever hope to learn. Remember that the next time you try something stupid!" Catiline says, lifting the slave by his shirt and slamming him into the wagon. "Now, we can either continue this or we can make a deal." He pulls a small purse from inside his armor.

"Just what have you got in mind?" the other slave asks, peering from the other side of the wagon. "What kind of deal are you talking about?"

"Simple. You give me the location of Marcus Gratidianus, and I will handsomely reward you. Kill him for me, and I will reward you even more," Catiline says, revealing several gold coins from the purse.

"Four gold talents apiece, and we will tell you where he is," the slave who had the rod utters, wiping blood from his lip.

"Six gold talents, and, as the possessor of proscribed property, I will also grant you your freedom when you bring me his head."

The slaves accept the counteroffer with a smile, and they run toward the house. Catiline hears a commotion inside, as items in the house come crashing down—until only silence is heard. Throwing his hand over his eyes to shield the sun, Catiline notices the two slaves emerge from the house, with one of them holding their master's head. As if magnifying their treachery, the slaves run back to Catiline, holding the head high in the air and presenting their gift in exchange for their freedom.

"We even brought you his signet ring!"

"Yes, I recognize this ring. Both of you have done very well," he replies, giving them the purse. "I now have all that I need, so I will return to Sulla and get him to sign over the property to me. Then I will be able to free you legally, but as far as I am concerned you are free as of this moment." Catiline looses the horse from the wagon and then walks to the wagon and places the two heads in a bag.

"So you will return with our papers of release?" one of the slaves says nervously as he helps Catiline mount his horse while the other ties the bloody bag to his saddle.

"But of course. Wait here and allow me to go to the Forum and back. Sulla knows that I am coming here, and he is expecting me back." He pulls the reigns and quickly rides off.

Half a mile from the house, Catiline meets six of Sulla's soldiers patrolling the city's boundaries. "Help!" he cries out, waving his right arm frantically to get their attention. "Two slaves at the house just up the road just murdered their master, his wife, and son and were shouting that they are free now. They robbed me—it was all I could do to get away from them," Catiline slyly utters, gasping for his breath as if fatigued.

"We've had to deal with rebellious slaves in the past, and these will be no different," the commander utters, pulling on his gladius.

"After seeing those bodies mutilated, if I had been better prepared I would have killed them myself!" Catiline cries, wiping a tear as he continues, "It was if it were my son and wife lying there."

Another soldier speaks up. "No slave kills a Roman and doesn't pay the highest price. We will see to that." They spur their horses and ride as fast as they can to the house of Marcus Gratidianus.

Catiline's eyes follow the soldiers all the way to his brother-in-law's house, knowing that he has double-crossed the two men, but the head in his bag was well worth the empty promise he has made. He begins his journey back to the city, where Sulla and his reward await him. Returning, he passes the tombs of long-dead Romans now splattered with the fresh blood of their relatives who clung to them for refuge and mercy. He makes his way through the gates of Rome. There is no shame on the face of Lucius Catiline as he parades his way up the Via Sacra, being hailed by those around him. Many even mention his bloody bag and congratulate him on his finds.

◆          ◆          ◆

The Forum is bustling with activity as various people come to the dictator to claim their prize. The once-beautiful center of Roman politics is now covered with blood, as even the temple steps are spattered by those hoping to seek refuge among the gods. The senators safe from the proscriptions stand in the doorway of the curia and watch as the thriving city is brought low. It is in this atmosphere that Catiline makes his way through the crowd. He stands below Sulla as he conducts his business, hearing the names of the murdered citizens and the rewards being issued for their murder.

"Dictator, I bring the head of your enemy, Marcus Marius Gratidianus!" Catiline shouts, holding the bloody head high for the group of scoundrels to see. Stepping closer to Sulla, Catiline continues, "I also have the head of my wife, who is the sister of Gratidianus, for your viewing pleasure."

"You disgust me, Lucius Catiline. I see you achieving great things because of that. If I remember correctly, you wanted to marry Lady Aurelia, correct?" the dictator continues.

"Yes, mighty General, I did, and with your permission I shall complete my plans," he says, placing the two bloody heads at Sulla's feet.

"Go, Lucius. Your new bride awaits you," Sulla states, holding Gratidianus's head up and looking it in the eyes.

Bowing to the general, Catiline makes his way through the crowd and turns aside at the pool of Apollo. He washes his hands of any trace of his filthy crimes, much to the disapproval of the watching priests, who fear Sulla too much to stop him. Looking up, he notices the priests, and he reaches in his purse and pulls out a coin for them. "Tell Apollo that I said thanks for the use of his pool. Let it never be said that Lucius Catiline was stingy." He throws the coin to the priests and walks off to celebrate his triumph.

# 4

# *Public Lies and Private Ambitions*

## 70 BC

Twelve years have passed since Catiline had secretly murdered his family and turned their heads over to Sulla for the love of a woman. In 79 BC, after resigning the dictatorship, Sulla had sat in his home conducting business as usual when a man had been brought before him for refusing to pay a debt, and Sulla had commanded the servants to strangle him. Sulla had shouted so violently that he had caused an internal rupture and, after passing a large amount of blood, had died a horrible death. Some say it had been the payment of his crimes. Rome had returned to the control of the Senate and the consuls and was beginning to see the rise of new politicians, who, following the example of Sulla, sought office for their own gains and not for the good of the people.

In the fall of the year 71 BC, the gladiator known as Spartacus had been destroyed by a joint effort of Pompey and Crassus. As a result, the two generals had returned to accolades in Rome, with Pompey earning a triumph for saving Crassus and for a victory over rebels in Spain; both had been a disappointment to Crassus. The crowds had lined the streets as Pompey's army had begun to make its way through the streets of Rome to receive its honor. Flowers and garlands had been thrown to the victorious general as he had waved from his chariot and saluted each senator he noticed. During this, a slave had whispered, "Remember that you are a mortal," in his ear.

Columns of Roman soldiers had paraded through the streets behind him, holding banners and shouting honors to their general, while young boys and girls had danced before him and musicians had played their best songs. Waiting at the steps of the Senate house, the leaders of Rome had watched with nervous anticipation, wondering if this would be the next Sulla. Crassus had envied Pompey bitterly, along with his new protégé, Gaius Julius Caesar, an up-and-coming politician and lawyer. Hungering for his own triumph, Crassus had wallowed in his bitterness, knowing that any power he acquired would be with the help of Gnaeus Pompey.

After bringing his chariot to a halt, the triumphant Gnaeus Pompey had stepped down and gallantly presented himself to the senators to receive his baton of victory. As he accepted his baton, he had announced that he was laying down his army, much to the relief of the aristocrats, Crassus, and even Lucius Catiline. This single action would pave the way for many schemes and plots for power in Rome.

It is now August, 70 BC, and for the past twelve years Catiline has hidden his atrocities from the public and enjoyed his marriage built on lust and murder, all the while deciding on what his next accomplishment should be. His political career had taken a near-devastating blow when three years before he had found himself before a jury of Roman knights for allegedly having sexual relations with a Vestal Virgin, something forbidden by Roman law and thought to bring consequences from the gods. Once again, his connections with the dregs of Rome and carefully placed bribes had earned him an acquittal, and the virgin, Fabia, had been buried alive for her promiscuity. Lucius Catiline had walked the streets of Rome, freely consorting with prostitutes and the drunken crowd. Murder and deceit have not quenched his appetite, but politics and power definitely could.

The Sergii clan has not supplied the Republic of Rome with a consul in three hundred years, and, in his own perverted mind, he is the one to fill the gap. Talk fills the streets among the lowest of Rome's citizens, as prostitutes live in nicer homes, drunks imbibe more wine, perverts more filth, and veterans of Sulla a chance at new proscriptions with a consulship headed by Lucius Catiline. After a short campaign, Catiline finds that his own private funds have begun to run dry, and creditors are knocking on his door. The budding politician knows that there is one option open to him: he must run for the office of praetor, which will get him a governor position in which he can bleed a province dry, canvas for votes, and be seen in the law courts.

In several areas of the Forum, cases are being disputed as orators plead their clients' cases, ranging from simply theft to murder. Recognizing one of the orators Catiline approaches the Basilica Sempronia clad in his toga, the attire for the Forum, and unknowingly sits in on one the most famous of cases underway in Rome—the case of abuse of power by Gaius Verres, the governor of Sicily. Curious, Catiline listens intently as the trial comes to an end as Verres's prosecutor, Marcus Tullius Cicero, makes full use of his skill in oratory and sarcasm to humiliate and convict him. From across the room, Crassus notices the trials' newest observer and makes his way over, finding a seat next to Catiline with another man following him.

Now in his mid thirties and slowly balding, the orator with the powerful voice and medium build is far different from the young soldier that Catiline remembers fighting alongside years ago. With the characteristically aggressive speech it is no doubt that this is the same man though time has obviously taken its toll. The black hair of the orator with its slight graying seemingly sways with every word spoken as Catiline runs his fingers through his own which has managed to keep its color adding further to his youthful and attractive looks.

Those next to Catiline quickly recognize Crassus, who is serving as consul for the present year, and give up their seats to him and his friend, as Crassus kindly thanks them and takes his seat.

"Lucius Catiline, it seems like it has been forever since I last saw you," Crassus whispers, noticeably flaunting his rings and gold-bordered toga, signs of his increased wealth.

"Yes, Consul, about eight years or so. That's how long it has been since Sulla passed," Catiline replies, moving his eyes from Crassus to the trial and back again.

"I have someone I would like you to meet, a newcomer to politics, much like yourself. Gaius Caesar of the Julii Caesars, meet Lucius Catiline. Catiline fought with Pompey and me under Sulla."

"How could we ever forget the great Sulla? He wanted me to divorce my wife, and unlike Pompey I refused. But that is another matter," Caesar replies. "The consul tells me that you are interested in running for a praetor's spot and possibly the consulship."

"I certainly am. I feel that I am exactly what Rome needs," Catiline replies, leaning back in his seat with a look of arrogance.

Crassus smirks as he says, "You must remember, Catiline, that post-Sullan Rome is full of men who feel the same way."

"My campaign will champion the poor, the destitute, and the average Roman citizens who need a voice."

As they both rise from their seats to leave, Caesar comments, "We could do a lot for each other, Lucius Catiline. Our goals are very similar. I hope that you will keep me in mind, as I will you." Caesar comments as they both slowly rise from their seats to leave.

"It was a pleasure meeting you, Caesar, and to see you again, Crassus," Catiline states.

Crassus leans over to Catiline and whispers, "If you want the consulship, don't do anything stupid and listen to me. I can get you anything you want." As Crassus and Caesar walk out, they draw the attention from many in the court room.

Cicero turns to the departing Crassus and proclaims loudly with a scowl on his face, "Furthermore, I am so glad that our beloved consul has made an end of his business so that the courts of Rome may finish with their business." Crassus smiles and waves as he is escorted out by his lictors.

Cicero continues, "Judges, I now make my address to you. Gaius Verres is evidenced not just by hard facts but from the mouths of witnesses. He is a political monster and a menace that Sicily was all too ready and willing to remove itself." Cicero faces the crowds, judges, and lastly Verres himself. "Verres has stolen, pillaged, and literally raped the island of Sicily, to the point that pirates were free to come and go as they wished. All of which, need I remind you, took place under this man, who has arrogantly denied any wrong doing." The orator faces Verres directly. "Gaius Verres," he continues, "you are proven to be a thief, a liar, a cheat, and a public disgrace to the people of Rome."

"Yes, and you, Marcus Cicero, by your trumped up charges, have proven yourself ignorant and of the worst possible character," Verres smartly replies, drawing laughter from the courtroom.

"Point taken, Gaius. It seems funny, however, that a man with a son who acts little better than a male prostitute should accuse me of having bad character." Cicero faces the crowd with his hands clasped behind his back. "Perhaps you should save that speech for when you see him again instead of wasting it here. Not only this, men of the court, but he tried his best to get an ex-slave of his, a practicing Jew by the way, to tell of his glory. It seems an irony to me that in the Latin language *Verres* is the word for boar. It begs the question, 'Why would a Jew testify for a pig?'" Cicero draws a snicker from everyone but Verres himself, who sits sullen in his seat.

Pausing for a moment, Cicero slowly unfolds a portion of his toga and drapes it over his head, as one who is making a sacrifice to the gods. "Great Jupiter, mightiest of the gods and generous protector of Rome and its people, I implore you to avenge yourself upon one who has robbed your temples and disgraced your image!" Cicero shouts, startling the crowd and drawing the judges' full attention. "Queen Juno, you also have suffered at his hands, and I beg you to repay the damage he has done with the utmost severity." The orator stretches his hands high in the air, pleading with the various gods. "I call upon all of the gods of Rome to rise up with indignation against the thief before you and avenge yourselves. Put a mind to convict in the hearts of our judges this day!

"Judges, it is your duty to find this man guilty. The gods will it and will not tolerate his insolence any further. I charge you to allow yourselves to be influenced by them as you decide," Cicero states, drawing his toga and folding it as he stands reverently before those who must now decide Verres's fate. Cicero walks past the crowd, who stand as he leaves the courtroom, Catiline forcefully makes his way out to get to him. As Cicero exits the basilica, throngs of people present themselves to him, some out of respect and others curious on his feelings of a verdict. The Forum buzzes with activity as senators and civilians go about their daily tasks in the shadow of the great temples and monuments of the Roman Forum. Standing near the shrine of Venus Cloacina and surrounded by lictors, Crassus eyes Cicero. Shielding his eyes from the sun, he shouts, "Marcus Cicero! May Marcus Crassus have a word with a great orator?" much to the recipient's displeasure because of his recent disruption in court.

Offering a sigh and a hasty smile, Cicero makes his way over to Crassus, who also notices Catiline leaving the basilica and motions him over as well.

Placing his hands on Cicero's shoulders, Crassus states, "Splendid job in there, Marcus. There's no way the judges will acquit Verres. You are certainly becoming a voice in the republic, and I offer my congratulations."

"My duty is to the state, Consul, but your remarks are appreciated, and I hope that mine were not perceived as disrespectful," Cicero replies, bowing to Crassus as Catiline walks up.

"You motioned for me, Consul. How may I serve you?" Catiline utters, almost out of breath, as he has hurried to Crassus's side—eager to gain favor as well as out of curiosity.

Cicero instantly recognizes Catiline and takes a few steps back from him, endeavoring to distance himself from him.

Crassus steps in to introduce them. "Lucius Catiline, I want you to meet an acquaintance of mine. This is Marcus Cicero of the Tulii Cicerones from Arpinum. Marcus, this is Lucius Catiline of the Sergii, an apprentice of mine in Roman politics. Catiline bows to Cicero, though continuing to draw contempt from the orator.

"It is a pleasure to meet you, Cicero," Catiline exclaims, offering his hand in greeting. "I thoroughly enjoyed your speech in the basilica—"

"I know very well who this man is. Unfortunately, Consul, I have made his acquaintance in years past," Cicero snidely remarks, cutting Catiline off.

Startled by the sharp reply, Catiline forces back a reaction and holds his composure, though desiring to lash out against the man who is two years his junior. Straightening his toga and clearing his throat, Catiline looks Cicero straight in the eye as he says in a cold voice, "The Social War was a hard time for all of us, and I was very young then. Please do not hold any mistakes I made against me, Marcus Cicero."

"You are worse then I thought, then," Cicero replies, drawing a puzzled look from Catiline. "I care little about the Social War. I am speaking of Fabia the Vestal, whom you killed. She was my wife's half sister."

Catiline replies through gritted teeth, "That was a tragic accident for that young lady, and I am sorry that it affected you so severely, but, when a Vestal breaks her thirty-year vow, she must pay the price."

"You deflowered a Vestal Virgin and murdered my witness who watched you, or you would be dead as she is," Cicero harshly responds, moving closer to Catiline.

Backing up, Catiline clears his throat and bows to Crassus and Cicero. "Consul, it was a pleasure to see you again, and I hope you will allow me to call upon you again. Cicero, I am glad to see you as well. I will be running for praetor next year. I do hope that I can count on you for support."

"Anything that gets a man such as you out of the city and into the middle of nowhere has my support," Cicero replies as Catiline musters up a faint smile and walks off.

Crassus crosses his arms and remarks, "Was that necessary, Marcus? He is a passionate young man, and the trial did prove he had nothing to do with it."

"No, Consul, the bribes of a rich politician and an adulterous murderer proved he did nothing wrong," Cicero responds, drawing a glare from Crassus, who knows the comment was directed at him and Catiline. "That man will be the downfall of the republic if he gains office in Rome, and I stake my name on that." He bows and leaves the consul's presence.

A safe distance away, Catiline begins to fume over his embarrassing encounter with Cicero as someone runs up to meet him.

"What was all that about?"

"The fool remembers who I am, Sura. When and if I make consul in the near future, Cicero is going to share the same accident that his witness suffered before Fabia's trial," Catiline replies as they round a corner and head home.

"I have Manlius working up the vote among Sulla's veterans to put you forward for a praetor position next year and I've been passing out the usual favors to everyone I could as well" Sura states visibly pleasing Catiline.

"That's just what we need. The veterans will tip the balances in our favor, and, with these lower citizens of Rome, it equals victory for us." Catiline tosses a coin to a beggar in the street, along with an encouragement to vote for him.

Meanwhile, several streets away Cicero finds himself escorted home by a small but loyal crowd of admirers who desire to learn from his famed ability. After dismissing them with kind gestures and blessings, two slaves come to meet him: one with a cup and another eagerly waiting to remove the cumbersome toga all males are forced to wear in the Forum. His two young children, Marcus and Tullia, are waiting for the right moment, and, as soon as his toga is removed and the slaves finish with their master, the politician succumbs to his biggest fans. As the two children wrap themselves around him, he looks up at his wife, Terentia, as she soaks up the image of her beautiful family.

"Well, if it isn't the great orator who brought a conviction to Gaius Verres," she touts, walking toward Cicero. "How does it feel to be the big man in the Forum, my husband?"

Pausing long enough to take a sip of his drink, Cicero smiles, surprised that the news has traveled so fast in such a short time. "How on earth did you know that already?"

"People are proclaiming it from the rooftops, how you insulted Verres. But you really should check your comments, dear," she cautiously advises, much to his displeasure.

"Children, I need to talk with your mother for a moment. I'll play again later," Cicero remarks, as the children run out of the room.

"Marcus, I hate how you do that. I really wish you would be more careful. Your sarcasm and insults could get you killed with the ruffians that have been in the city lately." Terentia walks closer and takes his hand in hers and kisses it.

"I have some bad news and some half good-half bad news, depending on how you choose to take it," Cicero replies, once again changing the subject, hugging her as a sign of affection and distraction. "Consuls Crassus and Pompey have asked me to go to Sicily and correct what Verres has done there. They want me to leave immediately, so I have Philologus packing my things now."

"I suppose that is the good news? What could possibly be the bad news? Do you have to leave because Verres is going to kill you?" she asks.

Finding a seat, Cicero becomes much more serious. After running his fingers through his thinning hair, he leans forward, resting his chin on his fist.

"Lucius Catiline is here in the city. I thought he had left after Fabia's trial, but he stayed. He has paired himself with the former Consul Publius Cornelius Lentullus, the one Sulla began calling Sura and who was expelled from the Senate for immorality," he states, with deep concern in his eyes to match the concern in his voice.

"Marcus, we have to let that go. The trial determined he was innocent and she was guilty. The price was paid, and I am just glad Mother and Father did not live to see it."

"Terentia, he was and is guilty, and had he not murdered that slave he would have met the same fate," he replies as his wife wipes tears brought on by the subject.

"Something is getting ready to take place. I can feel it. Catiline is a revolutionary. I can see it in his eyes and hear it in his voice. And you should see the company he keeps: Gaius Manlius, a centurion of Sulla who murdered Marius's men; Publius Lentullus, a man expelled; some new man named Gaius Caesar, who acts just like him; and lastly Consul Marcus Crassus, the richest man in Rome, who is most likely bankrolling everything." Cicero counts off the names on the fingers of his hand.

"If you feel this way, then why did you agree to leave Rome?"

"Because the consuls and the state need me, and what's more the people of Sicily need me." He moved close to his wife and embraced her.

At that moment Philologus, one of the family's slaves, enters the room with Cicero's bags and alerts him to the fact that the transport is ready to take him to his ship.

"My friend Atticus will be stopping by occasionally while I am gone. I asked him to check on things while he is here in Rome in the letter I posted to him this morning. I should be back relatively soon." Cicero kisses his wife on the cheek.

"I think we will be fine without your brother's brother-in-law checking in on us, Marcus."

"Yes, but I would feel better if he did with the way things are becoming in the city," he adds, heading to the door. "If business permits, I will write as often as possible. I love you, Terentia," he states as he heads out the door and to his waiting carriage.

"Greetings and salutations to the great orator Marcus Cicero!" a familiar voice shouts belonging to a portly man in his late forties who is a far cry from the strong centurion that he once was under Sulla.

"Cethegus I don't have time for this right now. I will speak with you when I return from my trip," Cicero sharply remarks as he climbs into his carriage.

Undaunted, the man stops the slaves and pulls back the curtain to where Cicero is seated. He continues to press himself on the rushed man. "But I really must speak with you about your property, Marcus," he continues, drawing an impatient glare from Cicero.

"Gaius Cethegus, if I've told you once I told you a thousand times that I've changed my mind about selling my villa in Pompeii, and besides that I don't like you anyway. You are making me late, now leave me be."

"Listen to me Cicero this is business.; I have a very wealthy client that who is interested in purchasing that piece of property and will certainly pay top price for it if you agree to sell it," Cethegus states, reaching into the carriage grabbing Cicero's arm. Jerking his arm back, Cicero takes a moment to adjust his cloak and gets in Cethegus's face.

"Yes, therefore rendering you a handsome commission for the sale. No deal, and if you so much as knock on my door ever again on this matter I will have the consuls arrest you, because if you remember I am quite close to both of them. Now good day," he states, pulling the curtain closed and motioning the slaves to begin their journey. Enraged, Cethegus storms off in the other direction.

However, in a house near the Forum, quite a different atmosphere exists: one of plotting and scheming. It is midday, and the house of Lucius Catiline is abuzz with the lowest forms of Roman society: actors, pantomimes, dancers, prostitutes, bankrupt citizens, and disenfranchised soldiers of Sulla. In one corner a group of soldiers pass a prostitute between them, while another group sits drunk on the other side of the room. In the atrium, groups of men gamble for what little possessions they have, while on a bench in the same room a group of young beardless boys take part in their first drinking bout—all courtesy of Lucius Catiline. The house of Catiline is known as a place where the down and out can come and find what they need in exchange for allegiance—a place where age, gender, and position are cast aside, along with morals and values. Here the most dignified become the lowest of creatures.

Through the cursing and drinking, Catiline makes his way through the crowd, making sure everyone gets what they need, all the while keeping his trademark smile and warm courteous attitude. Making his way to his *exedra* with Publius Lentullus, the two shut the door, keeping the prying eyes of the dregs out of his private business.

"These people are filthy, Catiline. How can you stand to be around them, much less in your home? What does Aurelia have to say about all of this?" Publius asks, wrinkling his nose up while Catiline sits smiling with his arms folded.

"My dear Sura, it is democracy in action. I can't believe that a former consul and ex-member of the Senate can't see that," Catiline says smiling turning up his cup and sipping its contents.

"I wish you would quit bringing that up. The stupidity of the Senate irritates me enough without you reminding me of it."

"Then use it for the whetstone for what we are to accomplish. Next year when I run for praetor and rule a province, we will have enough funds to push for a consulship. Through that, we can purge this Senate that you hate so much," Catiline answers, bringing a smile to Publius's face. As the two men converse, a knock is heard at the door. Publius walks to the door to see who is there.

"I want to see Lucius Catiline, if he is here," a voice asks through a crack in the doorway. Opening the door, Gaius Cethegus nods to both men in greeting. "I understand that you are the man people come to who want things changed in Rome," Cethegus remarks, bringing a wary look to Catiline's face.

"Who told you that, and who exactly are you?" he replies. Publius slowly draws a dagger hidden in his clothes.

"My name is Gaius Cethegus, and I am a veteran of Sulla. I was a realtor until I was fired this afternoon for being unable to procure a piece of property for my client," Cethegus replies, as Catiline nods to Publius, who replaces his dagger.

"I am campaigning for praetor, Cethegus. If you wish to join my campaign, I would be more than happy to grant you a paid position on my staff," Catiline touts, baiting the newcomer.

Looking Catiline in the eye and then turning to Publius, Cethegus begins to pace about the room. He makes his way to a nearby table, takes a cup, and drinks it, after Catiline gives a nod of approval. "I want Marcus Tullius Cicero dead. Are you the man who can get this done, or can you not? I am not in the mood for games." He looks at the cup while Catiline snickers loudly.

"That is exactly what I was hoping to hear from you, Gaius Cethegus," Catiline utters. "I see hate in your eyes that only Cicero can inspire; and besides that I know all about your recent run in with him" Catiline continues as a surprised Cethegus listens. "I have a couple of silent partners, and we are looking for drastic changes in Rome, particularly a consulship followed by a purge of the Senate and proscriptions. I have the same problem with Cicero that you have, and I promise that if you help me gain office as praetor I will see to it that you get your wish." Catiline draws his listener in with every word he speaks.

"Tell me more," Cethegus whispers as he leans back in his seat.

# 5

## *Let the Consuls Die First*

### 66–65 BC

Day after day and year after year, republican Rome continues to change as policies introduced by new and radical politicians take hold and tear down the constitution. Much has taken place in the past four years. Before even allowing his conviction, which was certain, Gaius Verres voluntarily went into exile, thus escaping the wrath called upon by Marcus Cicero at the hands of the judges. Pompey and Crassus, after a turbulent year as consuls, laid down their powers on December 31, 70 BC, but only after being encouraged to make amends as their final official act before laying down their office. Throughout their consulship, the two men had sought nothing but how to supplant the other and win favor for themselves: Crassus for political power and prestige in the city, and Pompey for military command and legions.

The year 69 brought new campaigns, including that of Lucius Catiline to be one of eight praetors in the city of Rome. Bribes and promises had filled Catiline's campaign, and in the summer of 69 his bribes paid off, much to Cicero's dismay, and he had been elected praetor in 68 BC, along with another notable—Gaius Antonius Hybrida famous mostly for his brutal acts in war. Forgoing the practice of taking a provincial governorship, Catiline had stayed in Rome and involved himself in politics; the next step on the Roman political ladder for an ex-praetor was the consulship, and this had definitely been within his sights. Knowing that his reputation was questionable, Catiline had kept his fraternizing secret and had played his political role to his best efforts. He had endeared himself to some during this time and had won over some who had doubted him. But to others, he had still been a radical who could not be trusted. Between carrying out his duties and attending meetings of the Senate, Catiline and his men had continued to infiltrate the populace and earn support by whatever they deemed necessary.

While Pompey, the now great military leader, had been away in Syria installing Antiochus XIII Asiaticus as king, Catiline had fulfilled the position granted to him by day but had continued to secretly scheme at night with his band of loyal followers on how to become consul. His rogue warriors now included Publius Cornelius Lentullus "Sura," Gaius Cethegus, Gaius Manlius, and Quintus Curius, who, like Sura, had been expelled from the Senate in 70 for improprieties. With these followers, Catiline had made sure that his promises were kept and that gold, wine, and sex flowed among his constituents and found their way to those whose allegiance was not yet secure.

The beginning of the year 67 had seen Manius Acilius Glabrio and Gaius Calpurnius Piso elected as consuls and Catiline setting foot as praetor in his new province of Africa for the first time. After leaving his comrades with orders not to do anything stupid and to win the populace over with promises and parties, Catiline had set sail for Africa with greed in his eyes and a lust for money in his heart. Once there, he had begun to rule gently in order to win the people to himself but also to gauge exactly how much he could profit in the forsaken land. The area once known as the great and powerful rival of Rome, Carthage, had been in the grip of a money-hungry politician who would stop at nothing to satisfy his needs.

A couple of months after he arrived, taxes had begun to be levied without the Senate's knowledge. Every attempt that was made to notify them had been destroyed by Catiline's temporary army of enforcers, who had been bought upon his arrival. His gangs had used torture, rape, and destruction to exact his high taxes—even to the point of selling citizens into slavery if need be. As his coffers filled, so had the streets of his province with prostitutes selling their bodies to pay taxes as well as poor drunks who barely made enough to pay taxes, let alone buy their wine. Again raids had been made against those trying to reach the Roman Senate with evidence of the atrocities that Catiline was committing, and one by one they had been discovered, tortured, and killed—in the name of treason against a governor of Rome.

Even on the day that he had left his province in early May of 66, he had determined that his name was not to be forgotten in the province, and a handful of cities were wiped out by his guards as evidence that his power could still be felt should anyone wish to inform the Senate after he left.

After a month's journey by sea, his ship has landed at Naples, where he is picked up by Lentullus Sura and swiftly taken back to Rome to begin his campaign for the consulship of 65, as the deadline for entering in June is quickly approaching.

"How was your journey, Lucius?" Sura asks, spying the trunks being unloaded by slaves and taken to Catiline's wagon.

"Well, as you can tell, it was very profitable. With the extra money we raised for Rome while I was there, I should get a warm greeting in the Senate," Catiline says as he and Sura make their way to the wagon. "The contents of these crates will more than finance our political endeavors."

Making their way up the Via Appia from Naples, the two men trade stories of what has occurred in Rome and in Africa, quickly passing the time on the journey.

Sura says, "I almost forgot to tell you—Consul Lucius Volcacius Tullus said that he wanted to see you at his home when we returned. He said that he had some news for you."

Catiline makes notes in his ledger as they ride. "Was he in good or bad spirits when he said this to you? I haven't always had a good relationship with the old man. He was my teacher, and I always hated him."

"I really don't know," Sura responds. "He didn't tell me himself. He sent one of his lictors over to deliver the message, and you know how they can be."

"Yes, I do. They followed me everywhere as praetor. It became quite tiresome after a while. So tell me, Sura, what are the elections like so far?" Catiline asks, slipping off his outer robe and replacing it with a cape as they near Rome.

"Well, it looks like Publius Sulla, the dictator's nephew, is going to run, as well as Publius Autronius Paetus, Lucius Aurelius Cotta, and Lucius Manlius Torquatus."

"Excellent. My name will make a grand addition to that lot, and coupled with a few hefty bribes we should be guaranteed a spot on the ballots," he states, but then his face turns serious. "What about Marcus Cicero? What is he doing?"

"Causing trouble in the Senate as usual, but he is not running for consul—that's what is important."

As they pass through the gates of Rome, Catiline replies angrily, "Do you think I couldn't beat him if he did? What does a foreigner from Arpinum have that I don't?"

"I never said that. But you know how smooth a talker he is. He *is* more gifted than you in that area, but you have more support that he does, especially with the veterans. Look there's Publius Sulla campaigning. Shall we go home and get your white toga first?" Sura asks, endeavoring to change the conversation to something more pleasant.

"No. I need to see what the consul wants first. That way I can announce my intention to run. Then I'll get my toga." Catiline jumps from the wagon and adjusts his cape. "If I recall, his house is just up the hill here. I will stop by and give my greetings, and then I will be home," he continues as he once more adjusts his cape.

"I will take these items home and await your arrival," Sura replies, patting the chests as he moves the wagon toward Catiline's home.

Making his way up the street, Catiline is greeted by familiar faces: the drunks and greedy young men who frequented his home before he left. Nodding his head and occasionally speaking, he walks by confident in what the consul has for him. He thinks that before long he will no longer have to rely on the dregs for his power. Soon he will have real power as consul, and the city will be under his control. Some find pity as he walks by, and they kiss his hand, earning a smile and a perhaps a sesterces from his pocket with promises for more if he can count on their support. Stopping, he looks ahead and sees the consul's home with half of his lictors stationed outside. He urges his followers away as he approaches, wishing to seem more dignified than he is.

He announces himself to the lictors, "Lucius Catiline, ex-praetor and former governor of Africa, to see Consul Lucius Volcacius Tullus, at his request." The lictors allow him to pass as he makes his way up the steps to the stately home. As he enters, he finds children at play in rooms of beautiful frescoes and mosaics.

The atrium is a wonder, and a glorious fountain overtakes his vision. Pausing for a moment, he notices a slave has approached him with a drink, which he refuses. He states that he was invited upon his return from Africa. The slave turns to another room and comes back as fast as he went. "The consul will see you, Master Lucius," the slave utters, ushering him into the consul's office. As he is introduced, Catiline bows to the consul, who stands at his entry.

"It is an honor to be received by you, Consul. How may I be of service?" he asks, meeting the eye of the elder statesman.

"Sit down, Lucius. This is no time for pleasantries. I know the game you play, and I am not in the mood for games," the consul bluntly states, drawing a surprised look from Catiline.

"Is that so? Well, I was going to compliment you on your beautiful home, but since you wish to be straightforward, Consul, state your business. I have better things to do than sit here and be insulted," Catiline replies, staring the consul down.

"I received an envoy from your province two weeks ago, and their tales of what you did astonished me. Never in my career have I heard of such despicable behavior from a Roman statesman abroad, and quite frankly I am ashamed. They said many others tried to escape to Rome but you had them killed. Is that true?"

"I went to Africa and raised more revenue for the city of Rome than any other governor, and this is what I come back to?" he shouts as the lictors step forward but are dismissed by the consul.

"Yes, and you lined you own pockets while you were there, didn't you?" Consul Tullus asks.

"Listen to me, you old fool. I did nothing wrong, and you have no proof—other than a couple of worthless men who didn't like to pay what they owed Rome. I challenge you to prove it."

"I fully intend to, Lucius. Next week you are going on trial for extortion in the Basilica Sempronia, and I look forward to hearing your defense."

"Consul, if I may, the deadline for the elections is the end of that week," Catiline replies, softening his looks.

"Yes, and if you are innocent as you say then the trial should be finished with plenty of time for you to register," the consul replies as Catiline grinds his teeth in anger.

"Consul, I bid you good day. I shall see you in the basilica." He bows once more and turns to leave, drawing a nod from Consul Tullus.

Storming out of the house and running down the steps, he flags down a group of slaves carrying an enclosed transport. Paying the fee, he steps inside and draws the curtains, not wanting to be disturbed. "Who does that fool think he is?" he mumbles under his breath, and he bites his nails nervously "I won't let that old man rob me of my chance to be consul—no matter what it takes!" All the way to his home, he continues to stew, but he suddenly brings himself back to reality by biting his nail too close and covering his bottom lip in blood. At that moment, the transport comes to a stop at his home, and he is met by Sura and Cethegus, whom he pushes out of the way. Running to his office, he begins to throw objects across the room.

"What in the name of Jupiter is wrong with you?" Sura asks, drawing a murderous look from Catiline.

"That old fool wants to put me on trial, for extortion of all things! Imagine the audacity of trying me for such a thing!" Catiline shouts as he slumps to the floor, clenching his fists.

Slowly Cethegus walks over. "Master Catiline, you are better than this. I could easily take care of the old man for you at a moment's notice."

"I would like nothing better, Cethegus, but right now we need to call upon our supporters as witnesses. If he died, everyone would know I had something to do with it, and I cannot afford that," he replies as Cethegus helps him up from the floor. "I need some men who can say they served with me in Africa in my administration, as well as accountants who can go over the books and make sure everything is in order and change anything that is not. Now is the time for clear thinking if we hope to get this trial over in time for the elections," Catiline states, gathering his wits.

Sura and Cethegus leave to find Manlius and Quintus Curius and to share the plans with them. The group begins to canvas for anyone willing to sell their integrity and testify on behalf of Catiline for a handful of gold. Those who agree are given fake traveling papers from Africa and clean garments, as well as a hefty alibi to back up their lying claims.

Within a few days, the time comes for the trial. Commoner and statesman alike flood the Basilica Sempronia, waiting what is sure to be an interesting trial. Catiline sits nervously, knowing that the deadline for the election is the next day. If he can get the trial over, he will still have time to announce his candidacy. Marcus Crassus walks up behind him, drawing a surprised look from Consul Tullus, and takes a seat beside Catiline. The whole courtroom takes notice of the richest man in Rome. "Don't worry, Lucius. We have everything under control," Crassus whispers, drawing a faint smile from Catiline. He notices that Gaius Julius Caesar is stepping to the judge's platform and will be presiding over the case.

Looking at the jurors, Consul Tullus jumps from his seat and rushes toward Caesar. "What are you trying to do here, Caesar? This is a courtroom not a circus! Every one of those jurors is either allied to Crassus or is known members of the Populare party," the consul firmly whispers, drawing a smirk from Caesar.

"What do you want me to do about it, Consul? These are the jurors whose turn it was to sit. I can't go about changing the laws simply because they don't fit your agenda."

"How would you like me to throw you in jail, Caesar?"

"On what charges, Consul? For administering a court as it should be and not how you want it to be?" Caesar replies, drawing a furious look from Tullus. Caesar nods to Crassus and Catiline.

Throughout the trial, which lasts long into the night, witness after witness is called, and the group of envoys from Africa tell their story as Catiline watches. Across the courtroom, sighs are heard as the atrocities are retold, but Crassus remains next to Catiline, leaning over to advise him on his answers, much to Consul Tullus's dismay. Catiline is given his opportunity to respond to each and every charge and to offer his own witnesses, all of which agree totally with his testimony. Furious, the consul storms out of the courtroom, much to Catiline and Crassus's delight, as Caesar notifies the jurors to make their decision based on the evidence they have heard. One by one, the jurors hold up their tablets. Each one reads "absolvo."

Crassus leans over to Catiline and whispers, "What did I tell you? If you don't do anything stupid and stick with me, I will help you get what you want." Then he rises, shakes hands with Catiline, and leaves the courtroom.

Catiline graciously bows to the jurors, and, with all of the flare of a veteran politician, he turns to the crowd and waves. Then he turns to shakes the hand of Caesar, who has come to congratulate him before he leaves.

The day is gone as Catiline leaves the basilica. He notices the torches along the Forum streets have been lit, and night begins to fall, bringing a cool summer breeze through the streets. Noticing the consul at a distance, Catiline rushes forward and greets him, bowing in acknowledgment of the other statesmen.

"Consul, as there is still time, I wish to put myself forward as a consular candidate for 65 before the morning deadline," he states. Tullus excuses himself from the others, leaving the two of them alone.

"I am pleased to see that the courts have found you not guilty as you said you were, Catiline. Your friend Gaius Caesar does a fine job conducting a court."

"Consul, I am putting my name forward as a candidate as the deadline has not yet passed." Catiline repeats himself as the consul stares off into the distance, not paying any attention to him. "Did you not hear me, Consul, or is there some sort of a problem?"

"Of course I heard you. Do I need to spell it out for you? I have decided not to take any more candidates. Four names is plenty," Tullus replies, fixing his eyes on Catiline.

"You can't do this. This is an outrage, and you have no right!"

"You forget that I can, and I just did. I am senior consul and in charge of elections, so I can do what I want—just as your friend Caesar got you acquitted," Tullus snidely remarks.

"You will pay for this insult," he mumbles, pointing his finger at the consul.

"What are you going to do about it? Have one of your dregs murder a few people?"

"If I do, I can assure you that you will be the first to go," Catiline states as he turns to walk off, "Have a good night, Consul."

Walking across the Forum, center and passing the Lake of Curtius and then the Temple of the Castors, Catiline wallows in his anger, furious at the old man who wields absolute power and how he snidely uses it knowing that he himself has better plans for such an office. Storming up the steps to his home, his wife Aurelia comes to greet congratulate him at his news of his acquittal, but he brushes past her without so much as a smile, and enters a room with Cethegus and Lentullus, following and closes the door. As she walks toward the door she hears the lock snap keeping would be eavesdroppers from hearing their business. and she then turns, hanging her head wondering why she has been shut out as she makes her way to her bedroom. Long into the night, garbled conversation is heard from behind the door as the three men drink and plan the next move, and as usual sleep until early afternoon.

Early the next morning, the Roman tribes gather in the Field of Mars, an exercise ground for troops and the central voting location. The various men running for office stand by as men cast their ballots. Patrons and slaves alike urge men to vote for them. Consuls Tullus and Lepidus also standby, keeping a close eye on each candidate to make sure fraud or bribery does not take place and that so much as cup of water is not given by a candidate to induce a vote. Long into the afternoon, Roman men endure the heat of a July day as they slowly make their way through the lines in support of their favorite candidate, many waiting until the votes are counted.

Later that afternoon in the home of Catiline, the three men begin to awaken from their late night of scheming. Aurelia knocks on the door, calling her husband's name, until he finally opens it. She is startled by his rough appearance.

"What have you been doing, my love?" she asks as he blinks his eyes repeatedly, still waking up.

"We merely stayed up too late. What do you need, Aurelia?" he replies, opening the door to reveal the other two slumped on the floor against a wall.

"Well, the servants have made lunch, and I was wondering if you wanted anything," she adds with a concerned look drawing astonishment from him.

"Lunch! That means we missed the elections in the Field of Mars!" he shouts, startling his companions.

"Yes, that was the other thing. Quintus Curius is here with news on the elections."

"Send him in. I want to see him immediately."

At that news, the three scramble to make themselves look presentable, as this might be the news they are waiting for. "Nice to see you are an early riser, Lucius," Curius says with a chuckle.

"I am not amused, Quintus. What news do you have of the elections?" Catiline replies.

"Publius Sulla and Publius Autronius Paetus have been awarded the consulship. Gaius Julius Caesar is aedile, and Marcus Crassus is censor," Quintus adds as Catiline finds a seat.

"Well, aside from the consuls, that is very good news. I am sure Caesar and Crassus will be very productive in their offices."

"As a matter of fact, Caesar is hosting a gladiator show in the Forum today in celebration of his victory. He made a speech announcing that he will be hosting many more," Quintus states, also pulling up a seat.

"Gentlemen, how do you feel about an expedition to the Forum today to congratulate our friends and enjoy the festivities?" Catiline asks. With a groan from one and a sigh from another, Cethegus and Lentullus stir from their seats and they all make their way out into the warm summer sunlight. Taking a deep breath, Catiline puts on his best smile and enters the Forum greeting people and shaking hands. He again becomes the skillful politician. The sunlight beams down on the Roman Forum as citizens make their way through the crowded streets, enjoying the generosity of an elected aedile who has not yet taken his post and won't for another six months. Children laugh and play, while street merchants sell everything from cheap trinkets to costly imported clothes.

"Hail, victorious Aedile!" Catiline shouts to Caesar. "My comrades and I bring our warmest wishes on your victory. May your office bring much good to the people of Rome."

Caesar grasps Catiline's arm and pulls him close. "Lucius, I accept your kind words and trust you and your friends will enjoy yourself today. I heard what Tullus said to you last night. Meet with Gnaeus Piso. He has some information I am sure you would like to hear. I told him you would be home later this afternoon. He could see you then if you like," Caesar quietly whispers, drawing looks from those around him.

"More than happy to, Aedile, and again congratulations to you," Catiline says loudly, hurrying off with Cethegus and Sura.

"What was that all about?" Cethegus rudely asks.

"As if it pertained to you. Caesar told me that Gnaeus Piso wants to meet with me later. So I may walk around here for a few more minutes, but then I must be home to see him" he says keeping a smile on his face.

"Caesar shares our feelings, Cethegus," Sura replies as the three walk closely together, eyeing senators and watching gladiators as they prepare for battle.

Catiline faces the two men and says, "Gentlemen, I'm afraid I may have to pardon myself already, as there are a few things I would like to take care of before he arrives. If you would, please notify Curius and Manlius of this new piece of information and meet me at home for dinner," Catiline states and turns to go.

Upon returning to his house, he sees a man sitting on his steps, anxiously awaiting him. He knows about Catiline, but Catiline does not know him.

Catiline cocks his head to one side as Piso stands up. "Piso, I presume?"

"That I am. It is a pleasure to finally meet you, Lucius Catiline. Gaius Caesar has told me very much about you. He says that you would be interested in what I have to say."

Catiline smiles. "If it involves money and power, my friend, I am interested." Catiline takes Piso by the arm and escorts him up the stairs and into his house. Once inside, a slave runs to his master's side with drinks and hands them to both of them as they hurry to a side room and close the door. "Make yourself at home, Piso. Whatever my slaves can get for you, please feel free to ask. Now what is it that you have to share with me?" Catiline takes his seat behind a writing table and reclines with his drink.

As Piso removes the burdensome toga he wears, he says, "I have heard through excellent sources that Publius Sulla and Publius Autronius Paetus are going to lose their office due to bribery. They got sloppy, and the Senate plans to expose them in the morning." He fans himself while he drinks.

"That is most interesting news, but, as Tullus refuses to accept anyone new, where does that leave me?"

Now Piso smiles. "I have a plan, Lucius, that I am sure Sulla, the dictator's nephew, will not take part in but Autronius will. The day that the new consuls, whoever they will be, take office, they will be the first of many to die. You will take one position and Autronius the other."

Catiline wrinkles his brow. "That is very kind of you, Piso, but what do you gain from this? Besides, we are just three men. What is that against a Forum full of citizens? There is no way it could happen, but I like the way you think."

"Lucius, I may look stupid, but trust me I am not. Between your men and mine, and the army of slaves that I have at my disposal, this will be nothing. And after you have served your year as consul, I will serve after you," Piso replies as he stands and begins pacing the room.

"Armed slaves? I may be low, but that is something I could never do, Piso. It is against everything that is Roman!"

"So is treason, Lucius. But if you sign on to murdering consuls, you are signing your death warrant, just as if you armed your own slaves" Piso sharply replies, turning to face Catiline.

"When will you know for certain that you will go through with it?"

"After I talk to Autronius tomorrow, while he is still angry over his banishment from the Senate which is certain to happen," Piso replies quickly.

"What about Marcus Cicero?"

"What about him? He is nothing but a foreigner from Arpinum."

"Yes, but this foreigner knows things and he can smell trouble a thousand miles away. You had better see to it that he does not hear of trouble," Catiline replies as Piso begins to fold his toga around him.

"Let him come. Let him try to make something of it. After the consuls die, he will be next." Piso states emphatically.

"No, Tullus needs to die after the consuls, then Cicero. I made a promise to Tullus, and Lucius Catiline does not break his promises." Catiline escorts Piso out of the house. "I will be at the meeting of the Senate in the morning, so once you have heard from Autronius, please come to my home and give me his answer." Catiline takes Piso's cup and hands it to his slave.

"I will, Lucius, but I can assure you that he will do it. I know him well enough. He will want to avenge his shame, and with Pompey out of Italy it will be easily done," Piso states as he exits Catiline's home adjusting his toga as he leaves.

"Who was that, Lucius?" Aurelia asks as she steps out from behind a corner where she had been listening.

Catiline replies harshly. "What is it to you? Why are you so curious about my business?"

"I am afraid you are getting into something dangerous. I know how you get when you haven't been sleeping well, and your face shows it," she replies.

Resting against a pillar in the atrium, Catiline's face contorts. He grabs Aurelia by the throat in one fluid motion. Almost growling, Catiline whispers, "Listen to me, you filthy whore. I owe you no explanation for anything that I do. If you know what's best for you, you will look the other way when my company comes to this house!" He shoves her to the ground. "If you want to be the wife of a consul of Rome, then you will heed my advice." He hurries back into his office and slams the door, leaving her on the floor.

All night long, he looks down to the Forum, eyeing the Senate house. Throughout the night, his tortured mind is flooded with murder and bloodshed. As he grows more weary, images of his enemies come before him, and he sees them beaten, bloody, and begging for mercy at his feet before he strikes the final blow. The Italian sun begins to rise over the city of seven hills and on a virtually comatose Catiline, whose eyes are bloodshot as he sits against a wall.

A knock is heard at the door as Sura walks in, and he is stunned by the shell of a man that he sees on the floor. "Lucius, what have you done to yourself? You have to be at the Senate in thirty minutes!" Sura shouts as Catiline, still facing the Forum, lethargically turns to look at Sura.

"When I am consul, Sura, there will be no Senate. I will be the only Senate Rome needs," he mumbles. As Sura pulls Catiline up from the floor, he takes hold of Sura's arm. "I am all right, Sura. I just couldn't sleep last night, so I sat in here thinking. Give me a minute or two, and I will be fine." He gathers his wits and prepares to change clothes. "We need to meet back here tonight with everyone. Piso told me that they are planning on ousting Publius Sulla and Autronius because of bribery."

As Catiline strips to his tunic and puts on a clean toga, Sura replies, "What does that have to do with you? Tullus wouldn't add any names, will he?"

With Sura's help, Catiline folds his toga into position and continues, "On January 1 when the new consuls take over, provided Autronius will go for it, we will murder the replacement consuls and any senators we can find."

Sura looked down. "That sounds dangerous, don't you think? I want you to get a consulship, but if we die there is no going back."

Before walking out the door and making his way to the Forum, Catiline remarks, "Last night, Sura, I made up my mind that I was going to do whatever it takes to become a consul. If you are to join me, then you must have that same determination. This first conspiracy of ours will be the proving ground for my supporters. It will separate the faithful from the unfaithful, should there be a need to abort."

Down in the Forum, lictors line the streets in one of the grandest scenes aside from a triumph that Roman citizens have ever seen. From all parts of the city, senators make their way to the Senate house some carried by slaves and others, like the stoic Marcus Porcius Cato, merely walk on foot. Noticing Cato, Marcus Cicero makes his way toward him, shaking his hand. Cicero also notices Crassus, Caesar, and Catiline entering the house together.

Cato remarks sarcastically, "That is an alliteration that I am not fond of at all, Cicero." They watched Crassus wave to the public.

"I agree, but the one who disturbs me most is Catiline. That man is evil, and, by the look on his face, he's working on something," Cicero replies as the two make their way into the Senate chamber. They approach Tullus. "What is on the agenda today, Consul?" Cicero asks as he shakes Tullus's hand and greets him.

"You will have to ask Crassus. He has asked for first speaking privileges this morning. He said he had something very important to take care of today before normal business is handled," the consul replies, drawing a confused look from Cicero and Cato, who are unsure of what Crassus has up his sleeve.

With each senator taking his respective seat, Catiline notices Cicero across the room. He nods in courtesy, receiving only a sneer from Cicero, who turns away from him, which brings a smile to Catiline's face.

Crassus begins his speech, extending his right hand high in the air, the traditional gesture of an orator. "Fathers of the Senate, I know that I break tradition by speaking first, but our esteemed consul, Lucius Volcacius Tullus, has so graciously granted me this privilege." At that moment, slaves enter and hand papers to the various senators. "Once again, you are witnessing a strange occurrence, but I assure you that it is well justified. You will find in these papers hard evidence that Publius Sulla and Publius Autronius Paetus are guilty of bribery. I recommend that they be disqualified from the consulship and that Lucius Aurelius Cotta and Lucius Manlius Torquatus be given their place," Crassus continues. He makes his way back to his seat while Sulla and Autronius sit infuriated at the charges. The Senate erupts with calls for prosecution and punishment.

Tullus rises from his seat and steps to the floor. "I saw the evidence before it was presented here, and I recommend as consul that Marcus Crassus's opinion be adopted immediately."

Publius Sulla shouts out, "Marcus Cicero! I implore you to defend me in this charge at trial!"

Standing to his feet even though he is urged by his fellow senators to sit, Cicero walks to the main floor. "Publius Sulla is a fine young man and much different from his uncle the dictator. I will gladly undertake his defense," he replies to the relief of his new client.

"What of you, Autronius?" Tullus remarks, drawing a glare from Autronius.

"I will not beg like a dog before anyone. If you want to prosecute me, I dare you to come after me!" he shouts as he leaps from his seat and storms out of the Senate hall, followed by Gnaeus Piso, who happens to be watching the proceedings along with other common citizens at the door.

As the atmosphere in the Senate calms, Catiline turns to see Piso and Autronius conversing privately in the doorway. Autronius steps back, **nods** his head, and then hurries off. Catiline turns to leave. "Gentlemen, if you will excuse me, I am sure this stuffy group of men we call a Senate can do business without me today. I have some business of my own to tend to, if you will excuse me." Catiline hastily states as he rises and turns to leave and is followed by Cicero's eyes as he goes. Running out of the Curia Hostilia, Catiline frantically looks for Piso. He sees Piso standing near the Lapis Niger, across from the curia.

"I have been waiting for you, Catiline. Your reflexes will have to be quicker if you hope to join our plan." Piso crossed his arms and smiled at Catiline.

"Well, if it had not been for avoiding the stares of Marcus Cicero, I would have been here sooner," Catiline replies, running his fingers through his hair.

"Autronius is more than happy to join. He thinks it is well overdue," Piso states, bringing a smile to Catiline's face. "Go home, think it over, and talk to your men. If you decide to join, I want you to be over there at the Comitium with a sword visible under your toga on December 29, just before the kalends of the new year. Until then, do not contact me. I will contact you after that date."

"Very well. I can promise you that I will be there. I will talk it over with my men, as I am sure that we will get 100 percent cooperation." Catiline bows to his new partner.

"I look forward to seeing you again," Piso replies, rushing away from the Forum.

Pausing for a moment, Catiline stands and looks over the Forum; before he realizes it, he becomes lost in the grandeur of where he stands.

"Catiline!" a familiar voice shouts to him. When he turns, he notices Marcus Cicero headed toward him in a fury. "What were you doing with Gnaeus Piso?" Cicero bluntly asks.

"My, my, my, if the star orator of the Forum hasn't come all the way from his seat in the Curia Hostilia to speak to me. What can I do for you, sir?"

"You know exactly what I want, Lucius. I know you are up to something. You have been up to something ever since the first day I met you, and when I can prove it—"

"Yes, when and if you can prove it, Marcus. The trouble is, you can't because there is nothing to prove. What we have here is a simple man from Arpinum who wants to make a name for himself. This time it will not work," Catiline says, enraging Cicero.

"Listen here, you son a whore, I will mark every move you make, and if you so much as breathe wrong the Senate will know," Cicero whispers under his breath as passing citizens begin to notice the confrontation.

Catiline feigns a laugh and throws his arm over Cicero's shoulder, nearly choking him. "Yes, and if you so much as come near me I'll have your slaves murder your family while you watch and then slice you to pieces and toss you in the Cloaca Maxima that runs under the city."

Cicero stood still. "I will stop you, Catiline, you monster."

"You go ahead and try. The republic is dying, and I'm just here to help it finish its course," Catiline says. "Let's keep this between us, shall we? Have a pleasant day, Marcus," he continues as he heads home.

Cicero returns to the Senate meeting. Making his way back to his seat, Cicero's friend and fellow senator Marcus Cato clears his seat and notices the concerned look on Cicero's face. "What's wrong, Marcus? You look as though you died and went to the underworld."

"Catiline is in league with Gnaeus Piso to do something terrible—so terrible that he threatened to murder Terentia and my children if I interfere," Cicero solemnly states drawing a look of anger from Cato.

"Marcus you must interfere. Can you prove this? If you can, we can take it to Tullus privately. He hates Catiline anyway."

"That is the problem, my friend. I can't prove it. All I can do is wait him out and strike when he is exposed," Cicero replies, turning from Cato and focusing on the Senate and its business.

Over the next five months, Catiline continues to hold his all night meetings and floods his house with the same drunks and perverts he was accustomed to before he left for Africa. Across the city, the partisans of Piso and Catiline begin to gather weapons in small caches. All the while, Lucius Catiline continues to play the innocent, budding politician in the Forum. He never gives his friends, enemies—and most of all Cicero—any occasion to suspect him, and he is always seen with his trademark charismatic smile, although a sinister mind lies deep inside.

The month of December is now upon the people of Rome, and, with the beginning of the ides, the fifteen-day gift giving festival known as the Saturnalia begins and passes with Catiline, Cethegus, and Lentullus Sura watching the events of the Forum with great anticipation.

"My friends, it is time," Catiline utters confidently to Sura and Cethegus. "Today is the day, men. With my movement, we are committed to change in the city of Rome." Sura begins strapping the sword to Catiline's side and folding his toga over it.

"Lucius, I believe it is concealed enough to pass an inspection by Sulla himself," Sura comments.

"Yes, but I want a portion to show for Piso or whomever he has watching for me," Catiline replies, moving toward the door.

Braving the cold winter air of the Forum, Catiline nods to the few people that he passes and makes his way past the Lake of Curtius and Shrine of Cloacina to the Comitium, the round, sunken area near the Senate house where the common citizens gather to hear political news. As he walks down the steps, the few people who are in the Forum notice the unusual spectacle and look curiously, as there is no business taking place to justify his being there. Satisfying their curiosity with brief stares, they move along as Catiline stands motionless in the sunken area. Then, he slowly opens his toga to reveal the handle of his sword and, turning in every direction, he calmly covers it and makes his way out. He knows that he has forever changed the path of his life, and as casually as he walked into the Forum he now makes his way home, leaving those watching wondering what he was doing, only too soon to find out.

A cold winter breeze blows across the seven hills of Rome on the kalends of January, as citizens from every sector of the city, both rich and poor, gather in the Forum, excited about the day's events. As the people throng the Comitium, the doors of the Curia Hostilia, where the Senate meets, slowly swing open. At the head of a mass of senators, the new consuls, Lucius Aurelius Cotta and Lucius Manlius Torquatus, proudly walk out to meet their public. After a few brief words, the new consuls are escorted up the Via Sacra to make the traditional sacrifices and vows to the gods for the safety of the people and for wisdom with which to guide them. Following closely behind them, Catiline surveys the crowd for Piso, as well as Marcus Cicero, who he is sure will show up for the festivities.

Patrician and plebeian alike gather along the road to greet the new consuls and give their best wishes; among them is Gnaeus Piso and a small group of his men, who nod to Catiline as the procession makes its way down the road. Murder is in the air, and, after several late night meetings since Catiline's appearance in the Comitium in December, the plot has grown in strength and determination. Not since the times of Marius and Sulla has there been more determination by a group of citizens to shed the blood of other citizens than there is today. With swords hidden under their togas, the group, numbering close to a hundred, makes its way through the streets, waiting for the signal from Catiline to begin the assault.

Making his way through the crowd and pressing closer and closer to the new consuls, Catiline is suddenly grabbed by the belt of his sword, which had once been securely hidden. Fear grips his heart, and a lump comes to his throat; he knows he has now been caught by Cicero, and his new enemy has the proof to send him to the Tullanium and to his death. Turning slowly, Catiline is surprised to see that Gaius Caesar, the aedile on his way to sacrifice, is the one holding his belt. A puzzled look comes over his face, as he suspects Caesar of changing his mind and revealing the plot.

"Don't do it, Lucius. Trust me, we have a better way—one that won't get you killed by an army of lictors," Caesar whispers, pulling Catiline close. From the roadside, Piso cranes his neck, curious at what is taking place and certain that they have been caught. Not noticing Caesar, he and his men slip back through the crowd and go home, as an alibi.

"What do you mean, Caesar? Now is the time I've been waiting for. If it is not done now, where I can leap to the Rostra and deliver my speech, then when?"

"Crassus has worked out a deal with the Senate to send Piso to Spain to secretly raise an army and come back to Rome before Pompey returns. This is to our benefit, but today's actions are not. Trust me," Caesar replies. In disappointment, Catiline covers his sword, nods to Caesar, and continues in the procession to consecrate the consuls.

Confusion clouds the mind of Catiline as the adrenaline disappears and a sense of loss overtakes him. With his countenance low, he pauses in the middle of the procession and turns to go home when he is met by Marcus Cicero.

"Sad that it is not you being consecrated, Catiline? Perhaps you were planning on taking their place?" Cicero snidely utters, knowing that his sharp words are merely serving to enflame his rival. With a snicker Cicero brushes past Catiline. Cicero's comment serves only as a catalyst to cement his purpose no matter the cost. In a vicious rage, he turns toward Cicero, ignoring all around him, and glares at him with unrelenting hate. Feeling that he is being watched, Cicero turns and receives the full force of Catiline's stare, which visibly pierces his soul, as he again turns from Catiline and continues in the procession.

Catiline casually makes his way home, allowing the citizens to have their party and the consuls their day. It would not be long before he was at the helm, and Rome would bow to him. When he arrives home, Cethegus, Sura, Curius, and Manlius notice a change in the man they have trusted to lead them to victory in Rome; a more sinister approach surrounds him, and in his eyes there is a look of death and destruction unrivalled by any. Such a fear comes over them that they hesitate to follow him into his house until he urges them inside without a word being spoken.

Once inside, the crew makes their way to Catiline's office, where once more the door is closed and locked. Planning begins.

"Plans have changed, gentlemen. We can no longer rely upon Piso, as he is a fool and will get us all killed," Catiline mumbles as he sits behind his writing desk. The others find their seats near a window or on the floor. "Caesar has told me today that Crassus will send Piso to Spain under the guise of putting out rebellion to secretly raise an army and return to Rome. I have decided to give it one more year and to begin my campaign for consul in 64. I can no longer wait on help. We will do it on our own," Catiline continues, pouring a cup of wine and downing it quickly.

"Will we join with Piso should he return?" Quintus Curius asks, bringing a smile to Catiline's face.

"That simple-minded fool will get himself killed in Spain. I guarantee it. Crassus is no idiot, and he knows Piso has no self control. So the answer is no. We will do what we see fit to do without him," Catiline replies, bringing the men to nod in approval.

For the next few months, the city is quiet. The Senate carries on as usual, and Catiline's house continues to be a hot bed for immorality, under the guise of campaigning to the masses. Late into the night, parties draw prostitutes, those in legal trouble needing false witnesses, and those so deep in debt that the only way out is to sell their souls to Lucius Catiline. His followers continue to pass out gold and favors, buying votes and trust. Day after day, they persuade the veterans that the only way for peace in Rome is to have Catiline as consul.

# 6

# *Consecration, Conspiracy, and the Consulship*

## 64 BC

Gnaeus Piso is dead. His men are left without a leader, and Catiline without competition. Not long after he arrived in Spain touting his newfound praetorian powers, Piso had found himself jerked from his horse and stabbed multiple times; he had died the same way that he had lived: without mercy. Rumor had quickly spread around Rome as to who was responsible; some said it had been a plot of the ruling class to wipe out a radical. Others said he had merely lost favor with Crassus, who had arranged for him to be sent to Spain in the first place. One thing had been certain: Catiline no longer had a kindred soul who shared his ideals beyond his own followers; but perhaps time would change all of that, or so he now hoped.

The new year brings the end of the consulship of Lucius Manlius Torquatus and Lucius Aurelius Cotta and starts a new term for Lucius Julius Caesar and Gaius Marcius Figulus, as well as fresh plans for consulship by Lucius Catiline. It wasn't long after the consuls took office that Catiline is the first to announce his candidacy and thus remove any chances of rejection. Once again a smile replaces his worn looks as he joyfully hears that he is accepted. He can finally hold his head high in the Senate because a member of the Sergii family will be in the running for a consul's position for the first time in three hundred years. But by April of that same year, all of that comes to a screeching halt, due in part to the proscriptions of Sulla twenty years ago and in part to a member of the Optimate party, the quaestor Marcus Porcius Cato.

It is a cold January evening in the torch-lit Roman Forum as Catiline makes his way to the home of Consul Gaius Marcius Figulus: the second consul to visit in his efforts to run for the consulship next year. Sura and Cethegus watch as he walks down the path from the ornate Roman home with a spring in his step and a smile on his face large enough to swallow the whole of Italy.

"They have accepted me, gentlemen! At long last a Sergii has received the honor that our clan is due!" he comments as he makes his way between the two men. "It is a cold but beautiful night in the city of Rome and if only Cicero were here so I could laugh in his face—that would be the only way it could be any better!"

"Where are we headed, Lucius?" Sura comments as he and Cethegus struggle to keep up with Catiline.

"First I must go to the Pool of Curtius, as I wish to make an offering in thanks for my fortune and say a prayer that I would be as bold as he was," Catiline remarks as the trio make their way among the citizens out for an evening stroll on the ides of January, specifically the thirteenth day. All along the way, Catiline and his men are greeted with warm smiles, which are promptly returned with reminders to vote for him for the consulship in June. A cold winter breeze runs through the Forum as Sura and Cethegus wrap their togas tighter, but Catiline continues to make his way, seemingly unaffected even by the elements.

"Goddess Fortuna and great Curtius the brave warrior, I ask you this day to shed your light on my path and to embolden me to do great things for Rome and my ancestors!" Catiline states as he pours a flask of wine and throws a coin into the deep hole in the center of the Forum, directly in front of the Basilica Sempronia where he had stood trial only a few years before. Pausing for a minute, he bows his head and whispers a few inaudible words before he is interrupted by Sura.

"It looks like you got your wish, Lucius," Sura states as he tugs on Catiline's toga, interrupting his silent conversation with the unknown bringing a look of anger to his face until he sees why he is interrupted. Making his way home from the Forum, Marcus Cicero walks with his followers from the basilica but makes a detour upon seeing his favorite Roman.

Catiline takes advantage of his opportunity. "Marcus Cicero, there must be gods on the Capitoline because only a few moments ago I was hoping that I would get to see you," Catiline states with a smirk as Cicero's face tightens. Sura and Cethegus fold their arms and guard Catiline.

"Well, if it was anyone else I would say I am flattered, but being that it is you I will simply say that I am less than amused."

But Catiline is not finished yet. "I, Lucius Catiline, have been accepted as a candidate for the consulship, and I just wanted to make you aware of that, as I just came from the consuls' homes," he states haughtily, endeavoring to rub his victory in his adversary's face.

"Well, then what are you doing here? Trying to appease the gods, or are you giving your little daughter something to drink, as she lies at the bottom of the pool of Curtius?"

"You have no right to say that, Cicero. I had nothing to do with her disappearance, and I still grieve her loss."

"Maybe not, but I do have a right to say this: I will certainly enjoy running for the consulship against you."

Catiline takes a step back, and he begins to sneer at his opponent. Turning his back to Cicero he looks to Sura and Cethegus, and they look back at him, unsure of what to say at the news. Turning back to Cicero, Catiline furiously bites his nails as Cicero watches curiously. Catiline suddenly twitches, as he once again draws blood.

"You really should check that vice of yours, Catiline. It is quite unbecoming of a potential consul to have unkempt nails—especially when they bleed everywhere," Cicero dryly comments.

"How can you run for consul? You are the new man in the Senate. They cannot allow a foreigner to run for the highest office! This is an outrage!"

"Well I can, and they did. The Optimates have chosen me to represent them, and it is my privilege to do so."

"That is something we shall see about. Have a pleasant evening," Catiline replies as he walks away from Cicero. "That stupid fool has another thing coming if he thinks I am going to play on his terms," Catiline grumbles as the three men walk off, leaving Cicero chuckling at what just took place.

Catiline no longer shows his friendly side to those around him but merely shoves his way through the crowd, anxious to get to the safety of his home where he can ponder his next move.

"Cicero is a crafty one, Lucius. You will need to watch him very carefully," Cethegus remarks, causing Catiline to stop in his tracks and grab him by the toga.

"I am well aware of how he is. I have watched him longer than you have been walking, and I have fought along side him in war. I am fully capable of discerning his techniques and even more capable of responding to them when they arise." He pushes Cethegus back. "We will plan, gentlemen, and then we will plan some more. This campaign will be very carefully engineered to eliminate failure and maximize my finer points to the citizens of Rome," Catiline continues as the three arrive at his home.

As they enter Catiline's sparsely lit home, Sura draws his sword and shouts, "Who are you, and what are you doing here?" Several men sit comfortably in his office.

"Sura, put your sword away. I have been waiting for the proper time to introduce all of you, and that time has apparently come," Catiline calmly remarks, removing his toga and tossing it in a chair. "You should actually recognize some of these men, as they are currently serving in the Senate of Rome."

"I know Publius Autronius Paetus, Gaius Manlius, and Quintus Curius, but the others I am unsure of," Sura utters as he and Cethegus scan the faces in the crowded room.

"Then allow me to introduce you to Lucius Cassius Longinus, Servius Sulla, Lucius Vargunteius, Quintus Annius, Marcus Porcius Laeca, and Lucius Bestia, all of the senatorial order, along with young Appius Fulvius, son the distinguished senator of the same name." Catiline gestures to each man, who in turn nods to Cethegus and Sura as their name is called. "Of the equestrian order I am pleased to introduce Marcus Fulvius Nobilitor, Lucius Statilius, Publius Gabinius Capito, and Gaius Cornelius. We all have the common goal of victory, along with a couple other friends who wish to remain anonymous."

"Why? What are they afraid of?" Cethegus asks.

Catiline smiles and closes the door. "Nothing. It has merely been deemed safer for them to remain unknown. That way the strings they control can be pulled without any unnecessary repercussions. For a time I have tolerated the useless politics of Rome and have endeavored to run a fair campaign, but with the news of Cicero running that is all out the window. You are all brave men and we have had our private conversations in the past, and I believe that we are of one mind and have one common goal. If you will help me achieve my dream, I can promise you that the iron hand that we have all lived under will finally be removed. Rome will be able to achieve greatness under my leadership. Now each of you have your individual orders, and starting tomorrow you will need to carry them out. Thus far is it Marcus Cicero, Gaius Antonius, and myself who are running for the consulship. I could easily tolerate serving with Antonius, as he has a pliable mind, but Cicero is too clean for his own good. We will meet back here on the kalends of June, the first day of the month, at ten in the evening, but for now I want you to memorize your orders and destroy them before you begin your work," Catiline remarks as each man nods in acceptance of his commands.

Catiline now stands at the door, which is lit by a single candle, and embraces each man as they leave until only Sura, Cethegus, and Gaius Manlius remain. Closing the door once again, Catiline takes a seat at his desk. "Gentlemen, it has begun. I will accept nothing but total victory, and you as my friends and closest allies will share in my glory when I am consecrated before Jupiter Optimus Maximus on the Capitoline Hill." Catiline raises a cup and toasts his comrades in arms. "Manlius, I have a special assignment for you. Do you remember the men that you served as centurion over?"

"I do, Master Lucius."

"Excellent. They are living in Faesulae, where they were given property by the Dictator Sulla, and are in need of a new leader. I have been in contact with them for sometime and have even visited them on various occasions. They respect you, Manlius, and are anxiously awaiting you to go to them as I promised. I need you to prepare them should we need their assistance, as well as their weapons cache here in Rome."

"I shall leave in the morning if you like."

"Yes. The quicker we move with the veterans of Sulla the closer we come to victory in Rome," Catiline replies as they all head to their own homes to sleep off the events of the day. Catiline, however, passes the night in the same sleepless fashion that has recently overtaken him, depriving him of rational thought, as well as mercy and human kindness. The inner demons that Catiline has catered to for so long have begun to grow stronger—to the point that they are driving him on, pushing him to either victory or destruction.

Slowly, the Italian winter trades its cold breezes for the warm rains of spring, and fresh grass grows in the plains and vines of acanthus begin to grow in the Forum. The Forum once again becomes the center of life as the earth breathes new life into the region. Within a matter of days, priests and servants are seen outside their temples cleaning the grime in preparation for the feasts, celebrations, and sacrifices that are to come. Aged senators and scholars bask in the warm sunshine as they are thronged by crowds of admirers, eager to capture a single wise word that might happen to fall.

It is in this atmosphere on the nones of April, or the fifth day of the month, that Lucius Catiline, clad in his best toga, makes his way to the Forum with Aurelia at his side and Cethegus and Sura standing behind him. Following an old practice, he watches as members of his crew distribute small bowls of grain to random citizens, each bearing his name as well as a reminder to vote for him in the upcoming elections.

Word begins to spread quickly through the streets of Rome that Lucius Catiline is a generous candidate. With a handshake and a smile, he and his wife parade themselves around, showing kindness all under the guise of merely being out for a morning stroll.

"The gods bless you, Catiline!" a beggar woman shouts from a shop window bearing torn curtains and tiny Romans with dirty faces.

"The gods have, my lady, and that is why I wish to bless you!" he kindly replies in his usual charismatic way, smiling beautifully as his wife looks on. Turning to Sura, he says, "Sura, be on the lookout for my little friend, if you don't mind. I am having a pleasant day and would certainly hate for him to ruin it for me."

"I already sent some men to his home with a dispute for him to decide for them. One of them is a Greek actor, so I am sure he will take up much of his time," Sura replies with a chuckle.

"If you did, then why are they walking this way?" Cethegus asks turning Catiline's smiling face to a look of cold stone.

"Sura, you idiot, what have you done?" Catiline snarls, drawing a wide-eyed look from Sura.

"What are you two doing here? Didn't I send you to Cicero's house?" Sura shouts as the men cower behind each other.

"Cicero wasn't home, Master Lentullus. There is a meeting of the Senate today," one of them replies. Sura raises a hand to strike him but is held back by Catiline.

"I was wondering why the curia doors were closed. Gentlemen, take Aurelia home. I'll be home once I find out what is going on." Catiline runs across the Forum square. Upon his arrival at the curia, the two slaves outside the doors open them as he slowly enters. Avoiding his normal seat in the front, Catiline finds a place in the back of the Senate, where, to his surprise, Crassus is also sitting.

"What is going on? Why wasn't I notified of a meeting today?" he whispers to his rich friend.

"You were notified, but you had already left your home this morning by the time the announcement had been made. Marcus Cato the quaestor has called a special meeting but has not yet got up to speak," Crassus whispers in reply.

"Do you know what it is about?"

"Not the slightest. But when a man as reserved as Cato requests a special meeting, it must be something big."

With that the conversation filling the Senate house begins to die down as the consul presiding over the meeting rises from his seat and makes his way to the center of the room, in front of the Altar of Victory to speak.

"Conscript Fathers, I bring you greetings and thanks this day that you have responded to the call to meet as so many of our forefathers have on matters of great importance. I wish to bring to the floor the quaestor, Marcus Porcius Cato, as it is at his request that you have been gathered here," Consul Gaius Marcius Figulus states, drawing his toga and extending his right hand as he motions Cato to step forward. Gathering a few papers, Cato straightens his toga and walks slowly to the floor with all eyes in the room focused directly on him not knowing exactly what he has in mind.

"I bring forward a proposal that I wish the Senate to consider," he states, his voice loud and clear in the audience of so many. "For over twenty years our memories have been filled with the bloody time of proscriptions under Lucius Sulla. As a young man I was considered a confidant of the dictator. Many times, though his age and experience overruled my opinion, I tried to get him to forgive and avoid proscriptions, but as you all know I apparently failed. We can do nothing about what took place twenty years ago, but we can rectify the fact that those who willingly profited in murder have gone free. Fathers of the Senate, I urge you to consider prosecution against those who are not only among us here but who for a handful of gold spilled Roman blood. For too long I have sat and watched those guilty of murder avoid their punishment, and it is high time that this be addressed by the Senate," Cato states calmly as he walks back to his seat. Nervous senators squirm in their seats, anxious to be the first to speak.

"Do you have a list of those who fit this category?" an aged senator rises to ask Cato.

"I do."

"Then allow the Senate to review it," another voice calls as Cato turns his head to answer it.

"The names will be announced once prosecution has begun. For too long these names have been the subject of political advantage and favors; therefore they will remain hidden until the proper time."

"My name is on that list, isn't it, Quaestor?" Catiline stands, looking in the direction of Cicero, who happens to be watching his every move.

"Sit down, Lucius. Let the business run its course," Crassus whispers, tugging on Catiline's toga, urging him to sit down. He harshly jerks away from Crassus.

"I do not have to sit down, Marcus Crassus," he shouts. Then turning to Cato, he states "I have a right to know if my name is on that list!"

"It is," Cato coldly replies amid an uproar of conversation, as senators all across the house turn to one another in amazement.

"This is a plot by the competing party to stop my bid for the consulship. You will find this charge very hard to prove indeed!" Catiline replies, shoving his way out of the Senate. "Fathers, this is a travesty of justice and a breach of all that is good and decent!" he shouts as he storms out in protest. All across the house, senators ask if their names are listed, which is met with silence by Marcus Cato. Optimates and Populares alike shout both in joy and disgust over the announcement as the leading man of the Senate, Quintus Lutatius Catulus, steps to the floor, endeavoring to regain control.

"You've really done it this time, Cato," Cicero whispers as he places his hand on Cato's shoulder. "You finally succeeded in bringing life to this stuffy Senate house."

"Marcus, it was the only way to get Lucius Catiline out of everyone's mind for the consulship. I trust him about as much as you do, and if we can at least condemn him in a court of public opinion, if not a court of law."

"This is a disgusting political move, and I ask the Senate to defeat this proposal," Gaius Julius Caesar shouts from his seat. "Certain politicians do not have what it takes to win on the campaign route, so they manipulate the laws how they want them!"

Much to the pleasure of the hardliners seated around him, Cicero shouts, "No, Caesar, it's just that certain politicians don't have a bag of gold to support them or cover up everything they do!"

"You have no right to accuse me of anything, Marcus Cicero!" Crassus shouts across the room to Cicero.

Cicero laughingly replies, "Whoever said I was speaking of you? His name wasn't mentioned, so it must be a guilty conscience that is driving our beloved Crassus to admit his guilt, my fellow senators." This draws a chuckle from various areas of the room.

Caesar replies to his insult. "Marcus Crassus is a fine senator and a well-respected Roman, Marcus Cicero. I think this body would agree that you owe him an apology."

"So are you now Crassus's queen, Caesar? I thought you belonged to King Nicomedes. His highness might be upset by this sudden change of his lover's allegiance, don't you think?" Cicero replies without even rising from his seat, as those around him laugh. Caesar and Crassus both storm out of the assembly.

"I have never been so insulted, especially in front of the Senate! How could Catulus allow such a thing?" Caesar asks as the two head toward the door.

Crassus replies, "You have to know Cicero. It was an insult, yes, but allow it to roll off. Cicero is a powerful man in Rome, and if you can get him on your side he will be a valuable asset." The two nod to citizens as they go, still endeavoring to keep their political face even after all that has happened.

"Crassus," a voice whispers from a corner as the two men walk past the Tullanium, a structure that serves as the Roman prison, which is no more than a roof over two chambers dug out of the ground.

Turning to see who called him, an arm with lightning speed grabs him by the toga and pulls him into the alleyway.

"What was the meaning of that? I thought you had that pompous fool under control!" Catiline shouts directly in the face of Crassus as if he could tear him apart.

"Take your hands—"

"Just be glad my hands aren't around your throat! Now you listen to me, you stupid old fool I have listened to you, and all it has gotten me is embarrassment. Either you reign him in, or I will. Believe me when I say that," Catiline mumbles as Crassus is visibly struck by fear at his now-crazed associate.

Caesar steps in. "Catiline, we were all insulted in there, but you have no right to manhandle a former consul like this."

In reply to Caesar's rebuke, Catiline exclaims, "He has no right to play games with a future consul, either." Then, turning back to Crassus, he states, "I am running for consul, and I will not see myself shot down due to a handful of conservatives who want their way in the Senate. You have helped me thus far. Please do not disappoint me again." Catiline releases Crassus and straightens his toga for him. His crazed look returns to a smile, and Catiline turns and calmly walks off in the other direction.

"So what are you going to do now? I think our friend has gone quite mad," Caesar asks a bewildered Crassus.

"We are going to get Cicero to defend him."

"How hard did he grab you?"

"Hard enough. Cicero may not like Catiline, but he has to admit that he would greatly advance his consulship bid as well as the number of supporters. If Cicero is as smart, as I think he is he will gladly accept the offer," Crassus replies as the two begin to make their way up the street.

The next few weeks pass uneasily for Catiline, as he rarely leaves his office. Sura and Cethegus join him in trying to compile a defense and work up enough false witnesses for the events twenty years ago—mainly the strange disappearance of his family and his known murder of Marcus Marius Gratidianus, his brother-in-law.

Across town, however, at the house of Cicero, a much different atmosphere prevails as a strange visitor arrives: Marcus Licinius Crassus. The slaves immediately recognize him and forgo the usual waiting period. They usher him directly into the atrium of the home which is decorated with all manner of art ranging from busts and sculptures from Greece to works by famous Roman and Greek authors courtesy of the library of his close friend Atticus. Following his usual custom, Cicero is reading one of his favorite works and being massaged by the family slave.

"Marcus Licinius Crassus to see you, Master," the middle-aged slave announces as Cicero continues reading and then pauses, laying his book aside. "A former consul is visiting the home of a foreigner? To what do I owe this great honor, Crassus?" Cicero states as he rises and bows to Crassus.

"I have a proposal to make to you, Cicero, if you can be serious enough to listen."

"Merely jesting. Now what can I possibly do for you?" Cicero replies, offering his guest a seat with a wave of his hand as the slave returns with a cup for the guest.

"I offer aid to your consulship bid in exchange for defending a client of mine in the upcoming prosecutions that Cato is proposing."

"Who might this client be?" Cicero asks with a solemn look.

"My client and I recognize that you have earned yourself quite a reputation for your skills in the courtroom and think that you are the ideal man to help."

"Who is it, Crassus?"

"Lucius Catiline," Crassus mumbles.

"Let me think it over. My answer is no. Thanks for the visit, Crassus. Now I am sure you know the way out," he quickly replies, beginning to walk off.

"Think of the possibilities. You both want to win, but with you being the new man in Rome there is some doubt over your head, and he has a questionable past. You both have your downfalls but can benefit from each other," Crassus states, walking over to Cicero and throwing his arm over his shoulder.

"I will consider it and let you know within a day or so."

"Very fair and very kind of you, Marcus. You are showing yourself to be the bigger man," Crassus replies, straightening his toga as he turns to leave the house. "I will check back in a day or so. Thank you for your time."

"Marcus, what was that about?" Terentia asks, peering around the corner with a curious look.

"Why do you ask? I am well aware that you were listening in on our conversation," Cicero replies with a raised eyebrow and a grin.

"I am concerned, Marcus. Anything to do with Catiline is dangerous business. You know that," she states, gently embracing him. "The rumor is that he killed his whole family to be paid by Sulla and to marry Aurelia and—"

"They are just that, my dear, rumors. They make excellent weaponry in the Senate and in public speeches, but beyond that they are still rumors."

"What about how that his daughter's body is in the—"

"They are rumors. Nothing more, nothing less. If I could prove it, and I would love to, I would happier than you could ever imagine. But the fact is that I cannot, so I must deal with what I know."

"So you are going to defend him?" she asks, pulling slowly away from him with a concerned look.

"I have not decided yet. I gave Crassus my word that I would think it over, and I will do that. Until then, say an extra prayer for me and offer an extra sacrifice that I might make the right decision."

Finding a carriage, Crassus hails it outside of Cicero's home and directs it toward the Palatine Hill district of the city, as night begins to fall in Rome. Within a few minutes, which Crassus passes by rehearsing his speech to Catiline, the carriage arrives. Tipping the slave, Crassus makes his way up the steps. He is greeted by Quintus Curius and Gaius Manlius outside of the home he would not dare to frequent except under the cover of night. Making his way inside, Crassus makes out drunken figures lying on the floor, most of whom are young beardless boys who have already sold their soul to the demigod in whose house they dwell.

"How goes the defense, Lucius?" Crassus utters as Catiline turns his eyes up at him but does not moves his head.

"What can I do for you, Crassus?" Catiline utters in a cold, monotone voice.

"I have found the man to defend you, so you need not worry yourself any longer."

"Let me guess—is it Marcus Cicero?" he replies, leaning back in his chair with his arms crossed.

"How did you know?"

"I may have drunken supporters, but I am not an idiot, Crassus. Cicero is the obvious choice politically, as we could benefit from each other and he is the only one skilled enough to get me off."

"He told me that he will notify me in a couple days as to his answer," Crassus states as he begins to sit.

"Did I say you could sit?" Catiline asks as two men step out of the shadows and move towards Crassus. "As you can see, I have men everywhere, even in the shadows, so why would I need Cicero? He is a hindrance to me and will serve me no good."

"Cicero is extremely skilled in oratory. If you are smart you will accept his offer if he accepts mine."

"I don't need your offer or his, Crassus, because I have something even better. Gaius Julius Caesar will be presiding over the court that will try me, and that is better than all the Ciceros in the world," Catiline replies with a smile. "Gentlemen, if you would, kindly escort Marcus Crassus to the door, but be gentle and bow as he leaves, as he is a former consul."

"You need me, Catiline, and you know it," Crassus states as he is ushered out.

"One day, my friend, you will come to me and that will be my line, but for now, pleasant dreams. I have work to do."

After much preparation, the day that he has waited weeks for arrives and spectators and jurors alike begin to crowd the courtroom as Catiline and his supporters prepare for a day of grueling testimony and merciless accusations mingled with lies and treachery. Just as he suspects, Cato goes for the throat the instant the trial begins, and Catiline sits emotionless, occasionally glancing at Caesar, who throws a short wink and a smile to Catiline. With the jurors on his payroll instead of Crassus's, Catiline knows that he has earned more supporters instead of sending them to Crassus as he had so foolishly done in the past. For hours the testimony goes on, as the details of Marcus Marius Gratidianus's murder is laid out before the jury, and the speculations are made of how his wife Gratidia was murdered by his own hand to earn a reward.

"This man, men of the jury, ruthlessly drove the gladius that he fought for freedom with into the breast of his lovely wife, and then heartlessly cut off her head to present it to the unfeeling Sulla as an offering," Cato utters fiercely displaying all of his power in oratory that he can possibly muster.

"Number one, men of the jury, Cato did not ever know my wife, so how can he possibly know whether I killed her? How is it that a grieving husband cannot bring the head of his murdered wife to Sulla and seek revenge for her slaying without being accused of the act?" Catiline replies, rising from his seat long enough to ask the question.

Cato did not take the bait. "Your act will not work here, Catiline. We have witnesses who say you are lying."

"Yes, but I have witnesses who say you are lying," Catiline remarks, leaning back in his seat, drawing faint laughter from the crowd. "I swear before mighty Jupiter that I had nothing to do with her murder or the disappearance of my children. Choosing to hide my grief in a new life does not make me a criminal, and I charge you to prove otherwise. Gentlemen, the case against me is weak and cannot be supported. How can a case built on speculation be expected to stand?" he states, maneuvering away from his table and making his way past Cato to address the jury. "Cato has proven that I killed Marcus Marius Gratidianus, but that was done on orders from Dictator Sulla. As you well know, you cannot disobey the order of a dictator, especially when that dictator was Sulla."

"But you could have at least refused the pay!" Cato shouts from across the room.

"He paid me for the slaves of Gratidianus, which, as part of his family, became mine. But I didn't want them."

"Yes, and as I recall they were murdered also."

"What a man does with his property is his own business, but it was Sulla's soldiers who killed them, was it not?" Catiline replies with a smile.

"Enough of the useless bickering. Jury, you have heard the facts. Now make your decision based on the case presented before you," Caesar exclaims as he rises from his seat and faces the jury, which promptly rises and leaves.

Now turning and walking back toward his respective desk, Catiline takes his seat to wait for what is sure to be a long deliberation for a trial that has lasted from ten in the morning until after six at night. Shuffling his papers in an effort to get things in order after his lengthy ordeal, he feels a hand gently fall on his shoulder but ignores it.

"Crassus, I told you I didn't need you. It seems as though I have made it just fine," he quietly states as he continues to work, not looking up at his supporter.

"You are doing a fine job, Lucius. Don't let them use speculation as fact if it is not," Cicero states as Catiline turns, surprised that his adversary would approach him.

"Thank you. You are certainly the last one I would expect to hear that from."

"You know why I could not defend you, don't you, Catiline?"

"Of course. For the same reason that I would not have if it were you in my place. It is a compromise of our individual principles that neither of us is willing to break."

"Cicero, what are you doing?" Cato shouts, rushing up to Catiline's desk.

"Making a gentlemen's agreement to disagree. Good luck in your campaign, Catiline. May the best man win." Cicero walks off as Cato rushes back to his own table.

Within an hour the jury returns and gives its decision that Lucius Catiline is not guilty of murder, much to Cato's dismay and Catiline's joy. Another barrier has been removed to allow him to pursue his consulship bid, as well as his aim of absolute power in Rome. A look of sickness comes over Cato as the verdict is read, and Catiline, joined by his supporters, is led triumphantly out of the courtroom. The smile on his face is too much for Cato, and against his better judgment he pushes through the crowd and confronts Catiline face to face.

"How can you live with yourself, allowing all of this pomp and celebration, when you know as well as I do that you are guilty beyond a reasonable doubt. Yet you aim for the highest legal office. You make me sick," Cato whispers to Catiline and is overheard only by Sura, Cethegus, and Manlius.

"If you are sick, perhaps you should see a doctor, Cato," Catiline replies with a smile. "The simple fact is you know I'm guilty, I know I'm guilty, but apparently the jury didn't. Now get out of my way. I have an election to prepare for, and if I need a philosopher I'll give you a call." He shoves past Cato, donning his characteristic smile for the public eye.

Cato looks around the courtroom for one person in particular. Once he sets his eyes on him, he too, like Catiline, begins to shove people out of his way. "Cicero, what was the meaning of that spectacle? I thought we were on the same side, and yet you turned your back on me. Why?"

"I could never turn my back on you, my friend, but the peace must be kept," Cicero replies as the two take a seat in an almost empty corner of the courtroom. "Catiline is a monster, both you and I know that, but he is smart and must be handled carefully."

"I know you have a point, but right now I am not seeing it," Cato replies with a look of disgust still on his face.

"If this courtroom would have seen the same Cicero it saw outside of the Senate house a few months ago, then they would have been convinced of a plot to stop him by our party. However, if they see a man sympathetic in his intentions, embracing his enemy and uttering a kind word—"

"Then you have transformed yourself into the acanthus with the serpent hidden under it," Cato finishes for him.

"Exactly. The key to launching a plot to keep the dangerous people under lock and key is to convince them that there is no plot," Cicero says with a smile as the two exchange looks of confidence in each other.

"I am sorry that I doubted you, Marcus. I should have known better. I hope you will forgive my insult," Cato says, bowing his head.

"No apology is necessary. You have done an important thing today, and that is letting him know that people suspect him of what he has done in secret. Now just help me keep a close eye on this man so that all of Rome is not destroyed by his lust for power," Cicero replies as the two shake hands and go their separate ways.

For the time being, every obstacle has been removed that might possibly hinder Catiline from obtaining his goal of consul. He lives thinking that the gods have favored him, as he has now dodged two attempts at prosecution as well as numerous disruptions to what he wishes to accomplish. For the next month and a half, Rome remains much the same, as Catiline, Cicero, and their contender, Gaius Antonius Hybrida, make their way about the city touting promises and passing out political favors to earn the votes they need. While Cicero and Hybrida stick to conventional promises, Catiline turns to the radical approach and attracts the most attention—both good and bad.

Endeavoring to appeal to a wider range of people, Catiline begins to toss about the promise of absolving all debts in Rome, much to the delight of Sulla's veterans, who accrued high debts—some from being gone for so long and others from having no fiscal responsibility. Catiline has seemingly found the key to gain success, but this same key also causes opposition in creditors who want their money, including those in the ruling class and in the opposition party. By the strict hardliners, Catiline is deemed a dangerous threat in matters of money.

As the campaigns near their deadlines, the Senate keeps a close eye on Catiline and his supporters, watching as bribes are visibly passed out by Catiline, Caesar, and Marcus Crassus. Being cautious to stay within the Calpurnian law, which strictly monitors election bribery, the trio pass out favors and occasionally some gold to secure a vote. Cicero and Cato watch in amazement that the Senate would rather debate bribery than do anything about it and that the tribunes of the people also indifferently watch the corruption that is going on. On the last day of May, just before the kalends of June when the election speeches are made, one brave tribune makes his way to the Senate, and from this day forward things will not be the same.

As the Senate is coming to order on the morning of May 31, the consuls, Lucius Julius Caesar and Gaius Marcius Figulus, stand in the speaker's area as the president of the Senate, Quintus Lutatius Catulus, is seated and looks over the list of proposals to bring to the Senate. Dismissing his two bodyguards, Cicero casually walks down the center aisle and takes his usual seat on the front row near the speaker's area, alongside Cato, who has been saving his seat. Amid commotion from outside, Catiline and his followers who are still members of the Senate make their way in as Cato sneers, Cicero smiles, and Crassus and Caesar both carefully eye them.

As he stands before the Altar of Victory surrounded by the consuls, Quintus Lutatius Catulus states, "Conscript Fathers, may I have your attention. It is time for the Senate of the people of Rome to come to order. As our tradition dictates, do the former consuls have a word to bring to the Senate to open our meeting?"

"We both wish to bypass any comments today, Catulus," Lucius Aurelius Cotta stands and answers, seconded by a nod from his partner in last year's consulship.

"I have a word, Master Catulus," Gaius Marcius Figulus, the current consul, states from behind the seated Catulus. "I wish to allow the Senate to hear the proposal of Tribune Servius Sulpicius Rufus and Senator Marcus Tullius Cicero."

Confused, Catiline leans down to Crassus and Caesar, who are both sitting below him. But he is only given a confused look, as the move has taken them both of guard.

"Senate of the people of Rome and honored Fathers, today I bring to you a proposal suggested by my friend and senator Marcus Cicero in response to the rash of bribery that has not only plagued our elections but has filled our courts with an abundance of cases," Rufus states, looking at the mixed appearances of the senators and noticing Crassus and Catiline in particular.

Now it is Cicero's turn. "Conscript Fathers, what we are proposing is a penalty so harsh that one would think twice about committing election bribery or fraud, and should they dare they will be exiled from Rome and its elections for ten years." Cicero stands with his right hand extended, gazing about the room as he speaks.

"The Senate is not a law-making body, Cicero, merely an advisory board," Caesar shouts out, as he looks for approval.

"Fathers, something must be done about this rash of bribery, and I recommend that we ratify it and make it law," Cato states, not even rising to give Caesar's comment respect.

Angry at the whole process Catiline sits silently in his seat seething in his fury at times slouching in his seat and nervously biting his nails. The whole debate goes on for over half and hour until, unable to take much more, Catiline leans over and tugs on Crassus's toga. "This is about me, isn't it? Cicero knows something, so he is trying to exile me with this stupid law of his, isn't he?"

But it isn't Crassus who answers; it is Caesar. "Clam down, Lucius. We haven't done anything that normal Romans haven't done. It's just that Cicero fights by using the law because he can't afford to fight with bribes."

Cicero continues, "We have heard the debates, Fathers of the Senate, and I ask you to approve this law. The republic needs solid laws that places all on the same level and preserves the respect and honor due to our beloved institution." Cicero walks toward his seat. "This law will also serve to take the weapon that is currently being forged against the republic out of the hand of an enemy that is among us," he exclaims as he takes his seat.

From somewhere in the room, an aged voice cries out, "What enemy is there that the Senate does not know of? Explain yourself, Marcus Cicero."

"I agree. If there is an enemy wishing to destroy the republic, the Senate must know of it immediately!" Lucius Volcacius Tullus, consul, shouts out to the applause of many of the aged senators around him.

"I do not yet have the proof that I need." Cicero stands. Crassus, Caesar, and Catiline begin to chuckle as their adversary is seemingly humiliated. A look of embarrassment washes over Cicero's face until he catches a glimpse of Catiline laughing at him. "Hear me, Fathers!" he shouts, startling the body of men. "Mock me if you wish, but I swear upon all that is honorable that I know who is planning something, when they are planning it, and what it is they are planning. They are sitting in this room, and I ask that if this body had the confidence to put me forward as a consular candidate that you also have confidence in my judgment when I say that we are under attack." His eyes focus directly on Catiline for a moment, allowing Catiline to know what he suspects without tipping the Senate off.

Slowly Cicero straightens his toga and takes his seat among the astonished senators, who all gaze in his direction as he stares straight ahead. Clearing his throat, Cato stands, pulls his toga up uncovering his left arm, turns to his friend, and begins to clap. Within moments, others stand and join him, along with the current consuls and the president of the Senate.

"What is this, a rally for Cicero?" Catiline hatefully mumbles to Crassus.

"Shut your mouth, put on a smile, and join me as I stand and clap—unless you want to incriminate yourself," Crassus remarks as the whole group surrounding them join in the ovation for the brave man from Arpinum.

Focusing on his adversary, Catiline catches the eye of Cicero. In an act of defiance, Cicero returns this look of hate with one of confidence, as the two adversaries exchange thousands of words in a glance that lasts only a few moments. Brandishing daggers in his eyes Catiline's look of murder is delivered with skill like only he can do across the crowded room as Cicero's warm smile answers his decree of death with a promise to elude, uncover, and destroy his plot before he has time to destroy Rome. For the next few hours, debates continue in the Senate as Catiline plans, oblivious to the discussion in the Senate until the meeting is dismissed. He calls his men closer, giving brief instructions, and turns to Crassus and whispers, "Cicero dies on election day," and then hastily makes his way out of the Senate to pass another sleepless night and prepare for his speech the next day.

With the arrival of the kalends of June, the Forum is filled with political hopefuls as well as pupils merely wanting to follow their heroes and learn the rules of politics in Rome. In gleaming white togas, Catiline and Cicero parade about the Forum square, each surrounded by their bodyguards, while Hybrida does his best to steer clear of both men and prepare for his speech that all are required to give on the opening day of elections from the Rostra, the tall platform adorned with honorary statues and situated in the rear of the Forum square.

A hush falls over the Forum as one of Rome's most respected citizens, former consul Quintus Lutatius Catulus, the leading man in the Senate, clears his throat and begins to speak.

"The kalends of June are upon us, my fellow countrymen, and with that comes the elections for the consulship next year. As our ancestors have deemed, each participant will be allowed to mount the Rostra and present his campaign to the people. Are the participants present?" Catulus asks, shielding his eyes from the sun and looking about the crowd for the characteristic white togas.

"I am here, sir!" Cicero shouts from just below the ledge of the Rostra, making his way to its steps.

"Gaius Antonius Hybrida is also present, honorable Catulus" Hybrida shouts as he waves amid his supporters, who usher him to the platform as he carries his nephew, Marcus Antonius, on his shoulders.

"Lucius Catiline, where is Lucius Sergius Catiline?" Catulus asks, searching the crowd.

"Here, Master Catulus," Catiline replies, standing directly behind him and beating his competitors to the platform. "Lucius Sergius Catiline presenting himself for the elections of the consulship of Rome," he further states, bowing to the respected senator.

"As senior among the candidates, the honor of being the first to speak goes to Gaius Antonius Hybrida," Catulus states as Hybrida straightens his toga and makes his way to the front of the Rostra to speak.

"My fellow Romans, it is with great honor and respect that I stand here before you today as a candidate of your consul," he states as scattered groups begin to applaud him in the middle of his speech, which he silences with his raised hand. "I have served with honor in the legions of Rome, suppressing the dreaded slave rebellion, and furthered my service with the dictator Lucius Sulla. I will make my speech very short in respect to my fellow candidates and merely say that I will give Rome my best as I serve as your consul, should you honor me with the office, which you alone have the power to bestow upon me." He closes his speech and makes his way down from the Rostra, joining his supporters and family.

"Lucius Sergius Catiline, step forward," Catulus calls out as Catiline smiles and proudly steps forward with Cicero watching his every move as well as scanning the crowd.

"Like my fellow candidate, I am honored to stand before you today as a candidate for the consulship. It has been my dream to be the first Sergii in three hundred years to have the title, and the ability to do good for the people of Rome. I too have served under Lucius Sulla and actually had the privilege to have dealt a blow to Gaius Marius the Younger, following him back to his fortress and then removing the traitor's head for Sulla and thus ending civil war in Rome. I have also served, previous to that, under Gnaeus Pompey the Great's father in the Social War, alongside my fellow candidate Marcus Cicero. However, unlike Hybrida, I will mention what I am for in case you haven't heard. I believe that Romans are too heavily in debt due to causes beyond their control. Therefore if elected I promise a total absolution of debts in Rome!" Catiline shouts, much to the approval of the crowd. The senators watch, shaking their heads in disbelief and frowning in disgust.

"Veterans who have served Rome away from their families should not have to come home to outstanding debts that they cannot pay. Honest people should not be at the mercy of greedy moneylenders, some of whom are sitting in your Senate! I also propose an increase in grain allotments to citizens, as well as allowing it to cover a wider range of citizens. Elect me to be your consul. I have made my promises to you, and Lucius Catiline never has and never will break his promise to the people he loves!" he shouts as thunderous applause fills the Forum. Catiline casually bows to the people and makes his way past a smiling Cicero. He stands at the bottom to hear Cicero's speech, wondering how he could ever top it.

"My name is Marcus Cicero, of the Tulii Ciceros from Arpinum. I am a new man in the Senate, and considered by some if not most to be a foreigner. I come from a humble background, but one that taught me respect for those around me, respect for myself, and respect for my country. I want to be your consul because I can do great things for Rome if allowed to serve. However, it would be far more fitting if Catiline and Hybrida were elected to serve together instead of me," he states, drawing a gasp from the crowd, a look of surprise from the senators present, and confusion from Catiline.

"Just their names and backgrounds alone prove that they are more fitted to serve together than either of them and myself. Gaius Antonius was so murderous and cruel that even Sulla distanced himself from him, and, after torturing an entire town of Roman citizens, he earned the nickname "Hybrida" as a testimony of his bloodlust. The subject of cruelty then brings me to Lucius Catiline, who killed his brother-in-law and his wife, and, being that his children are nowhere to be found, probably them too," he continues, regaining confidence from various senators and enraging Catiline and embarrassing Hybrida.

"I ask you, Romans, how can you elect a man who tortures citizens like yourself? What do you think he will do to you when his policies are not passed? What about a man who proudly carries his wife's and her brother's heads through the streets with no remorse? I ask you how can you elect men who have murdered so many and seem to care nothing of it? I can promise you today that I will not always do what you approve of, but I will do my best for Rome. Allow me to be your consul and the lesser of the two evils to serve with me," he exclaims, closing his speech and stepping aside, but not leaving the platform as he notices Catiline at the bottom of the stairs.

Fuming in anger, Catiline's face turns a deep shade of red and he clenches his fists, wanting nothing more than to kill Cicero in front of everyone, no matter the punishment. Regaining his wits, Catulus reminds the people of the elections in the morning. Catiline takes the left sleeve of his toga and wipes his nose and then his forehead, attracting the attention of Lentullus and Quintus Curius.

"What is he doing?" Curius asks upon beholding Catiline's strange activity.

"It's a message. Tonight is the night we have been waiting for. Get Cethegus and help me spread the word that we are to meet at Catiline's home at midnight. Tell them Catiline expects them to be on time," Lentullus Sura states as he smiles at Curius, who makes his way off through the crowd. Sura then looks at Catiline and returns his signal with a nod.

"Marcus Cicero," a middle-aged soldier calls out as Cicero lingers on the platform, still waiting for Catiline to leave. "Marcus Tullius Cicero, might a soldier have a word with you?"

"Of course you may, young man. How might I be of service to you?" Cicero replies, making his way down the steps of the Rostra as Catiline leaves, still enraged by the orator's comments.

"My name is Marcus Petreius. I served as a young officer under Sulla. I understand that you know a man named Andronicus?"

"Why yes, I do. We served together along with Gnaeus Pompey under Pompey's father in the Social War. Do you know him? Is he doing well?"

"I did know him. Unfortunately he died many years ago in Marius the Younger's first attack on Sulla's camp. He told me about you and encouraged me to meet you if I ever got the chance."

"Well, I am glad that you have, though I hate to hear about Andronicus. What brings you to Rome? I notice you are in your soldier's garb."

"I am currently serving under Pompey and am on leave for the next few months, due to my wife having our first child. When I heard that you were a candidate for consul, I wanted to rush over here before going home in case I should miss you."

"Well, my friend, I am glad that you did. It is nice to know that with the way things are right now that I have at least a couple friends in Rome," Cicero remarks as the two begin to leave the crowd of the Forum and walk toward Cicero's home.

The two stop for a minute. Petreius asks, "What do you mean? Doesn't the Senate have everything under control?"

"Unfortunately, no. We cannot prove it yet, but there is a conspiracy to destroy the republic and murder consuls and senators alike."

"Who would do such a thing?" Petreius replies as Cicero shakes his head, unwilling to spread a rumor he cannot prove by mentioning anyone's name. "Lucius Catiline. It's Lucius Catiline, isn't it?"

"What did you say?" Cicero asks, unsure exactly how Petreius came to his conclusion.

"Lucius swore to Marius's son before he cut off his head that he would rise in his footsteps and conquer Rome. I was the only one in the room, and I didn't think anything of it as he had been drinking, but now I know it was real."

"We must get Pompey back to Rome before he does, Petreius. Catiline is sick and cares nothing about the people he will have to murder to get his way."

"You will have to do something in the Senate then, Marcus, because Pompey will not come back until the war is over."

"Then, my young friend, you will need to say an extra prayer for us. We will need all of the help we can get," Cicero replies as the two shake hands and part ways.

The rest of the day, Catiline is unseen. Not even Sura knows where he is until later that night when he walks into the *exedra* and sees Catiline staring out the window overlooking the Forum. The two men stand silent in the dark room, which is lit only by two flickering candles that barely allows enough light in to see and occasionally reveals the frescoed walls with their scenes of debauchery. Letting out a sigh, Catiline turns and looks Sura in the face revealing his bloodshot eyes. The look of madness once scared Sura, but now it barely fazes him.

"Tonight, my dear Sura, we find out who is with us and who must die for knowing our plot," Catiline mumbles. "Not only will we be consecrating ourselves, but I have a young man who heard too much and now wants to be a part of our plans. I promised him we would include him tonight," he continues, staring back out over the Forum.

Sura tells Catiline the reason he has come. "Everyone is here, Lucius. They are all on time, but they wanted me to come in and make sure you were ready to see them."

"Enter, my fellow citizens! Enter and allow your consul to entertain you!" he shouts as the men file in, filling the small room and then closing the door. "Of all of the men I know, you alone are my friends. I have served in the Senate with most of you, and others I have fought alongside in war. It is my honor to be here with you tonight. Tomorrow, my loyal followers, we shall win, but if we do not then we have a great undertaking to perform, and I will need your help. Rome has been bogged down by useless and ineffective men for so long that the people will rejoice to see us set the wrongs right. It is time for change, my friends, and when I become consul we will proscribe the rich and take back what they have taken from us! Sulla will be proud when blood once more flows in the streets as our haughty oppressors are banished to the underworld forever!"

As Catiline quickly swallows the contents of a cup, Sura asks, "Senator Quintus Annius, would you be so kind as to remove the cover from the table beside you?"

A feeling of shock comes over the men, including Sura, as they see what they did not expect. Resting silently on the table beside them, a young man in his late teens lies lifeless with his abdomen split open and Catiline's gladius laying on his chest, stained in blood. In the silence, a low maddening chuckle fills the room. The men turn and see Catiline, who is rocking in his chair, playing with a stylus in his right hand. Rising from his seat and still laughing to himself, he walks over to the body, takes the gladius, cuts a portion of the boy's intestine out, and lays it on a plate over a candle, where it begins to sizzle and fill the room with a putrid odor.

"As of a few moments ago, you are all now guilty of this boy's murder. You are present in the room where it took place, and due to the lack of lighting you didn't notice his blood all over the floor—which by now is on your robes and your shoes," Catiline states, watching the entrails cook and cutting them in bite-size pieces. As the men look on in horror, Catiline takes his gladius and makes a new incision on the body, drawing fresh blood into a cup. He then cuts the palm of his left hand, squeezes his own blood into the cup, and hoists it up in the air.

"We take an oath tonight, gentlemen, to follow each other to death or to glory, whichever comes first. I speak a curse on any one of you who partakes and then reveals our plans. You are then an oath breaker, and therefore needlessly assisted in this boy's murder," he states, allowing his speech to sink in. "In this cup is my blood, mixed with wine sacred to Bacchus, and the blood of this sacrifice to Apollo, who was killed with a sword I stole from the temple of Mars. Each of us will drink of it and each of us will eat of the sacrifice, or else the shades from the underworld will claim you as we speak," he mumbles as the men debate who will be first to partake.

"I will proudly join you in this sacrifice, Lucius," Sura states, stepping forward and eating and drinking with Catiline, who welcomes his friend with an embrace and a smile. One by one the men step forward, take their due, and consecrate themselves to Lucius Catiline, kissing his cheek.

"I am proud of you tonight, men. Nothing could prove to me more that I chose the right men then what we have shared tonight. We have worshiped the gods of Rome in the most sacred way possible, and it is a beautiful thing," he states. Every man present has mysteriously come under his power, and all are willing to die for him. "Tomorrow, my friends, we are going to the Field of Mars for the elections. If we lose, that is the sign from the gods that we are to strike hard. If I lose, by this time tomorrow Marcus Tullius Cicero will be drowning in his own blood." He takes the cup of blood and wine and swallows every drop, allowing the filthy mixture to run down the sides of his mouth.

Early the next morning the group of conspirators finds themselves awakened from their drunken stupors with their robes soaked in the boy's blood and the sound of flies buzzing over Catiline's sacred offering. In one fluid motion, the whole group jumps from the floor in disgust, and each notice Catiline sitting on his desk, laughing at their realization of what has taken place in that room.

"Good morning, my friends. Are you ready for a day of victory?"

"Our clothes are stained. We cannot leave the house like this!" Lucius Cassius Longinus shouts, holding his robe away from his body and looking at his companions, who all share the same feeling.

"Relax, my little children. I have sent my slaves to your homes with the alibi that you had a meeting last night and would need your togas for the elections this morning. They should be here shortly."

"What about the body? Where is it?" Servius Sulla asks as he steps to the forefront of the group.

"Once again, you need not worry. Last night while you slept, I took the sacrifice and threw it in the hole that was once the Pool of Curius. No one would ever think to look in there—especially for someone who would never be missed," Catiline says, leaping down from his desk and walking among them.

"What have we done?" Lucius Bestia asks, looking at his hands, which still bare the crusted remains and putrid odor of blood and cooked entrails.

"What have you done? Why, Senator Bestia, you have sold yourself to Catiline. You belong to me now," Catiline replies as he slowly raises his eyes, looking across the room with a smile. "My slaves are at the door. Change your clothes, meet in your predetermined groups, and go to the Field of Mars. Once there, wait for my signal, should I lose, to kill Marcus Cicero," he continues as each of the men make their way from the room, change their clothes, and proceed to the elections, ready to serve their new master.

It is a bright summer day in the Field of Mars as candidates, senators, and common citizens gather for an exciting election two days before the nones of June. The madness is gone from Catiline's face, and a politician's smile has taken its place as he meets the public, embracing some and waving to others before he takes his place among Cicero and Hybrida to watch the elections in plain view of the senators, who are monitoring for fraud and bribery. Out of Cicero's view, Catiline's followers position themselves behind the candidates while others come close so that once the signal is given they can easily join the action. If Catiline should for some reason lose the election, he will stand and shout that he is taking the consulship and then will thrust Cicero out of his chair. Gaius Cethegus is to have the pleasure of the first blow to his body. It is a day that Cethegus has waited for ever since Cicero embarrassed him and caused the loss of his job. He has consecrated his sword and cannot wait to hear the man cry out as the blood runs from his body.

For the space of three hours, the candidates wait as the citizens cast their ballots and watch as the censors come forward to tally the votes and eventually proclaim a winner. A smile comes over the face of Catiline as he is certain in his victory, but he cannot decide which victory will give him more pleasure: will it be losing and watching Cicero die or winning and watching his disbelief? Either way, he daydreams for a moment or two and then unconsciously lets out a chuckle, which catches Cicero's attention.

"What is so funny, Catiline? Or do I dare ask what you have up your sleeve?"

"I was just thinking about how much I shall enjoy being consul," he replies with a sarcastic smile.

"It's nice to see that you're so positive, but what makes you think that if you win I would not be your partner? Not only that, but the Senate would make me the senior consul because I have more political acumen. You have not even tried your first case," Cicero states, easily wiping the smile from Catiline's arrogant face.

"You had better hope you lose, Cicero, because if I lose, you die," Catiline replies as he leans close to his enemy and carefully whispers his threat, bringing a smile instead of fear to Cicero's face.

"I have thirty-five bodyguards surrounding this platform to protect me. How many do you have? I have only counted about sixteen. Surely you have more than that?" Cicero replies as Catiline leans back in his seat, visibly fuming but staring straight ahead. "You do have more than sixteen, don't you, Lucius?"

"You have the upper hand this time, but I will have another chance." Catiline rises from his seat, bows slightly to Cicero, and then shakes his head in the direction of Cethegus. "I am going to my home to await word of the elections. Have a pleasant day, Marcus, and you as well, Hybrida." Making his way past his fellow candidates, he walks down the steps of the platform and proceeds to leave the Field of Mars. He is quickly joined by a furious Cethegus.

"I thought we were going to do this!" Cethegus whispers impatiently in Catiline's ear.

"If you question my judgment again, I will take your sword and gut you myself," Catiline replies, pulling his own small dagger and carefully sticking it to Cethegus's side so as not to be seen. "Cicero has so many guards here it is impossible to get to him. It will be a lost cause."

"I want to kill him, Lucius, and I want him today!" he grumbles as the group walks off the election grounds where they can speak more freely.

Catiline turns to Cethegus. "Did you see those two women conversing with him while we sat up there?

"Yes, what of them?"

"That is his wife, Terentia, and his sister-in-law, Pomponia. They will surely walk him home today and when they do, kill them too if you need to—or if you just feel like it," Catiline sarcastically replies as he turns home for what is sure to be an afternoon of anticipation and nervousness. He has allowed his enemy to believe that he has won and for the time being will bide his time planning and scheming—capable of murder and on the brink of madness.

# 7

## *Julius Caesar Sends a Message*

### January to June 63 BC

The news came rather quickly to Catiline, and Cethegus unfortunately had to be the bearer of the news that would surely drive Catiline mad as if he wasn't already. Within an hour of his leaving the Field of Mars, the censors had announced that Marcus Cicero and Gaius Antonius Hybrida had been elected consuls for the following year. Not only that, but, acting on orders from their leader, Cethegus and Gaius Manlius followed Cicero and his female companions, only to find that it had been a trap laid by Cicero. The two ladies were male bodyguards, armed and ready for the attack. As a mark of evidence against them, one of the bodyguards, Publius Clodius Pulcher, a reckless noble that Cicero had taken under his wing to mentor, had swung his sword and cut Manlius across his face. As a result, Catiline had sent him away once again to Faesulae to the troops he had gathered, but this time for good, as his scar would be evidence of the plot Cicero had said was coming.

For the next six months, Catiline retreats to his home and basks in the support of the filth of Rome as he and his followers continuously fill the small office, offering plans, suggestions, and murderous schemes to get Catiline into the ultimate office of government. Time after time, the common denominator is Marcus Cicero; something must be done about this meddling consul-elect before something disastrous happens to Catiline and his plans. Just before dawn on the last day of December, the group meets once more, knowing that the next day will be filled with celebrations and sacrifices as the new consuls are consecrated and the Senate opens for a new year of business.

"I have a suggestion, if I may," Publius Servilius Rullus, the tribune-elect for the next year states. He is the new man in the conspiracy, yet holds much power for a young noble. "Pompey's troops are most likely coming back within the year, and I have been given the task to find a way to accommodate them with land once they return," he continues, pulling several sheets of paper from his robe and handing them to Catiline. "My idea, should you approve, is to put the idea forward for a commission of ten to gather land with the state's money for the purpose of settling the troops."

Senator Quintus Annius offers, "There is but one problem. When Pompey returns and finds out about our plot, we will be dead." Others in the room nod in agreement.

Rullus continues, "Yes, but the quicker we can get this through the Senate and the quicker we can get Catiline and Hybrida, who is supportive of us, on the commission, the quicker Master Lucius can control the land surrounding us, thus keeping Pompey at bay by not having any land to settle on, and giving Catiline unrestricted access to the treasury." A smile settles on Catiline's face.

As he lays the paper down and begins reasoning with his followers, Catiline exclaims, "This is how we all need to be thinking, gentlemen. The gods have placed each of us in positions for a reason, and that reason is what we are doing now. Use your power and influence to bring this commission to fruition in the Senate. Get everyone you can to support it."

Rullus replies, "I will bring this to the Senate tomorrow morning when we meet for the first time in the new year." With their way lit only by a few torches, the various conspirators make their way home, anxiously awaiting what will transpire the next day in the Senate. Upon returning to his home, Quintus Curius notices that most of the lights are extinguished, which is unusual as his female companion Fulvia normally stays up late. Upon entering, he notices slaves hurrying in every direction and then freezing upon seeing him.

"What in the name of the gods is going on here? Are my slaves robbing me while I am away from my home?" he asks angrily as the eldest of them walks toward him, trying to abate his anger.

"It was Mistress Fulvia. She told us to gather her things and—"

"Where is she?" he asks, to which the slave merely points. Curius walks into the room where she is. "What do you think you are doing?"

"I am leaving," she states as she tells a young slave girl what to pack. "I am tired of living like this with you. When I first came here, you gave me everything, but for the past few months you have done nothing but spend time with your friends, and have bankrupted yourself along with them. I can have a better life back with my husband who, by the way, would kill you if he ever knew I was with you," she continues, pausing long enough to chastise him before going back to ordering her slave.

"Leave us," Curius orders the young girl and shoves her out the door, slamming it behind her. Turning around in one fluid motion, he slaps Fulvia, knocking her to the floor. "The only one in this room who will be doing any dying is you if you think you are going to walk out that door!" he shouts, pulling his dagger from under his toga and holding it to her face. "I have been spending so much time away from you because I have a deal in the works that will allow me to treat you as the lady you should be treated as, without any worry of your beloved husband!"

"What do you mean?" she asks, holding her hand to her mouth, which is red and swollen from his attack.

"I mean that Lucius Catiline and several others are plotting to take over the government and make him consul. Once he is there, he will have a proscription of the rich, and as one of his partners we will share in his glory!" he states, helping her up and looking lovingly in her eyes. "I know I have not always been there for you, and at times I have lost my temper, but it is because I am trying to give you the best."

"So does this mean Cicero will finally die?" she asks with a smile.

"Yes, Gaius Cethegus has been given that privilege."

"I will stay, my love, but on one condition," she states as she walks to a desk and pulls out a sword. "This was my father's gladius. Give it to Cethegus and ask him to use it to kill that old fool."

"My pleasure," he replies, as they once again embrace. She leans over and blows out the lamp, thus allowing the two to make up for months of neglect.

Across town a very different situation is taking place as Cicero has summoned his partner in the consulship to his home for a late meeting before their consecration in the morning. Looking worn from a day of early celebration and preparation, Hybrida is escorted into Cicero's home by Cicero's slaves, handed a drink, and helped to a chair as Cicero sits quietly and pens a letter to his friend Atticus.

"I understand that you wanted to see me, Cicero. Intending on exercising your privilege as senior consul before we formally take office?" Hybrida asks, watching Cicero lay his stylus aside.

"Nothing of the sort. I had promised a dear friend that I would write him tonight, and I feel that I'm bound to that promise. Besides this is business I am sure you will approve of it."

"Well then, say on."

"I want to exchange provinces with you, Gaius. I will gladly take Gaul and allow you to have the more profitable Macedonia to recoup your financial losses in the election," Cicero remarks, leaning back in his seat and accepting a cup from his slave.

"Why the sudden act of kindness? After that speech of yours, there must be some sort of catch to all of this," Hybrida remarks, setting his cup down and looking Cicero in the eye.

"I know that you are supporting Lucius Catiline in what he is doing."

"If this wasn't in my favor, I would say you were trying to blackmail me, Cicero."

"I am a politician, Hybrida, but I am not Crassus. What I want from you is for you to cease your support of Catiline and to allow me to have the reigning hand in our consulship in exchange for Macedonia," Cicero replies, rising from his seat and pacing about the room.

"What if I refuse?" Hybrida asks, also rising and walking toward Cicero.

"Then you are an idiot and a discredit to your clan. Your ancestor the great orator would be ashamed of you if he knew you supported Catiline and what he is trying to do," Cicero sharply replies, turning instantly and facing Hybrida.

"Who said I am supporting him?"

"If you are not supporting him, why wait until now to deny it? A simple yes or no will suffice for an answer, Hybrida," Cicero remarks, turning his back to Hybrida and staring out the window toward the city.

"I accept your offer, but let's keep this support thing our little secret."

"Of course. Now tell me what you know of Catiline's plans," Cicero asks as the two delve into a conversation that will last long into the night.

The next morning a familiar scene fills the Forum as the new consuls, accompanied by senators and other newly elected officials, leave the Senate and make their way to the Temple of Jupiter Optimus Maximus to be consecrated for the new year. On Cicero's request, they immediately return to the Senate to begin working for the people, as there is a backlog of proposals and bills to debate. Lictors guard the two consuls as they make their way back into the Senate house, only to be stopped by Lucius Catiline and Gaius Julius Caesar, who promptly extends a hand of friendship to Cicero and warmly congratulates him on his victory. Catiline also asks to be considered for elections in the next year, which Cicero will preside over. With the greeting warmly returned and candidacy accepted, Cicero and Hybrida proceed into the Senate house, take their places in the speaker's area, and surround Catulus, the president of the Senate, as he is seated there.

"It is time for the Senate to come to order gentlemen," Quintus Lutatius Catulus calmly states as he sprinkles incense on the burner before the statue of Victory. "We have several articles to cover this day, and, if we can move quickly through them, we might get out of here by tomorrow morning," he continues with a smile, followed by scattered laughter in the house as late arrivals begin to take their places in the hall.

Gaius Antonius Hybrida remarks, "The first motion for the Senate to consider is allotment of land to the troops of Pompey upon his return. He states in his letter to the consuls that the war is going as he hoped and that he will be home within a year and will need land for his army once disbanded." Caesar and Crassus both share a silent comment and then a sneer.

"Pompey is a rich man. Let him provide land for his troops, or better yet let him stay where he is and take that land he has conquered!" Crassus shouts, amid the occasional boos of other senators.

Much to Cicero's surprise, Catiline stands and offers, "As a veteran myself, I know what these men have been through. As their advisory body, we need to accommodate them as best we can." Crassus cuts Catiline a hard look over his shoulder.

Publius Servilius Rullus, one of four tribunes, stands and offers, "I make a motion that the Senate allow for elections of a body of ten able men to buy Italian land to redistribute to those needing land, as well as to Pompey's troops. Furthermore, I recommend Lucius Catiline and Gaius Antonius Hybrida to be among those ten as candidates," he continues, drawing sneers from all across the house.

Cato stands and faces Cicero. "Sounds like the old money bag is behind this one again, Fathers of the Senate! We don't need another commission. The Senate can make its own decisions!" he shouts to the approval of the hardliners who surround him.

Titus Ampius Balbus, another tribune, offers, "I stand in support of this proposal. It is the only fair option to the Senate and the troops." He too stands briefly and is shouted down.

Cicero stands up. "Senators, may I be allowed to speak merely as a senator and not as a consul, though this is my first day of service to you? Why do a majority of you sit silent on this matter? Can you not see exactly what this is? It is nothing more than a plot by a select few who have consolidated their power and are aiming at even more!" Cicero proclaims, drawing the attention of the house, especially Crassus's section. "Three of the four tribunes have voted in support of this bill so where is the forth? In the pocket of those who are pushing its passage? I am not accusing him of misuse of power, but in the name of the gods I ask that he step forward and veto this bill that is not in the interest of the republic or its people!

"There was a time in our history when a rich man bought large quantities of grain and sold it during a famine at a cheap price. He was killed in our streets for being suspected of aiming for regal power. Is this not what is happening today? The only difference is that we are debating land and not grain! Senators, arise to your duty! Tribune, serve your people and your Senate! I have read this proposed law, though it is more of a hijacking, and its implications are disastrous. Imagine enjoying your villa when Rullus and his men walk up and inform you that it has been sold for the good of Rome! Rullus, you are a devil in a senator's clothing, and if I had my way I would have you thrown out this instant!" Cicero shouts, exciting the group and creating righteous indignation on both sides of the aisle.

Caesar stands and notes, "Cicero is afraid to lose his Tusculam villa. We need land reform, but it seems this Senate always finds a way to shut it down. Why is that?" People from the other side hiss and boo.

Lucius Volcacius Tullus stands and declares, "The land that our ancestors gave us is just that. No commission should have the right to sell it as they wish!" Caesar and Crassus share a chuckle.

As he makes his notes and looks up briefly for an answer, Quintus Lutatius Catulus calmly asks, "The arguments are abundant. What is the opinion of the Senate on the passage of this proposal?"

Tribune Lucius Caecilius Rufus offers, "Honorable Catulus, I wish to enact my power of veto of this bill and move for land allotment consideration to be made nearer to Pompey's return," as his three counterparts and Catiline's party mumble in disagreement but are forced to accept defeat by a tribune's veto.

"So ordered. A message will be sent to General Pompey. With that, we move on to the next order of business, a bill proposed by Lucius Caecilius in regards to Publius Cornelius Sulla," Catulus replies, passing the Senate's decision onto the scribe to be recorded in the cities records.

"Catulus, might I have permission to read a letter I received in regards to this proposal before debate begins?" Quintus Caecilius Metellus Celer rises briefly from his seat to offer his statement.

"Say on."

"Fathers of the Senate, I received this letter and feel it says what I have been asked to say better than I could say it."

---

P. Cornelius Sulla to the Senate of Rome:

I was made aware recently that my half brother, Lucius Caecilius, had written a bill hoping to alleviate the shame that I had recently suffered after having rightly had the Consulship taken from me for mistakes I made in my campaign. I willingly made those mistakes and have paid for them, but I was unaware that he proposing a law with my interests at heart. I have asked that this law be taken off the record, that no debate be made for it, and that it be treated as if it were never proposed.

Fathers, I hope to one day earn your trust, and as I pen this at my home in Naples that is all I am concerned with, along with the fact that I brought shame to the traditions and holy elections of our land. Please do not count his good intentions against my brother, as they were not a means of subverting our laws.

Your servant,
Publius Cornelius Sulla

Catulus replies, "So ordered. The Caecilian law is to be stricken from the record as if it never existed." Cicero steps forward, while Caecilius makes his way back to his seat amid applause for Sulla's sentiment.

"I would like the Senate's approval on a decision that I and Consul Autronius have made together," he states; his characteristically strong voice gaining attention in the house. "We have decided to exchange provinces that the Senate years ago voted to assign to the consuls of this year in which we are serving. With the Senate's approval, I wish to give my partner the more lucrative Macedonian province and take Gaul for myself. I am also toying with the idea of renouncing it all together, with the Senate's permission," he continues as members mumble among each other.

"Macedonia is a lucrative province, and in the hands of the Consul Hybrida extortion will run rampant. I vote that we deny the request," an aged senator calls out from the front row.

"Yes, but Gaul needs a man like Cicero to bring the tribes into submission to Roman power," Licinius Murena offers, standing among the newly elected young nobles.

"With the proper army even I could bring Gaul into submission!" Julius Caesar shouts much to the distaste of the hardliners.

"This is obviously a gesture of kindness and humility on the part of Cicero, and I vote that we let it be done," Cato remarks without even rising.

"Cato has spoken, let the Senate react. Is that how it is?" Crassus sarcastically shouts as he throws his hands in the air. "Senators, this decision must not be taken lightly. We must not act simply because the philosopher thinks it's the right thing to do."

"Sit down, Crassus. If your speech was as good as your money, the Senate might listen to you," Cato fires back as Cicero chuckles and Crassus takes his seat, visibly upset. Cato continues, "Fathers, as I recall it is the consuls' decision to do what they like with the provinces that they are given. Am I not correct? I believe that I speak for most everyone here when I say whatever the consuls deem necessary, then let that be done."

"So ordered. Without any objection it is decided that the consuls be allowed to exchange provinces at their own discretion," Catulus replies, shuffling through papers and endeavoring to keep a good pace in the Senate.

"It seems our friend Catiline is quite consumed with this run of bad luck this morning, Crassus," Caesar whispers to Crassus, who nods in agreement "I think I need to make the announcement today, don't you think?"

As the Senate goes about its business, unaware that plans of retribution are being plotted while it debates, Crassus replies, "If Catiline is planning like his face says he is, then he will force the Senate to invoke the ultimate decree. If you think your plan will work, then we must do what we can to protect him without getting involved."

"A word, Master Catulus," Caesar exclaims, interrupting the proceedings of the Senate and drawing looks from across the house.

"Once we are finished with the current business, you may have the floor but not until then, young Gaius," Catulus remarks coldly.

"Very well, but let the Senate think on this while I wait. I am announcing my intention along with Titus Labienus to indict Senator Gaius Rabirius on the ancient charge of treachery for the murder of Saturninus," he calmly remarks as he takes his seat and waits as the atmosphere of the Senate turns into a virtual riot.

"That was almost forty years ago! You were barely old enough to remember it! How can you sit here and call yourself a member of this body if you use its laws against another member?" Gaius Rabirius, now in his seventies, slowly stands, but with a strong voice denounces Caesar before the assembly.

Cato shouts, "The Senate is being high jacked today, one way or another. If the opposing party cannot get their way, it is obvious they will do whatever they need to do even if that means trickery!" Cato stands, pointing his finger in the direction of Caesar and Crassus.

"Call it what you like, but come next week Rabirius will be before a jury, and I am certain he will be condemned," Caesar replies as senators across the house endeavor to shout him down. "Come, gentlemen, we have business to tend to and a prosecution to gather," he continues as he and several others, including

Catiline and his party, Rullus, and Crassus, all stand and begin exiting the Senate House.

"The Senate has not concluded its business, Gaius Caesar." Catulus rises amid the fury of the hardliners.

"The Senate is underworked and overpaid. I am sure they can make it without us today," Caesar responds as the crew makes their way out the doors and disperses in the street.

"Rullus, come here for a moment, would you?" Catiline calls out as the tribune meets with two of his partners, exchanging papers and thoughts.

"I'm sorry for what took place in there. You know how the Senate and the Optimates can—"

"You failed me, you idiot. No one fails Lucius Catiline, do you understand that?" Catiline mumbles as he and Lucius Cassius Longinus, Servius Sulla, and Lucius Vargunteius pull Rullus to a side street and surround him. "I assigned it to you to drum up support for your bill so that it wouldn't fail. You allowed it to fall into Cicero's hands. That was the last place it needed to be."

"But I don't know how Cicero got it. I just wrote it out the other night before you saw it!"

"Then there are two options: you penned it with Cicero to make me look like a fool or you are a traitor."

"Catiline kills traitors, Tribune," Servius Sulla coldly replies, drawing fear from the face of Rullus.

"I'm telling you I don't know what happened!"

"That is what I will tell the Senate when they investigate what happened to you," Catiline remarks as Vargunteius and Longinus take Rullus by the arms and restrain him. "Throw him in front of a chariot, but do it quickly so you are not seen," he continues as he walks away from the struggling trio, seeing Caesar and Crassus nearby and trying to catch up to them.

"Don't look now, but I believe our friend wants to see us," Caesar sarcastically remarks to Crassus as the duo walks toward the Temple of Saturn.

"I know he does. I asked him before we left the Senate to meet me at my home. I want to know what he is up to," Crassus replies as Catiline runs up to meet them.

"You still wish to see me, Crassus?"

"Yes. Come with me to my home. I want to talk with you about some things, as does Caesar."

"Is that so? Well what do you want to know?" Catiline replies, stopping in front of the Temple of Saturn and taking advantage of the lack of spectators.

"I want to know what you are up to and when it is going to happen."

"Lucius, Crassus and I are concerned that you are treading on dangerous ground. We are asking that you exercise caution and think of the damage whatever you are planning would do to the party," Caesar states as Catiline fights back the urge to strangle both of them.

"My friends, I assure you that all I am doing is planning on winning next year's consulship," is the reply that comes from the characteristically charismatic individual.

"Word is that you want to kill Cicero." Crassus comes directly to the point as Catiline glances around for eavesdroppers.

"I want that fool's head on a platter. What is wrong with that?" he angrily grumbles, changing before their eyes. "I and my men have resolved that if I cannot become consul by votes then I will take it by sword."

"Lucius, that is suicide. There is no way it can work," Caesar remarks as Catiline begins to chuckle.

"My dear Caesar, you have no idea. I have told both of you enough. I will do my best to win with honor, but if I cannot then people will die—with Cicero being the first and you two second and third if you reveal any of this," Catiline continues, his eyes wildly darting between the two showing minute by minute the madness that has consumed him.

"Catiline, we would never turn you over. As a matter of fact, what you just witnessed in the Senate was on your behalf." Caesar's statement draws a confused look from Catiline. "The Senate will try to invoke the ultimate decree against anything you do. If we can dismantle that through Rabirius's trial, then that equals protection for you."

"Just warn me before you do anything drastic. Can you at least do me that much?" Crassus remarks as Catiline regains his composure.

"Of course. Anything for my two best friends who brought me where I am today. Now, if you will excuse me, I have some business to attend to. Have a good day, gentlemen," he continues, leaving the two men to their schemes.

"He is mad, Crassus. I don't recall ever seeing someone that crazed for power before."

"No, but just think of the possibilities of what he is doing. If he fails I will seal the power vacuum as dictator and make you my master of horse. If he succeeds, we will pull the strings of the Senate to make us dictator and master of horse to take him down. Either way, we can win and be a force for Pompey to reckon with when he returns," Crassus remarks as the two continue their walk through the Forum.

A night and a day are uneasily passed by the aging Rabirius, who now, after the previous day's events, feels even older than he did before. Rising from his bed, the old statesman greets his slaves tenderly by name, as he has known and loved many of them like family. He makes his way to the atrium, where breakfast is ready, amid a fountain with bathing birds and a beautiful view of the Roman countryside. "Marcius, I will miss this all terribly very soon. I hope the afterlife is something like this villa, so I will not hate to be there," Rabirius solemnly states as he eats his single egg and nibbles a warm biscuit.

"Master, you shouldn't talk like that. I am sure that men know you well enough to know that you are not guilty and will do what they can to dismiss these charges," Marcius replies, pouring a small cup of wine for Rabirius bringing a thankful look to the old man's face.

"Yes, don't talk that way, or else I shall have a terrible time trying to defend you!" Cicero joyfully remarks as he enters the atrium, walking to Rabirius and embracing him. "A group of us got to together, and they decided to ask me to defend you, which I gladly accepted."

"Marcus, we will not win, and you know that we won't. Caesar is becoming the Populare party's front man, taking Crassus's place. There is no way we can get past this one," Rabirius replies as he gazes out over his farm. "I hear that Caesar has already ordered a beam to be set in the ground for my cross to hang from."

"We are going to win, Gaius. We will not allow Caesar to take the day, nor will we let Titus Labienus make a name for himself at your expense."

"Do you know the punishment for this charge, Cicero? First they will scourge me and then they will crucify me. At my age those nails will tear through my skin like my teeth through this biscuit, not to mention what the flagellation will do." Rabirius wipes a tear from his eye as he tries to choke down his breakfast. His slave Marcius leaves the room, unable to see his master like this.

"Listen to me! We are going to win, but you are going to have to want to win. Men like Caesar must be fought, or else he will crucify us all one day if we don't," Cicero exclaims, grabbing Rabirius by the arm. "I just wanted to stop by to let you know the news. I will be back in three days to pick you up for the trial. We will ride with my lictors and give Caesar the spectacle that he didn't want!" he continues as the two embrace once more. Cicero makes his way home.

After the long trek into the country to Rabirius's rustic villa, Cicero finds himself back home just as the Italian sun begins to set, ready to greet his slaves and relax after an eventful day. His wife and children are away on vacation, and he works. Startled by lights inside his home, he sends four of his twelve lictors inside to investigate. They bring what appears to be a woman out of the house who occasionally struggles to get free then calmly walks with them before struggling again. Interested at the peculiar sight, Cicero steps from his litter against the lictors' suggestion and walks towards the lady, who pleads for an audience with the consul.

"Well, you have the consul. Now what do you want with him?" he replies as the lictors release her.

"My name is Fulvia. I am the mistress of Quintus Curius."

"Yes. He was removed from the Senate a while ago on immorality charges. What is that to me? I certainly will not do anything to reinstate him, if that is what you want of me."

"Curius is one of Catiline's followers," she states solemnly, gaining Cicero's undivided attention. "Catiline is planning on murdering you at the next election if he does not win, and this time he has the men to do it. Many more than the sixteen you saw at the last election."

"How did you know that?" Cicero asks, still unsure of whether to trust her but knowing that comment was only shared between himself and Catiline.

"That is what Catiline told the others that you said to him before he got up and left the platform."

"Come inside with me and my lictors. We definitely need to talk," he replies as they walk into the house. As they enter the house, the sight of Philologus warms Cicero's heart, as he is a reminder of the peace and safety that Catiline and his men threaten to destroy. "Now tell me what you know," he continues as the pair sits on a couch in part of the home where the slaves have been tending a fire for their master.

"All I know right now is that I was fed up with how much time Quintus had been spending with Catiline and how that he had virtually bankrupted himself when he came home a couple nights ago and caught me leaving him," she states.

"Tell me what happened next."

"Well, he told the slave girl to leave the room, and when she didn't move fast enough he shoved her out, slammed the door, and struck me, as you can see, knocking me down," she replies, pointing to the slight bruise on her face.

"How did the conversation go from there?"

"That was when he told me they had plans to murder you and that's why he hadn't been home much—because of the planning sessions. He went on to say how they had consecrated themselves to Catiline by killing a young boy and drinking a cup of his blood mixed with wine and Catiline's blood, as well as eating a portion of his entrails."

"Did he mention who was there?"

"No, he didn't. Just that Gaius Cethegus was the one who had the privilege of killing you when the time came," she continues as Cicero hangs his head in thought. "It was then that I gave him my father's sword and told him I would stay as long as Cethegus used it to kill you. I felt it was the only way to earn his trust at the time."

"Understandable; you are a brave and remarkable woman to be bringing this to me as you are in the snakes' pit as well as I am."

"After that he began kissing me, as if Catiline's perverse passions had gripped him to the point of arousal! Can you imagine what it was like having to make love with someone who was daring to do all of the things he had said, let alone the fact that he ate another human?" She pounds on the table, startling the lictors.

"No, my dear, I cannot imagine that. The republic is in a great debt to you, and I will see to it that you get the entire honor you are due when this is over."

For three hours the two continue to talk, as Fulvia tells Cicero everything that she can possibly remember for Cicero to take to the Senate. The two agree on a system of alerts to keep the consul up-to-date on the happenings at Catiline's house, hopefully turning Quintus Curius into an informant. With night now heavily upon the city, she carefully makes her way out of the consul's house and down the road to her own home, where her husband thinks she has been away on a trip, not in adultery with Quintus Curius.

Over the next couple days, light is rarely seen in the home of Lucius Catiline, as he has become infatuated with darkness; some even wonder if he thinks it can hide his murderous plots. Day after day he goes without eating and leaves his office rarely, entertaining only his followers, and mostly sitting in freezing cold conditions through the night, honing his body for extreme sacrifice. Following his example, his men begin to conduct themselves in strange manners, often alerting their families that something is afoot without saying a word.

It is a bright Friday morning as lictors shout to make way for the consul of Rome as Cicero and Gaius Rabirius make their way to the trial that Caesar hopes will not only protect Catiline but also disarm the Senate. Finally coming to a halt, the lictors pull the curtains as Cicero emerges and waves to those gathered to see him. Rabirius follows him, while members of the prosecution stand by, staring in contempt at the solidarity Cicero and Rabirius are showing.

"Look at them, prancing in here like he has been awarded a triumph, and that old mule Rabirius is playing right along with him!" Labienius crudely remarks as Caesar, Crassus, Catiline, and Sura look on.

"Yes, I can't wait to see the look on the old man's face when the jury passes down the guilty plea, thanks to Crassus," Caesar says as Crassus throws his arm over his shoulder.

"Don't forget the funds of Lucius Catiline and his followers. We lobbied hard to get that together for you," Catiline states, looking over his shoulder at Caesar and earning a nod of thanks from him.

In his usual fashion Cicero boldly escorts Rabirius into the courtroom directly in front of the group of antagonists, brushing them as he passes with no fear of their reprisal toward him. "Come, gentlemen, don't lag behind. I have a trial to win," Cicero comments, enraging Labienius, whom Caesar holds back as they all turn to enter.

"Just remember," Caesar comments to Labienius, "we are here to shut down the power of the Senate—not take on Cicero. There will be plenty of time for that later. Right now let's focus on crucifying that old fool Rabirius."

Finding their seats, Cicero familiarizes himself with the settings as he gazes toward the jury box and recognizes men who are patrons of Crassus. A sinking, sorrowful feeling comes over him, which he tries to hide from Rabirius.

"We are going to win, are we, Marcus?" Rabirius asks as Cicero stares at the jury. He fumbles for an answer.

"I will give it my best, my friend. I promise you."

"Don't bother, Marcus, because I'm going to die today. I know those Roman knights on the jury are friends of Crassus," he replies, causing Cicero to turn away. He knows that his task has now become harder—if not impossible—to win. Deep down, they both know that the trial is fixed; it is common knowledge that Rabirius isn't guilty. But the feeling is cemented even more when they see Caesar, who presides over the court as an elected aedile, walk to the judge's platform to observe the case, along with his half brother Lucius Caesar. As the custom is, the two judges take their seats, and at the wave of Caesar's hand the crowd is seated. Caesar begins to read the case against Rabirius.

"Gaius Rabirius, you have been indicted on the charge of disturbing the peace known as *per duello* by this court, with Titus Labienius prosecuting you and Marcus Cicero defending. Is there anything you wish to say before we begin?" Caesar remarks, shuffling papers aimlessly and trying to avoid eye contact with Rabirius or Cicero.

"I did nothing of the sort. This trial is fixed as a means of political leverage for a crime that the evidence will show I didn't commit," Rabirius remarks as Cicero smiles at Caesar, who, surprised by the remarks, glances up, unsure what to say.

"Cicero has graciously allowed the tribune Titus Labienius to begin this trial, if you would step forward with your speech," Lucius Caesar states, bringing a confident smirk to Labienius's face as he begins.

"It is the events of almost forty years ago that bring us to this place, men of the jury and citizens of Rome. Saturninus had blockaded himself in the Capitol and was prepared to fight his way out with his followers—until their water supply was cut," Labienius states, pacing the floor and casting glances across the room. "Gaius Marius had broken his deal with him and forced him out, under the provision of safe keeping in the Senate house, much to the dismay of the Senate, who declared him a public enemy. This, however, was not enough for the defendant. The evidence listed before you shows that Gaius Rabirius, then a young man, climbed on top of the building, ripped off the roof tiles, and struck all the men inside until they were dead. I ask you, is this any way for a Roman citizen of noble birth to perform?" He continues, drawing sighs from the crowd and looks of disgust from Cicero.

"It goes beyond this for me, as well as for some of you in this courtroom. My uncle was among those brutally killed in this attack, which finds its shelter and authority in the unconstitutional decree that the Senate refers to as the ultimate decree. 'The consuls are to see to it that the republic comes to no harm.' What harm was there in a handful of men speaking against the Senate? The harm was that the Senate thought their power might be hindered; therefore they declared the men public enemies and made provision for them to be killed by this heartless man, who robbed my cousins of their beloved father and robbed Rome of two great men. There is but one recourse of action to be taken here today: convict Rabirius of murder and let him suffer the consequences," he continues, as he takes his seat in a calm, collected manner, despite how active he was on the floor. "I spoke for only a few minutes, and as tribune I declare Cicero the maximum of half an hour to defend his case," he states, glancing at Cicero, who is expecting the move.

"The right of the tribune to restrict the allotted time as based on Roman law is recognized and so ordered," Caesar states as Rabirius hangs his head in frustration. Cicero clears his throat, rising to make his speech.

"Men of the jury and honored judges, I feel that it is my duty as well as an honor to stand here and defend my friend, Gaius Rabirius," Cicero declares as he walks the floor, turning and addressing the crowd. "You see before you a new man in the Senate, a man with humble upbringing who is about to make an impassioned plea to let justice be done unto another man of humble and gentle nature. I have known Gaius Rabirius for many years. He has always been my friend, and a friend of the republic and its people. The charges brought today are an undercut by a select few to hide their own crimes by persecuting and prosecuting another.

"What they are proposing is that this friend of mine that you see here, well advanced in years, is to be scoured and crucified according to our ancestors, but I beg you today to spare him from the humiliation of being led naked and shameful to a most disgusting death," he continues, turning and facing Labienius and directly addressing him with the accusation. "There are men in this house who want nothing better than to destroy all that is good about Rome, namely a good man and the friendship that he shares with those around him. The crime that the prosecution claims he committed happened so many years ago that ample proof cannot be supplied. There is no possible way that my friend can be fairly tried.

"In order that this may be accomplished, the less than honorable tribune has curbed my time, but in my few short comments I plead with you, men of the jury, to find compassion. The radicals have aimed their arsenal at this man in an endeavor to hide another, whose plans to destroy the republic are even now being forged," he continues, thrusting his finger at Labienius, visibly angered.

With a sigh, he walks back to his seat, collecting himself and adjusting his toga. "I have done my best to plead with you for the life of my friend. Men of the jury, please let justice be done. Set an aged man free and allow him to live out his last days free from torment and the suffering of a cross." He takes his seat, and Labienius, Crassus, and Caesar all breathe a sigh of relief that it is over before much real damage could be done to their plans. Leaning together to speak, Lucius and Julius Caesar make comments and write notes, preparing to deliver a verdict when the jury gives their vote.

"Men of the jury, you have heard the case, seen the evidence, and heard the pleading of each side. If you are ready to deliver your verdict, speak and let it be known," Lucius Caesar states while his half brother looks on.

"We declare Gaius Rabirius guilty and order him to be crucified according to the law of our ancestors," an elder among the jury states as Cicero mumbles something unintelligible and Rabirius begins to sob uncontrollably.

"Consul Marcus Tullius Cicero," Labienius states as he faces the two men, "would you kindly ask your lictors to bind your client's hands and take him to his destination?" Dropping his head, Cicero merely motions with his hand, and one of his lictors reluctantly walks to Rabirius, ties his hands together, and leads him out while those on Caesar's side share a moment of victory.

"Cicero, you tried your best. But you know as well as I do that this court was stacked. There was no way that you could have won," Quintus Caecilius Metellus Celer, a friend of Cicero and Rabirius, states, walking up to console Cicero on the loss as people begin to move about the room.

"These robbers are not the only ones with tricks up their sleeves," he states, smiling. "I need you to do me a favor if you want to save Rabirius."

"Anything."

"Run to the Janiculum and pull down the flag. I stationed one of my lictors there to wait for you, knowing this would happen."

"We only do that when enemies approach the city," he replies, confused at his friend's suggestion.

"Correct. Enemies *are* here, and, under our law when the flag comes down, all business ceases, including an execution."

"Understood. Consider it done!" Celer states as he tries to push his way through the crowd.

"Lictors," Cicero shouts, gaining the attention of the court room, and especially Caesar and Crassus, "make a way for this man!" They begin dividing the people, allowing Celer to rush to the Janiculum before it is too late.

"What is he doing Crassus?" Caesar demands, grabbing Crassus by the toga, causing him to answer with a confused shrug.

"That fool is going for the Janiculum! That's all he can do!" Labienius angrily exclaims, throwing his papers from the trial on the floor.

"Maybe so, but at least we got what we wanted: attention to the ultimate decree and the power of the Senate," Caesar notes as the others nod in agreement. "There are other ways of dealing with Rabirius and Cicero."

"You failed me," Catiline remarks as he approaches with his familiar, crazed look on his face. "With all of your power and influence, you have gotten nowhere. Now it is my turn." He rushes from the court room, passing Rabirius as he is brought in by the same lictor who took him off. The two friends embrace and share a moment of joy, rejoicing even more that Caesar and his group got to witness it firsthand. Protection for Catiline by dissolving the power of the Senate and the ultimate decree has failed. Fearing that Catiline is about to force the Senate's hand, Crassus and Caesar both begin to separate themselves from the revolutionary and look for ways to cover the fact that they once stood beside him.

# 8

## *The Final Insult*

### June–July 63 BC

A warm summer breeze sweeps through the Forum on a beautiful ides of June. Acanthus is growing lush in the sunlight, and the fragrance of wine mixed with spices and cooked oxen fill the air as the priests make their sacrifices to the gods. Catiline, Cethegus, and Lentulus take a casual stroll through the Forum, soaking up the sights, waving to voters, and marking for death those who found a place of disgust in their minds. Honorary columns loom overhead as the trio gaze at the Forum. For the first time in a long time, Catiline offers a genuine smile and a sigh of happiness as he gazes at the temples, columns, and statues built by generations long past.

"An equestrian statue of myself will look rather nice over there next to the grove of Marsyas, don't you think, Cethegus?" Catiline asks, gesturing toward a grove of fig tree and vines.

"Master Lucius, when all is said and done, if I were you I would fill the square with your monuments."

"I can't possibly do that. After all, we need a place for monuments to you, gentlemen. Besides, we also will need room for the executions to be carried out," he replies as the trio walks toward the Senate House, where groups are flooding in for the latest meeting. "I should only be a little while," he continues as he joins his fellow senators and enters the building. The hall is bustling with activity as the various senators find their seats. Offering salutations of his own, Catiline makes his way to his seat, bowing to Crassus and greeting Caesar, as Catulus, the president of the Senate, stands to call the meeting to order.

"Fathers of the Senate, this meeting is formally called to order," he declares as he turns and offers incense on the Altar of Victory, allowing the fragrance to fill the room. "The first order of business is to be brought forth by Consul Marcus Cicero."

"Conscript Fathers," Cicero states, walking from behind Catulus, "I wish to bring before us again today the proposal offered by Sulpicius Rufus in regard to bribery and campaign corruption. As you might recall, the provisions of this bill call for ten years of exile and disqualification from office for two years after that. The republic needs a law such as this to protect our foundations."

Marcus Cato stands. "I concur with the consul. Laws against corruption need to be as strong as this body and carry enough weight to ensure corruption will not be a practice in our politics." In the Senate, there are nods and vocal gestures of approval.

"Consul, might I offer a proposal to this law?" Catiline timidly states, rising slowly and standing before the crowd like a schoolboy on his first day.

"Lucius Catiline, candidate for consul who rarely offers anything to our debates, you are most welcome to make a contribution if you so desire," Cicero warmly remarks amid sneers from the conservative side.

"I wish to offer something to this law that is simple, quick, and will guarantee there will no longer be corruption in this house or our elections," he replies, walking to the main speaking area, much to Cicero's surprise.

"Which would be?" the puzzled consul replies.

"That the slaves would lock the doors and a massacre of the Senate be ordered," he exclaims amid gasps of disbelief across the house and a look of amazement from Cicero, who stands four steps from him.

"Have you lost your mind? This is a meeting of the Senate of Rome. We have no time for your silly ideas!" Cicero shouts. Catiline merely smiles.

"This is treason!" Cato shouts. "Consul, arrest that man, he's—" He suddenly stops to the sound of the doors slamming shut and armed slaves standing at the doors.

"Gentlemen, the time has come to purge this body," Catiline boldly declares as his followers stand and begin mercilessly slaughtering the members one by one and tossing their bodies to the main speaker's area. Cicero and Catulus stand in disbelief, too afraid to move but knowing that they must unless they wish to join the pile of bloody bodies. Turning to run, Catulus stops, noticing the blade of Catiline's sword shoved to the hilt into his body. He faces the monster. Catiline smiles, jerks his blade out, and strikes his head, killing the aged senator. Looking over his shoulder, he notices Crassus and Caesar both endeavoring to sneak out. He shouts to his companions to kill both of them and to cut off their heads as trophies for the people.

"What have you done, Catiline?" Cicero asks as he sobs before his enemy.

"I have purged this body of corruption. The republic will take on a new look under my consulship! Which reminds me, you have something that belongs to me!" he shouts, separating Cicero's head from his body and then kicking the bloody carcass out of his way. He and his followers make their way out of the Senate house, as their task has been completed. "People of Rome!" Catiline shouts as the doors open and the crowds stare in amazement at the bloody spectacle. "Lucius Catiline is your consul now. I am your dictator! Starting now there are new proscriptions, and everyone with wealth will die!" he continues, walking down the steps and into the Forum, as people run in panic in every direction.

Bodies continue to fall, and blood covers the pavement as Catiline makes his way to the Rostra to get a better glimpse at what is taking place. A man darts in front of him to avoid his pursuer, and Catiline strikes him down, stepping over his body and smiling at the bloody mess he has created. As he makes his way past the Pool of Curius, something catches his eye. A hand is coming out of the hole, and, as he turns to send his men to look, he hears a tiny voice call his name.

"Father, what's going on?" a pale little girl asks as she stands a few feet in front of him.

"Ser—Sergia? What are you doing here? How did you get here?" he stammers, slowly walking backward as the little girl follows him.

"Mommy said you were going to get yourself into trouble, so she asked me to bring you home. Don't you want to come home, Daddy?" she asks.

"To where? Where is home, Sergia?" he asks, trying to get away but unable to break through the men behind them.

"Down there, Daddy," she replies, pointing to the pool.

"No!" he shouts, turning and trying to run, but his men block his way. He falls to his knees in shock as the faces of his men have become skulls loosely wrapped in decomposed flesh. "What are you doing to me?" he shouts, turning to Sergia, who now holds the bloody head of Cicero. "Where did you get that?"

"I found it, Daddy. Can I keep it?"

"Throw it away! By the gods, what are you doing to me!" he shouts, as the sounds of death fill his ears.

"You are a dead man, Catiline," the bloody head of Cicero mumbles.

Catiline is brought back to reality by once again hearing his name shouted.

"Lucius, I have been calling you. Why didn't you answer me?" Sura asks, irritated at being ignored.

"My apologies. I was merely wrapped in thought," the weary Catiline replies.

"Did you finally get some sleep?"

"Catiline does not sleep, my friend." He hangs his head between his knees as he sits slumped against the wall. "There is much work to be done. Even if I could sleep I don't have the time to do so," he replies.

"You must sleep, Lucius."

"Don't you think I have tried?" he shouts, grabbing Sura by the shirt. "I can't, so I have determined to use it to my advantage. I sit in the cold dark alone, conditioning myself and strengthening my resolve that no one will beat me and no one will out endure me!"

"There is a group of men sent here by Manlius to see you. They are veterans of Sulla," Sura replies, standing and adjusting his clothes.

"Then I suppose I should make myself more presentable," he states, slowly stripping off his dirty tunic. "What have you heard of the early elections for praetor?"

"I won, Lucius. Now I can return to the Senate at your side next year. Gaius Julius Caesar also won the election for *Pontifex Maximus*; you should have seen the look on Catulus's face when he found out he had lost and Caesar had won. He was furious!"

"Nothing but Cicero's death could please me more, but that comes a close second." Catiline chuckles as he dons a fresh tunic and a richly embroidered robe of gold and purple to meet his guests in. "Whenever they are ready, my dear friend, please send them in," he continues as he takes his seat, motioning for his slave to fill his cup. A group of battle-hardened men in their late forties and early fifties, twelve in number, enter and bow their heads to their new commander. "Welcome, my friends. It is good to see that men who were once my comrades in arms long to be again!"

"We understand that you can bring us dignity that the politicians and money lenders have stolen," one of the men, obviously the highest-ranking by his military garments, states with sincerity, trying to discover Catiline's intentions.

"My friend, I not only can, but I promise I will. The money lenders beat on my door as well. Now it is time for Rome to serve us!" he declares, slamming his cup on the table. "What has Manlius told you?"

"He told us of elections, Cicero: murder, plots, proscriptions, and treason."

"In two days, the elections for consul are held in the Field of Mars. You men were judged by Manlius to be the best and bravest from your record of service under Sulla as well as current service under Manlius; you are to serve as my bodyguard. Tomorrow when the time is right, Cicero will die and I will seize the consulship. However, if things do not go as planned, everything is not lost. We will discuss these plans at midnight in this room. Understood?"

"Yes, Master Catiline."

"Excellent. My slaves will lead you to your rooms. If you would like some—company, let my slaves know, and they shall procure the best and most beautiful for you." Catiline rises from his seat and raises his cup to them. "To victory my friends. victory and proscriptions that Sulla himself would be proud of!" The men all nod in agreement. For the remainder of the day and on into the night, the soldiers of Sulla soak up the pleasures of Catiline's home, indulging in drink and the pleasure of prostitutes of both sexes, while Catiline sits silently in his office, seething in his anger and hatred, allowing his mad mind to plot.

As evening comes and the warm sun exchanges its penetrating rays for the cool moonlight, Fulvia makes her way down the streets of Rome concealed by her robe, which is neatly folded over her head, as she makes her way from Cicero's to her lover's. Knowing that it would mean death for Quintus Curius and possibly herself if she is caught, she avoids contact with everyone she passes. She cautiously opens the door to Curius's house. He sits at his favorite table as a female slave massages his shoulders while he reads and drinks.

"Good evening, my love. I'm sorry I'm late. My husband had a change of plans and left later than he was originally supposed to." She enters and removes her cloak before kissing Curius and sitting beside him.

"That's quite all right. I noticed his carriage pass by a few minutes ago, so I figured you would be by soon," he replies, dismissing the slave. "Catiline has brought in twelve of Sulla's veterans as bodyguards for himself and plans on taking out Cicero at the elections two days from now. Everything is proceeding just as he planned, and before long Rome will be a far better place to live." He smiles and pulls her close to him as she tries to look impressed at the news. "I have a meeting at Catiline's tonight, so I cannot stay here with you, but you are most welcome to stay until I get home."

"Well, then that works out. My husband said he might actually be back tonight, so I should probably go home just to be safe."

At that moment, a hard knock at the door startles both of them, unsure of who it might be. A slave casually walks over to open it, but the door is broken down by a group of lictors bearing the rods and axes of the consul.

"Marcus Cicero wishes to see both of you immediately," one of them comments as the group surrounds them and binds their hands. At the lictors' urging, the two make their way under the cover of darkness to Cicero's home, finding it well lit and heavily guarded. As they enter, Cicero sits at a desk, making notes and heavily involved in his work. "Consul, here are the people you wished to see," the lictor states as Cicero looks up.

"Leave us, please," Cicero says to the lictor.

Curius cannot hold back his anger. "What do you mean bringing us here in the middle of the night when—"

"Shut up, Curius. I have no time for your stupid tricks and acts of innocence! You will answer me and tell me what I need to know, or my lictors will persuade you to," Cicero replies, stacking his papers in a pile. "I know that you two are involved with Lucius Catiline. I want to know everything you know about what he's planning, and I want it now."

"I don't know what you are talking about, Consul," Curius replies as he looks away from Cicero.

"You lie, Curius. Unless one of you starts talking, you will spend the night in the Tullanium."

"Tell him, Quintus," Fulvia whispers. "We can't hide it anymore. Cicero knows. We've got to tell him."

"Your mistress is right, Curius. I know all about it. I merely want one of you to assure that I am right."

Curius hangs his head low in shame. "The most recent plans are for you to be killed in the Field of Mars on election day, after Catiline makes his speech," Curius replies. "After that there is to be full massacre of the Senate, and Catiline is to proclaim himself as consul. Our next meeting is tonight—to make sure we all know our roles."

"And what will your role be in all of this?"

"I have been assigned to kill Catulus," he mumbles. "But I wasn't going to. I was going to stay home sick. I could never raise a hand against Catulus!"

"Curius, if you help me expose this I will see to it that no prosecution comes to you. I will do my best to make you into the spy who infiltrated Catiline's home and revealed this plot and helped to save Rome, but you must help me see it through."

"I can use Fulvia here to relay the messages, if she will consent to that," Curius states, as she nods in agreement. The three stand to end their meeting.

"You feed me the information that I need, and I will do what I can to protect and praise you." Cicero begins to lead Curius and Fulvia out the back. Upon leaving the house, the two lovers cover their faces with cloaks they had hastily grabbed before going home and quietly make their way into the street.

"I don't have long before the meeting, so I am going to Catiline's home," Curius states. "I will try to contact you later when I can."

"You are going to help Cicero, aren't you? You're not going to tell Catiline, are you?" she asks, endeavoring to keep her face covered.

"I am going to tell Catiline everything. He probably already knows we were here, so if he thinks I'm hiding anything we both will die without a chance to explain. I am going to correct the mistakes I have already made by doing the right thing and try to stop Catiline. I will contact you later, my love." He quickly turns and walks toward the Forum, his way lit by a few mounted torches. Curius sees the home of Lucius Catiline, a place that has just recently become a place of dread, as he summons his courage and proceeds to either death as a betrayer or eternal life as a savior of Rome. Ghostly figures dance in the windows as the few candles Catiline has permitted light the way for his fellow conspirators to his office. From a distance, these figures seem like spirits of long-dead Romans who once sought power as Catiline does and have returned to empower the madman.

With his cloak pulled over his face, Curius walks up the steps and looks up to see Catiline and Sura talking in the moonlight, sharing a drink and a laugh. Curius sprints up the steps and removes his hood to avoid attack. He faces Catiline, who is smiling.

"You are early, my friend. Would you care for a drink before the others arrive?" Catiline holds his cup toward Curius.

"Lucius, Fulvia and I just came from Cicero's home."

Catiline withdraws his cup. "And?"

"He claims he knows everything and wanted us to tell him what we were involved in. He said that you even told him on the Rostra in the last election that you were going to kill him."

"What did you tell him, you cretin?" He steps away from Curius and Sura and faces the Forum.

"That we were involved in an election campaign and that we had just finished with Sura being elected as praetor. I told him that he must be crazy."

Turning swiftly, Catiline moves as close to Curius as he possibly can, looking him over, trying to glean any possible information. Through gritted teeth, Catiline says, "If you revealed anything to him, I swear I will gut you on his hearthstone!" He grabs Curius by the throat. "What is more, I will ravage and flay your pretty little mistress before your eyes if you are lying to me."

"Master, I owe no allegiance to anyone but you, and that is why I came here straight from Cicero's home. If I am lying and if I have betrayed you and broken our sacrificial oath I will flay her myself so that you don't have to," he replies, struggling to get the words out as Catiline continues to grip his throat. Catiline finally releases him.

"I know you are telling the truth. I was merely checking to see what you would say," Catiline once again withdraws and faces the Forum. "I have been having you followed as I know your tendency to talk. I know that you were taken to the consul by his lictors and that they broke in your door to take you there. Use this insult as your whetstone to see that fool stripped and flogged before all of Rome!"

"Lucius, I would like nothing more than to retake our oath using his blood and entrails."

"When we are finished, there will be plenty of blood to go around!" he joyfully states as he throws his arms around the two men, escorting them into the house. "We have the house to ourselves, gentlemen, as my dear wife didn't seem to care for the hours and company that I have been keeping so I sent her to her family in Naples until I need to recall her once I am consul," he continues. The trio walk into his office. "Gentlemen, if you would light all of the candles to help our other friends find their way," he continues, taking his seat behind his white marble desk as one by one the conspirators enter, commenting on the brightness of the room.

"Lucius, we have been able to secure six locations throughout the city, including my home, to store weapons for when you are ready to use them," Cethegus remarks, striding into the office with a confident look on his face. "Won't the Senate be surprised when they see our little army ready to remake the republic!"

"Excellent news, Cethegus. Sura, are we all accounted for?" Catiline asks as he gazes across the room.

"We are, Lucius."

"Gentlemen, if you are near a candle do be so kind as to extinguish it for me, except for those two by the door. I have something I wish to show you," he states, rising and walking to the front of his desk as the room gets darker to where men can barely make out each others faces. "I have most wonderful news for you, my loyal band of brothers. Gaius Manlius has sent me twelve of his finest soldiers, veterans of Sulla, as bodyguards and extra hands in our endeavors."

"Where are they then? I don't recall ever seeing them." Lucius Cassius Longinus speaks up from the middle of the cramped group.

"I thought you would never ask," Catiline replies, smiling devilishly. "Before you gentlemen arrived, Sura and I as well as our twelve new friends engaged in sacred rites here in the halls of my home, and they willfully consecrated themselves to Dis, the god of the underworld, in the name of our conspiracy. As I have stated before, the gods are behind us in what we are doing."

"So when do we get the privilege of meeting these bodyguards, Lucius?" Lucius Statilius asks, amid murmurs of agreement from others in the room.

"Right now." Catiline says as the candlelight barely illuminates his face but clearly marks the madness that has overtaken him. "Veterans of Sulla, my companions wish to meet those who now belong to the underworld," he states raising his voice as if calling the men from another room. An unnatural fear falls on all present as pairs of illuminated eyes begin to appear in the darkness behind Catiline, until twelve pairs are visible in the darkness. Nearly falling over each other, the conspirators begin to move backward toward the door. Finding it locked, they know that no natural men other than themselves were in the room when they arrived.

"This is witchcraft, Catiline!" Servius Sulla boldly remarks, as Catiline begins to laugh to himself.

"I have told you that the gods back us and have granted powers to us to accomplish great unnatural deeds."

"I assure you, my men and I are very real, Servius Sulla," the leader of the veterans states. As he steps from the darkness, his eyes change to natural appearance as he reveals himself. "Dis has consecrated us, and we belong to him in the name of Catiline."

"How did you know my name?"

"Nothing is hidden to the gods," he remarks. As he turns his back to the group, the illuminated eyes all vanish at once.

"In two days, gentlemen, I shall mount the Rostra and deliver my speech to the people of Rome. When that takes place and I pull my toga away from my breast, our followers will rush the Rostra, kill every senator that is nearby and restrain Cicero. I will proclaim myself as consul and make each of you partners in my administration!"

"All hail the consul of Rome!" Sura shouts, lifting a cup high in the air. Two slaves enter and distribute cups to all of the men, who toast their leader.

The next morning Catiline, Cethegus, and Sura venture to the Forum, surrounded by the veterans of Sulla as bodyguards. greeting voters and courting other politicians making a grand procession for all to see. Honorary columns that line the square loom overhead as the trio stops and gazes at the monument of power that is the Forum and for the first time in a long time Catiline offers a genuine smile and a sigh of happiness as he gazes at the temples, columns, and statues built by generations long since gone. The bustle of politics and daily Roman life sweep around the group of secret revolutionaries.

"An equestrian statue of myself will look rather nice over there next to the grove of Marsyas, don't you think, Cethegus?" Catiline asks, gesturing towards a grove with a fig tree and vines.

"Master Lucius, when all is said and done if I were you I would fill the square with your monuments."

"What did you say?" Catiline remarks, turning sharply toward Cethegus.

"I said that if I were you I would fill the Forum with your monuments. Why?"

"Nothing, just a passing thought about a dream I had. The Senate is gathering. I will meet you all at home tonight," Catiline replies as he joins the throng of senators entering the house.

Catiline makes his way to his seat, bowing to Crassus and Caesar as Catulus stands to call the meeting to order. As Catulus stands, Catiline's dream runs through his mind and he wonders if today is the day he has longed for. Putting his complete trust in the gods, he reaches down and feels the handle of the sword that he knows he did not bring.

"Fathers of the Senate, this meeting of the Senate of Rome is formally called to order," Catulus declares as he offers incense on the Altar of Victory, allowing the fragrance to fill the room. "The first order of business is to be brought forth by Consul Marcus Cicero."

"Conscript Fathers," Cicero states, walking from behind Catulus. "I wish to bring before us again today the proposal offered by Sulpicius Rufus in regards to bribery and campaign corruption. As you might recall, the provisions of this bill call for ten years of exile and disqualification from office for two years after that. The republic needs this law to protect our foundations."

Marcus Cato stands. "I concur with the consul. Laws against corruption need to be as strong and carry enough weight to ensure corruption will not be practiced in our politics."

"Consul, might I offer a proposal to this law?" Catiline timidly states as he rises slowly and stands, shaking before the crowd, fumbling with his toga as he rises.

"Lucius Catiline, candidate for consul who rarely offers anything to our debates, you are most welcome to make a contribution if you so desire," Cicero warmly remarks.

"I wish to offer something to this law that is simple, quick, and will guarantee there will no longer be corruption in this house or our elections," he replies, disappointed that his hands failed to find a sword under his toga, which had been there in his dream.

"Which would be what?" the puzzled consul replies.

"I recommend that the term of disqualification be lengthened to five to ten years. Rome does not need someone who has had ten years of exile to cultivate hate, with only two years to cool off before resuming office," Catiline replies, once again taking his seat.

"Well spoken, Lucius," Cicero replies, turning to the crowd once again. "What does the rest of the Senate say?" Cicero continues as Catiline, lost in thought, drowns out the proceedings of the Senate by plotting where to go from here. The placing of soldiers and alternative places to store arms crosses his mind, as well as exactly how he is going to treat his nemesis once he has taken over.

"If you are not planning something, Lucius, then quit looking like you are," Crassus comments, bringing him back to reality. Catiline jumps and notices that the Senate has been dismissed. Its members are slowly leaving, though Cicero is sitting across the room gazing at him with a look of disgust, which Catiline promptly answers with his characteristic smile as he rises to leave.

"My dear Crassus, if you only knew what I was planning you would have left Rome the day you met me," he remarks, passing by Crassus, who looks in the direction of Cicero with a look of terror, which urge Cicero to find the evidence he needs.

Walking out of the Senate House, Catiline is surrounded by his bodyguards, along with Sura and Cethegus, after hours of waiting for the Senate to adjourn. "Cethegus, get as many weapons as you can and stockpile them, increasing the locations wherever possible. Sura, I want you to have Gaius Cornelius gather a band of men together to set fire to the city, should we need to resort to that. Let him know it is up to him to arrange it. Today is our day, my friends. Rome will be ours in only a few hours." The trio parades down the Via Sacra, surrounded by the veterans decked in military garb, casting a sense of awe and wonder in the eyes of all who see them—all but Cicero.

The next day passes as Catiline once more spends the cold night facing the Forum with bloodshot eyes, pallid complexion, and an aura of madness that causes even Sura to hesitate in approaching him.

"Lucius, it is nearing time for the election speeches in the Forum," he remarks, trying to get Catiline's attention without getting too close.

"Thank you, but I am well aware of the hour. I am merely spending the time rehearsing my speech," he replies, looking up and startling Sura with his haggard appearance.

"You haven't slept, have you?"

"Lucius Catiline does not sleep. I must be ready at all times should my adversary offer battle, my dear Lentullus Sura." He staggers to his feet, clearly fatigued if not somewhat delirious, as Sura endeavors to dress his staggering master.

"The rest of the men are already in the Forum, waiting for you to arrive with the veteran bodyguards, Lucius." Sura continues helping Catiline to the steps.

"Then let us not keep Cicero waiting," Catiline replies as the two stagger out the door, met by his bodyguards.

Just across town and surrounded by his admirers, lictors, and well wishers, Cicero proudly walks down the steps of his home, turning to wave to Terentia as he makes his way through the streets of Rome. Waving to his constituents, he turns his head, smelling fresh bread, and as he motions to his lictors to pause for a moment he approaches the stand and places his order for what is sure to help him through a long day of politics.

"The gods be with you, Consul," a soft female voice utters as he, not turning to meet it, continues to watch as his order is filled.

"They are, my lady, and with you also I trust."

"The plans are for you to die in the Forum today, Consul, and the Field of Mars tomorrow if they fail. My lady's lover told her so last night. Veterans of Sulla surround Catiline, there are arms caches throughout the city under Gaius Cethegus's command, and Servius Sulla is in charge of setting the city on fire should the need arise. I leave you to your business. May the gods bless you," the lady continues as she hurriedly walks off with her basket full of bread.

Joining his lictors once again, Cicero motions them all close to him. "A slave belonging to my informant just let me know that there is a plot to murder me today in the Forum or tomorrow at the elections. Have your arms ready, and two of you alert Catulus as well as other bodyguards belonging to various senators to watch for danger," he remarks. Cicero makes his way into the Forum in plain view of all citizens, clearly protected by his staff of lictors.

"There he is, Lucius, surrounded by lictors with their swords drawn," Sura remarks, enraging Catiline.

"He knows something. But that will not deter me. I will watch him die today no matter what it takes!" he mumbles while still trying to smile and wave to the voters.

"But if the lictors surround him, then there is no way to get to him, Lucius."

"Then you had better find a way, Sura." Catiline separates himself from Sura and his bodyguard to mount the Rostra and wait his turn for his speech.

Catulus steps forward to make the introductions and to silence the growing crowd of Roman voters and onlookers. "I greet you, my fellow countrymen, in the name of the Senate of Rome!" Catulus shouts to the gathered people as they anxiously await to see what each candidate will promise and how many lies will be told this afternoon. "The four candidates in this year's elections are here before you to deliver their speeches. Lucius Catiline has been selected to go first, followed by Decimus Junius Silanus, then Lucius Licinius Murena, and finally Servius Sulpicius Rufus."

Catiline rises smoothly from his seat and bows to Catalus and his competitors. "People of Rome," Catiline shouts, "I am overjoyed that the consuls have granted me the privilege to stand before you once again to offer my services to you," he continues as scattered applause erupts from the crowd. "I am thankful that you did not see fit to elect me to serve in this current year, as it has allowed me to witness firsthand even greater suffering inflicted on the people and veterans of Rome who have proudly served our country." He clenches his fists, becoming animated, much to the displeasure of Cicero and the other senators who are standing by.

"For too long, my friends, rich men have ruled in Rome, and their policies have succeeded while mine and those like me have failed. I have seen debt relief bills and other forms of compassionate legislation tossed aside, while new taxes are levied and calls for mercy are shouted down. I promise that as consul there will be a general abolition of debts in Rome, so that men who work hard will no longer be sold into slavery to pay their debts, and veterans can hold their heads high, knowing that their service actually meant something to Rome!" He continues to draw applause from his crowd as Catulus hangs his head in shame. The other candidates look on in disbelief, as the popular favor seems to lie with Catiline. Throughout the crowd, senators are seen busying themselves, most petitioning Cicero, while others make their way to Cato, one of the staunchest of conservatives.

"The present consulship has brought no relief, merely more bondage. I will set Rome free and be the leader to the overlooked and underprivileged who are constantly walked on! Rally to me, unfortunates of Rome, carry my name to the election boxes, and I will carry you to prosperity!" he haughtily remarks as Cicero and Antonius make their way to the Rostra surrounded by Lictors and watching Catiline who is grabbing his toga and carefully watching his enemy. Silence falls as Catulus walks down and meets with the consuls, nods, and returns to the platform. Catiline surveys the crowd, waiting for the opportunity to give the signal for the massacre to begin but not getting the chance.

"At the request of the consuls and the Senate of Rome, this meeting is hereby disbanded in order to convene an emergency meeting of the Senate, due to the content of the candidate's speech." Catulus announces, leaving the Rostra and heading to the curia, leaving the candidates puzzled and Catiline clenching his fists, distraught that his opportunity to fill the Forum with blood had not arrived and now he must answer the Senate's prodding questions.

"Get out of my way!" Catiline mumbles as he shoves Lucius Licinius Murena aside and pushes his way through the crowd to endure a time of torment. "I told you to get to Cicero. What part of that did you not understand?" he quietly asks Sura, who has rushed to meet him.

"I did the best I could, Lucius, but there was no getting close to him. He had the lictors surrounding him so that not even a child could have gotten to him!" Sura replies as the group moves toward the curia. Catiline leaves them and enters with the other senators.

"Lucius Catiline, the Senate demands to know the meaning of that speech you delivered in the Forum!" Cicero shouts before Catiline even has a chance to take his usual seat.

"We are called on as candidates to deliver a speech, and I fulfilled that requirement. What is the problem, Consul?" Catiline replies, offering his characteristic smile along with his sarcastic response.

"He openly attacks the Senate in the Forum and has the audacity to pretend he has done nothing wrong! Let him be expelled!" Gaius Calpurnius Piso shouts and is seconded by various ones.

"I call on the consuls to enact a measure of discipline against Catiline," Cato calls out, drawing a chuckle from Catiline and those allied with him.

"Let the attacker of the Senate be expelled!" Lucius Volcacius Tullus offers, as Catiline laughs and waves his hand in the direction of Tullus, brushing off his comments.

Infuriated, Cato now stands, making his way slowly across the speaker's area in the direction of Catiline. "Lucius Sergius Catiline, you have unashamedly verbally attacked the Senate, which you are a part of, for no other reason than to incite the voters and earn favor among them, all the while acting as though the Senate does not have the right to launch its own attack against you. What do you say to this charge?"

"Marcus Porcius Cato, illustrious member of the Senate, known and respected for your philosophies, this is how I answer your question: the Senate may attack me, but rest assured that I will answer any attack it brings against me." Catiline rises from his seat and walks to meet Cato. Tightening his face in disgust, Cato turns and makes his way back to his seat, mumbling treason for all to hear, while Catiline stands emotionless, waiting for the next attack.

"To incite the commons in such a way is to break the peace. Time permitting, I am announcing my intention to take you to trial for breach of peace under the Plautian law!" Lucius Paulus shouts out from the other side of the room, amid agreement from various senators.

"You will find the charge will not stick because I have done nothing wrong."

"The commons are outside chanting for you, Catiline I believe that I speak for everyone here when I say that this body will not bend or bow to the body of people outside of these doors—no matter how much you wish to disgrace yourself or urge them on," Catulus rises from his seat only long enough to make a comment.

"It is funny that you mention that, most honorable Catulus," Catiline replies, taking his seat and looking toward the ceiling. "Is there something wrong with wanting to lead?" he continues as he turns to leave. "Conscript Fathers, I have answered your questions and proven that I have done nothing wrong but made statements that some of you disagree with. I am a politician, and I have an election to win. That is all I have done. Now if you are quite finished, I have business to attend to," he coolly remarks as he leaves the Senate House followed by all eyes in the place.

"Our illustrious consul, Catiline's greatest opponent, has kept silent. I wonder why?" Crassus sarcastically remarks as the supporters of Catiline share a laugh at the opposing party's expense.

"Because I wanted the private conversations that I have shared with this body to be brought to remembrance. I have been informed that there was a plot to murder me in the Forum, and since it did not take place it is to be tried again tomorrow," Cicero replies, pacing across the main floor of the Senate.

"And how do you know Catiline is behind it?" Lucius Bestia, one of the secret conspirators, asks from behind Cicero, causing him to turn sharply in that direction.

"Because one of his close friends, Publius Cornelius Lentullus Sura, tried to get near to me today. You should know, Bestia. He's a friend of yours too, isn't he?" Cicero replies. "The republic is in grave danger, Fathers of the Senate. If something is not done about Catiline and his group, Rome will be no more! I am asking the Senate to allow the consuls to make a formal investigation, to enact the ultimate decree, and to grant us the power to preserve the republic!"

"I fail to see where there is enough proof to warrant such action. Furthermore, I am inclined to think that these murder plots exist only in the consul's head," Gaius Julius Caesar replies amid whispers of agreement from the Senate.

Cicero remarks sullenly, "So say you all? I shall continue on my own time until I have enough proof to convince this body. Go home. This meeting is adjourned until further notice." The senators quietly file out of the building.

Walking up and placing his arm around Cicero's shoulder, Catulus states, "Don't be too downcast, Consul. We all know that Catiline is guilty of something, but without enough proof how can we threaten investigation or a decree against him?"

"I will get the proof we need. I just hope that we are all still here to see it."

All night long, Catiline's home is ablaze. The next day, all of Rome gathers on the Field of Mars to place their votes for consul. Slowly and meticulously, the plans are reviewed as men are assigned areas to oversee, while others are given the names of those they are to kill at Catiline's signal. Drinking into the night, the men fill the room with their outrageous plans while their leader urges them on, pouring his poison into their ears and filling their minds with murders and treason. Without a single moment of sleep, at dawn the group stirs and helps Catiline prepare for his election. The gang of thugs make their way toward their destiny in the Field of Mars.

As they arrive, each man is instructed to locate their targets and center their activities on Cicero, who, much to everyone's surprise, has not yet arrived. Puzzled at the consul's tardiness, the men begin to regroup and look to their leader; the consul has obviously failed to appear out of fear. Just as they begin to devise a new plot, a commotion is heard a few yards away, as a group of armed men appear with swords, surrounding twelve lictors who are also armed, who in turn surround Cicero. He readily displays a breastplate under his toga, serving to alert all those present of the plots against him.

"Citizens of Rome, rally to my aid. I implore you! Your consul needs you, as he is forced to come armed into the Field of Mars because of word that he is marked for murder!" Cicero proclaims for all to hear as he makes his way to the voting station, where he and Antonius can watch the voting take place. Seeing Cicero's boldness, Catiline makes his way toward the consul, pushing through the crowd, only to be stopped by Cicero's bodyguard.

"I am Lucius Catiline, candidate for consul. I wish to see the consul."

"And I am Publius Clodius Pulcher, the head of his bodyguard, and I say that as long as I am alive you'll only see him from a distance."

"That can be arranged if you're not careful, Pulcher," Sura coldly replies. Pulcher keeps his attention on Catiline, not allowing Sura to distract him.

"Yes, but this breaks any arrangements you try to make," Pulcher replies, holding his sword to Sura's chest. "Now stand aside. You are blocking the consul's way."

"Just inform the consul that I am here to check in. I am returning to my home to await the results of my victory," Catiline states before he turns around and leaves the Field of Mars; a handful of his supporters stay behind to observe the election and bring him news. Catiline passes the rest of the afternoon in solitude, not even allowing Sura to enter his office. Silence has filled the house, as Catiline has sent out all but the inner circle until favorable word has come, thus leaving his men somber and even more anxious to hear the news.

An exhausted slave of Catiline's runs as fast as he can on the stone streets, bearing news from the Field of Mars. "Master Lucius, where is Master Lucius?" He tries to catch his breath.

"I am here. What do you have for me?" Catiline remarks, standing in the doorway of his office. He slowly makes his way to the young man.

"The results are in, Master. You were beaten," the young man replies, hanging his head before his master. Catiline stands silent and motionless for a few moments, as all eyes in the room are on him, not knowing exactly what his reaction will be. Wondering what to do, the slave slowly raises his head to look at Catiline. "Master, are you all right?" he asks, as Catiline lets out a blood-curdling scream and swings his sword at the young man, striking through his right shoulder and through several ribs. He releases his sword and pants like he has finally lost his mind as the lifeless body hits the floor with Catiline's sword still embedded in it.

"This is it. This is the final insult," he remarks, tracing his fingers in the slave's blood and tasting it "I have tried to do things the proper way; the gods have determined that I am not to be consul by the proper means, so I will take it by armed resistance—even if that means marching on Rome itself. Sura, send a message to Manlius to be ready to take the field on October 27."

"What about Cicero?" Marcus Fulvius Nobilitor asks, drawing a scowl from Catiline.

"I will take care of him myself."

"Allow me to take care of him. I would love nothing better than to convene morning greetings to him and kill him in his home," Cethegus remarks bringing a smile to Catiline's face.

"I would love to join him, if I may, Lucius," Lucius Vargunteius adds.

"Excellent, my friends, but we must wait for a more convenient time. Aside from passing information periodically, our next official meeting will be at Marcus Porcius Laeca's home on November 6."

# 9

## *Denounced*

### October–November 63 BC

For the first time in a little over three months, Rome is at peace. For the first time since his return from Africa, the home of Lucius Catiline is silent. Shut up in his home like a sullen hermit, Catiline brews in his anger, to the point that he is about to boil over. For days at a time not even his inner circle is permitted to see him, but they content themselves with the sounds they hear behind his office door as evidence that he is still alive. At times he laughs and at others he cries and screams, but most of the time he shouts bitter words and curses against his enemies and pleads with the gods to grant him the power to kill them. On the rare occasions that visitors are permitted into his presence, they find a shell of a man wholly taken in madness.

Nothing is heard from Catiline in the political realm. While this should ease the fears of the Senate, rather it keeps Cicero wondering, as Curius and Fulvia have no information for him. Catiline no longer attends the Senate meetings; some say for shame at his loss, but Cicero and Cato claim it is due to a guilty conscience bent on murder and revenge. Cicero has fed the Senate news of Catiline so often that he finds himself mocked. People about Rome and in the Senate begin their conversations with "I have been informed," his trademark saying. Without even realizing it, Catiline is striking his opponent a deadly blow; his sudden silence has begun to lull the complacent Senate to sleep, and without action to back up Cicero's allegations has made him look the fool.

The late nights are no longer dominant in Catiline's home, but rather across town at the home of Marcus Cicero. Suffering from poor digestion, the consul finds himself trying to rationalize his enemy's silence. Four days after the ides of October, late in the evening, a gentle knock is heard at the door of the consul as the family slave Philologus makes his way to the door. The gentle knock becomes pounding and screaming, to which Cicero urges the slave to hurry. The lictors, present at Cicero's side, stand ready should this be a murder attempt.

"Cicero!" a man screams, running through the atrium, headed for the consul. "Marcus Cicero, I have what you have been needing!" The man, now revealed as Marcus Crassus, runs to Cicero's side, followed by two other gentlemen from the Senate: Marcus Marcellus and Quintus Caecilius Metellus Pius Scipio. Pulling a bundle from under his arm, Crassus tosses a stack of papers on the consul's desk. This irritates him, but he is willing to hear his intruder out.

"What is this, Crassus? I'm not in the mood for jokes," Cicero comments, knowing Crassus's friendship with Catiline and his ilk.

As Cicero thumbs through the stack and Crassus tries to catch his breath, Marcus Marcellus states, "It's no joke, Marcus. We were all at Crassus's home tonight and a knock came at the door about thirty minutes ago. A man identifying himself only as the slave of a man and his mistress handed Crassus these letters, each addressed to a different senator, and asked that they find their intended recipients."

"We came as soon as we could after I read the letter addressed to me and Scipio read his. It is a warning of a massacre that is about to take place. It says that if I hope to survive I need to leave Rome now," Crassus interjects, drawing Cicero's attention with his uncharacteristic sincerity. "What's worse is that it told me that Gaius Manlius was in Faesulae gathering troops and would take the field on October 27. That's only six days before the kalends of November."

"Marcus Licinius Crassus, Quintus Caecilius Metellus Pius Scipio, Quintus Lutatius Catulus, Gaius Julius Caesar, Gaius Antonius Hybrida, and Gaius Calpurnius Piso. Marcellus, it seems you and I were not to know about this," Cicero states, handling the letters carefully so as not to break the seals. "Gentlemen, there is but one course of action to take. We must call an emergency meeting of the Senate, hand these letters out, and let them break the seals and read them without my intervention, should someone accuse me of making them up. Lictor, if you would please be so kind as to locate messengers to notify the Senate of a meeting tomorrow at the curia."

"What if Catiline comes?" Marcellus asks as Cicero walks toward his guests.

"Let him. We will still follow this course of action and judge his reaction to it. You men have done me a great service tonight, and Rome will never forget it," he continues. He gracefully bows before the men. For the rest of the night, Cicero plans his next move, knowing that this is the crucial moment in which he can force Catiline to move if he is too careful or retreat if he is too forceful. He hopes, as he busies himself about his work in the late hours, that he can draw Catiline out and free Rome of his toxic mentality. Ultimately overcome with planning, his eyes grow heavy, and sleep conquers the man that Catiline cannot.

With roosters crowing in the backyard and young Quintus and Tullia running about, Cicero awakens to find notes stuck to his face where he had fallen asleep on them sometime in the night. Finding that he is running late for the meeting of the Senate, he directs Philologus to retrieve his toga. Quickly throwing it on, he awakens his lictors so they can hurry him through the streets. By the time he arrives, the Senate is buzzing with impatient senators who, while they have only been waiting twenty minutes, feel that the consul has inconvenienced them. Amid the animoisity, Cicero makes his way down the center aisle, holding the letters in one hand and the edge of his toga in the other.

"Honorable president of the Senate and Conscript Fathers, I beg your forgiveness for my tardiness. Had I not been up until very late preparing, I would have been here much sooner. Please forgive me," Cicero humbly states, easing the tension in the room. "I have here parcels for several senators. As your names are called, please be so kind as to take the letter, then read them in the order that you received them. You will find the seals intact, just as they were delivered to me by Marcus Crassus, Marcus Marcellus, and Quintus Caecilius Metellus Pius Scipio. Gaius Antonius Hybrida, Marcus Licinius Crassus, Quintus Caecilius Metellus Pius Scipio, Quintus Lutatius Catulus, Gaius Julius Caesar, and Gaius Calpurnius Piso, please come forward and take your letters," Cicero continues. The men file forward, puzzled at what is taking place, retrieve their letters, and return to their seats. Consul Gaius Antonius begins to read.

---

Consul Gaius Antonius Hybrida,

It is my duty to inform you that you are in great danger if you stay in the city of Rome. Within the next few days, a general massacre of the Senate will occur, and none will be spared. If you want to live, leave the city and don't look back."

"Mine says the same thing but addressed to me and not signed!" Catulus states, as the Senate, still taken aback from the reading, turns to face him.

"Same here, but addressed to me with no signature," Caesar states.

"My letter is worded exactly the same also," Piso states, as the men examine the letters and allow those around them to view them.

"Gentlemen, finally I have brought evidence that Catiline is planning his massacre. We are all marked to die. What more will it take for you to believe me?"

"I resent that charge, Consul!" Catiline shouts from the rear of the room "I knew you would be up to something. Those letters have no signature, and furthermore there is no mention of who will carry it out. The consul is deluded, trying to make my second loss for consul an even greater shame to me than it is already."

"What of your friend Gaius Manlius in Faesulae gathering troops? Word from that region is that he is gathering them in your name, but I suppose you know nothing of it."

"Consul, you are the madman, I am of the Sergii a family, which has served Rome well in politics and on the field. I have no reason to resort to what I am being charged of!"

"Then you won't mind if I ask the Senate to approve the ultimate decree and launch an official investigation into these letters, will you?"

"I will vote for it myself, as it will exonerate me. You will all see how foolish you were for choosing a foreigner as consul!" he replies, amid hisses for his verbal abuse of a consul. "I have done nothing, and to prove it I offer myself to Marcus Cicero to keep me in his home under house arrest, where he can watch me day and night." Several senators voice their approval, and some clap, bringing a smile to his face.

"Thank you, no. I believe I shall pass such a high honor to another citizen far more deserving of your presence, as I am already in danger with you outside of my house," Cicero replies.

"Very well, Consul. As you wish. Manius Lepidus, I surrender myself to you."

"I decline," Lepidus replies, rising to answer then sitting again.

"Very well then, a very distinguished one among us, Metellus Celer, will you consent to watch over me?"

"If it will serve the Senate and the republic, I will gladly welcome you to my home."

"Thank you, Senator. Consul, urge this body to pass the decree if you like, but I have done nothing to be ashamed of. I ask the Senate and those here who know me best to defend my name," Catiline replies, turning to leave the house in a dignified manner that becomes one who truly is innocent.

"You have heard it from his own lying tongue. You have had time to talk among yourselves. What is the decision in this matter? Will it be the decree or nothing?" Cicero continues. All across the house mumbles are heard, alternating between calls for decree and calls to investigate until the latter overpowers the former.

Catulus stands to deliver the Senate's view. "From my hearing, the Senate has chosen for the consuls to continue investigating. Pending more information, the Decree is a viable option, so say you all?"

Cicero is clearly upset by the inactivity of the advising body. "I pray that there is a Rome and a Senate House for us to meet in when the time comes," he says.

"So what happened?" Sura whispers to Catiline.

"Someone has written letters to Crassus, Caesar, Antonius, Catulus, and Quintus Scipio, informing them of our plans. They were read in the House. Right now the Senate is voting on whether to pass the ultimate decree against us."

"Don't you think you should be in there fighting it?"

"No, I voted for it. We must do everything we can to divert attention from us and to make this consul look like the fool he is," Catiline states, as the two march across the Forum, heading for his home. "We need to pack my things. I have voluntarily surrendered myself to Metellus Celer while the consuls continue to investigate the letters."

Sura is thinking of something else. "Curius did it. I'm sure of it! He's the only one stupid enough. We should have never included him in our plans."

Catiline shakes his head. "I don't think so. I have had four men watching his home in six-hour shifts, as well as Fulvia's home. Everything has been as it should. I don't believe it was him."

"I'd feel better if we tortured him to find out for certain," Sura remarks as the two men pause beside the Temple of Saturn.

"There will be plenty of people to torture once this is all over with, far better than Quintus Curius. Besides, I am planning on killing him in the end. As you stated, he is far too stupid to be left alive," Catiline replies as the two continue to Catiline's home.

For two days, silence reigns once again. Cicero tirelessly investigates each lead, ultimately finding that his adversary has done a better job than he could have thought possible. Even with huge rewards specifically aimed at those who follow Catiline, no information comes in. Late nights are spent researching and hoping that a new piece of information will reveal itself. Time is running out, along with any hopes of stopping Catiline from murdering indiscriminately. Finding him dozing off after midnight on October 20, Terentia encourages her overworked husband to rest.

"Marcus, please come to bed. This is the second night that you have been up this late. It isn't good for you." She walks up behind him, caressing his shoulders and relaxing the tired consul.

"Terentia, I have to find a solution. The Senate is getting impatient. They feel that if there really is a danger to Rome the facts should be easy to come by. So far they haven't been." He rubs his hands over his tired face and lays his head on his desk. "It's not only that. I have heard from Catiline's own lips what he intends to do, and he is delighted that no one is listening, and that I am running out of time to prove my case. People are going to die if I don't find what I need."

"Perhaps you should talk to someone. Perhaps you can write Atticus a line or two?"

"No, he wouldn't get it in time anyway," he replies, clearly exhausted.

"What about Quintus Arrius? I saw his wife today, and she said that he had just gotten back in town from visiting his sister in Faesulae. Perhaps you could—"

"What did you say?" he asks, interrupting her.

"Quintus Arrius. He's back from Faesulae. Why?"

"Lictor!" Cicero shouts, startling his protectors as they rush to his side, fearing danger. "Someone get me a litter. I need to see Quintus Arrius tonight!" he continues, haphazardly tossing some clothes over his bedclothes and preparing to leave. "My love, you may have just unlocked the door that I have been beating at." He kisses her cheek and rushes out the door with the drowsy troop of lictors. The band of men make their way through the dark streets of Rome, trying to find the home of Quintus Arrius. Finally recognizing it from memory, Cicero stops the procession and heads for the door, summoning the man's slave by knocking. "Consul Marcus Cicero wishes to see your master Quintus Arrius," he states through the slightly opened door to a slave who has obviously been stirred from deep sleep.

"Master Arrius is asleep, Consul, due to the hour."

"I am well aware of what time it is. Now get your master up and tell him I am here on matters that cannot wait until morning," he replies, pushing through the door with six of his twelve lictors. Hurrying off, the slave mumbles a few brief words, and within a few minutes the sleepy Quintus Arrius rushes into the atrium of the house to greet his guest, while the slave kindles the fire, warming the room for the men.

"Macrinus said this was urgent. What can I do for you, Cicero?" Arrius asks, taking a seat and offering the same to Cicero and his men.

"Quintus, I thank you for understanding. You know that I would not call on you unless it was desperately important. My wife said you have just returned from Faesulae, is that correct?"

"It is. I was visiting my sister there. Is there something wrong?" he replies, becoming concerned by the consul's tone.

"You are not aware then of what has been taking place here with Lucius Catiline, are you?"

"Only that he has lost the consulship twice, and of course the prosecutions he was under, but other than that no."

"He is suspected of a plot to murder senators and various citizens, as well as myself, very soon. What brought me here is the rumor that Gaius Manlius, one of Sulla's centurions, was in Faesulae training and gathering troops and—"

"Marcus, he is. I received a letter from my sister only a few months ago wanting to know about Rome, as there was such a troop gathering outside of town. That was part of the reason I visited her. I was very concerned for her safety."

"Did you see the troops, and do you still have her letter?"

"Yes to both. There was a rumor that her son had been asked if he wanted to join with a centurion of Sulla, but we brushed it off since we had never heard of such a thing."

"Well, it is being done. That army is going to march here and take Rome by storm, and we are all going to die. The only problem I am having is convincing the stubborn Senate, who refuses to believe it."

"The letter is here. I always keep my correspondence handy, should I need to reply about a subject," he replies, thumbing through a small box of papers. "Here it is," he states, pulling on out and handing it to Cicero, who carefully looks it over, smiling more and more as he does.

"This is exactly what I need. I'll need to take this, and I will also need you to be in the Senate tomorrow morning for your testimony, if you please."

"Yes I was planning on being there and would be most happy to testify," he states as the two men conclude their meeting.

"Quintus, you may have given me the weapon that I need to finally seal Catiline's fate," Cicero states, making his way out the door preceded by his lictors. "We will meet at nine in the morning. Please be sure that you are there my friend." As the consul leaves the home of his friend, he carefully directs two of his lictors to make their way around town accompanied by messengers to pass the word of his intention to have a special meeting to the various members of the Senate. Long into the night speeches are prepared and testimonies and evidence are set in order. Cicero may finally get the emergency power he needs to follow through with his investigation.

Early the next morning, on October 21, the body of the Senate gathers with rumors that the overzealous consul has more information. To those who have not taken him seriously, the joke continues to make its way around the house, with these senators greeting each other with the phrase, "I have been informed." Today Cicero waits for each senator to arrive, until, to the surprise of all who enter and see him in the house with his pile of notes.

Carefully scanning the crowd as they enter, Catiline and his fellows in the Senate are no where to be found, raising suspicions as to whether this is the appointed day. But Catiline finally enters, paying his respects and taking his normal seat.

"Fathers of the Senate, this meeting is officially called to order by the request of the consul, Marcus Tullius Cicero, and his colleague Gaius Antonius Hybrida," Catulus states, going through his familiar ceremony of offering incense before the altar in the front of the room.

"I have become the joke of this body of men. I am well aware of that, and I gladly accept the place that the gods have appointed to me for the time being. For in the end I am certain that I shall be known as the savior of the republic," Cicero confidently states, drawing a chuckle from some and sympathy from others. "I have in my hands the evidence needed to grant the consuls emergency powers to prepare for war against an enemy living and breathing within the walls of the city. I have here a letter from a common citizen who, not knowing what has been taking place, has identified Gaius Manlius by name, as well as his efforts to recruit the young men in the city of Faesulae."

"We have been informed that there is also a man to testify that he saw this with his own eyes. Where is such a man, Consul, if he does exist?" Lucius Vargunteius sarcastically asks, bringing laughter from those on Catiline's side and a nod from Catiline himself.

"Right here," Quintus Arrius states. A look of disbelief comes over Lucius Vargunteius's face. "I was visiting my sister in Faesulae. And being that I have been absent from the Senate the past few months, I was not aware that there was a supposed conspiracy or revolution. When I arrived, Conscript Fathers, I noticed that there was an unusually large amount of soldiers outside the city. When I asked my sister, she told me that even her son claimed that soldiers had been trying to recruit teenage boys for service, but we laughed it off until I realized it was serious," Arrius states.

Cato rises. "I vote for the ultimate decree to be passed immediately and that emergency powers be grated to the consuls to see that the republic suffer no harm." Others rally behind him, while allies of Caesar, Catiline, and Crassus try to drown them out with disapproval. After listening for over twenty minutes, Catulus rises and begins to speak.

"Fathers, we have debated, and the voices have been heard. It is my own opinion that the powers should be granted for the safety of the state, and from my hearing that is your desire as well. It is therefore decreed that the ultimate decree is to be passed, granting emergency powers to Consuls Marcus Cicero and Gaius Hybrida for the suppression of violence as well as preparation against."

"As the first order of business, I call your attention to Quintus Marcius Rex and Quintus Metellus Creticus, both of whom are outside of the city wishing to recommend Quintus Pompeius Rufus and Quintus Metellus Celer to be dispatched to Faesulae, Apulia, Capua, and Picenum respectively to deal with the situations arising there and to raise troops of their own to deal with Manlius, should he indeed take the field on the twenty-seventh as I have been told. I have also prepared a list and delivered it to my colleagues of the men who serve as watchmen on the walls of the city, and others who serve as an emergency group, should fires or other disasters occur. Conscript Fathers, the city is in good hands. We will preserve this republic against its enemies," Cicero states as the senators stand to applaud, while Catiline and his group sit by unimpressed but still stand to applaud the consul with everyone else.

As the senators leave after their relatively short meeting, Catiline's men begin to gather out of the sight of the other senators, toward the rear of the building. With some serving as lookouts, Catiline carefully delivers his speech to his men, urging them on to great things for all of Rome, as the republic needs a drastic overhaul. "My friends, you have heard it with your own lips. Our cause is discovered, and all that lacks being known is our names! Now we will prepare like never before, preparing for a revolution like Rome has never seen! We will meet next on November 6 at midnight at the home of Marcus Laeca to discuss the final plans. November 8 will be our night of uprising!" he callously states, bringing smiles to those perverted and sick conspirators before they all disband.

All the way home, Catiline's mind is wrapped up in the events of the next few days. Everything must be timed exactly right or else it will fail. He will never get to see the sight that he has so longed for—the head of Cicero resting on a spear in the Forum as his goods are auctioned for profit. Meeting him at the door of his home, Cethegus and Sura greet their leader with questions of the proceedings and what the next move is to be. "The Senate has passed the emergency powers decree. Though they have not named me, I assure you that we will all be under tremendous scrutiny," Catiline remarks.

"What about the weapons we have stored? Won't the consuls be searching for them?" Cethegus asks, reminding Catiline that it is at his home, where the arms are kept.

"Yes, but without knowing the day of the attack Cicero will wait to search for them so he might have his most powerful evidence at the end. Do your best to hide them. Make sure they are secure and continue to add to their number," Catiline replies as he removes his cumbersome toga.

"What of Manlius? If they mentioned him by name, is he not a liability?" Sura asks, staring out the window toward the Forum.

"Not in the slightest. My last word from Manlius was that he has two legions of men. I have sent Capito to him to help him get here by October 27, the date to begin hostilities, as there is no way Pompey will get back to Rome in time. The Senate has sent four men to Faesulae, Apulia, Capua, and Picenum respectively to gather troops, but Manlius has several months on them so there is no way they can recruit fast enough. By the morning of November 9, the three of us will be the ones Rome bends it knee to," Catiline continues.

"I have dismissed all of those from the house involved with our plans and have given orders to everyone to stay away from here in case Cicero has spies watching who is coming and going," Sura states, motioning a slave over to fill it once more.

For the next few days, all information gathering is at a standstill. Cicero continues to run into walls he knows have been constructed by Catiline to hide his true intentions from being discovered. Offers of freedom to slaves or rewards to freemen reveals no information, as Catiline's years of supplying prostitutes, wine, and sex have obviously paid off. No matter what he plans, nothing seems to sway their allegiance to him. Frustrated at the endless barricades he has faced, Cicero decides to clear his head with a walk through the Forum, taking with him only a single lictor instead of his usual twelve. The fresh air does him some good, and he enjoys his slow walk, taking in the sights, smells, and sounds of republican Rome.

The ever-vigilant lictor maintains a safe distance between the consul and other ordinary citizens. Out of nowhere a woman's cry is heard a few feet away, as a commotion erupts over a beggar trying to rob her, to which Cicero, now standing in an open area in front of the Rostra, urges the lictor to find out what is going on. As he leaves Cicero's side, the consul turns around to see Catiline looking him in the eyes with his trademark charismatic smile.

"You really should be more careful, Consul. Someone might have come up behind you and stabbed you with this," he coldly states, holding out a small dagger.

"You engineered that, didn't you?"

"You catch on quickly for a foreigner. If you are going to catch me, you had better get some evidence. You are running out of time," he replies, slipping through the crowd just as the lictor returns from arresting the beggar.

"Consul, was there any trouble?"

"No, but let's return home. I have had quite enough of the Forum for one day, and I have work to return to," Cicero replies as the two make their way through the crowd. They are joined by other senators who rebuke the consul for venturing out under such a light guard. Though it has been over a week since the emergency powers had been issued, as he prepares for the regularly scheduled meeting of the Senate on the kalends of November, the consul finds himself praying to the gods to grant him something, rather than give the Senate cause to revoke their decree. Today is the first day since October 21 that the Senate has meet for official business, and the consul fears that the complacent Senate will feel there truly is no danger and will revoke the power he needs to bring the conspiracy to light.

Once again, Terentia brings a smile to his face. Philologus wraps his master's toga for him, and she gently kisses his cheek before sending him on his way. Tired and distraught from fruitless investigations, the consul makes his way to his litter followed by his lictors, only to be stopped by a messenger. Taking the message, he issues the order for the slaves to begin their journey as he breaks the seal and begins to read. "Stop the litter!" he shouts as the startled slaves set the carriage down as the excited consul struggles to get out. "Lictors, I am victorious today. I feel like parading to the Senate House as a triumphant general!"

Making total use of his office, Cicero parades down the Via Sacra, instructing his lictors to clear the way so that all might see him as the protector of Rome and its people. His smile shines so bright he virtually lights up the whole of the house as he enters, bringing curious looks to the senators. Cicero ensures that everyone present gets a view of the letter that he holds in his hand.

"You seem to be walking in the clouds today, Consul," Catulus remarks, eyeing the paper Cicero holds in his hand.

"I hardly think you could catch me in any better mood. The only complaint I have is that it is bad news that makes me feel so good. I pray the gods will forgive me," he replies as Catulus open the meeting of the Senate, filling the room with incense. "Conscript Fathers, I bring you bittersweet words today. I received word not five minutes after I left my home this morning that Gaius Manlius has taken the field outside of Faesulae."

"Where is the evidence, Consul?" Quintus Annius asks. "Surely you have proof of such an action."

"If the Senate will permit me, I have a letter that I received from Senator Lucius Saenius, whom I sent to Faesulae for this very purpose.

---

Lucius Saenius to Marcus Cicero Consul, Greetings,

As I am certain you will read this in the Senate. I will spare the revered body the time that I would normally fill with greetings and pleasantries. I arrived in Fae-sulae on October 24 and investigated the situation as you instructed me to do. Not so much as two hours after I arrived I walked the streets in clothes befitting one suitable for service in the army and was approached several times by sol-diers asking if I would be interested in joining their cause, as they clearly did not know I was a senator.

The third time I was approached I resolved to look further into it and ask more questions. Upon doing so, I found that the purpose of the army was to make its way back to Rome to join a band of men already in the city and to there begin a revolution with proscriptions. I could get no names from the soldier, as he seemed not to know. At this posting on October 30, the troop was beginning to make its way to Apulia to make further recruits.

Your servant,
Lucius Saenius

---

"As you can see, there is abundant cause for what I have proposed. The action has been proposed, and now we the consuls have come for an opinion," Cicero continues, pacing the main floor addressing the body.

"I move that Gaius Manlius be rendered a public enemy and a traitor!" Gaius Calpurnius Piso stands amid sounds of agreement throughout the room.

"Let him be cast from the Tarpeian Rock and his body dragged with a hook to the Tiber River!" another senator calls out, drawing applause from the conserva-tive side and ridicule from the Popular party members.

"We should give Manlius time, should he see the error of his ways and wish to return for clemency," Julius Caesar adds with a nod from Crassus and a sneer from Cato.

"Caesar speaks of clemency, Fathers of the Senate, because he has financed this whole endeavor," Cato shouts. "Let the former proposals stand, and let the public enemy meet his fate when captured!"

"I find it interesting that the man around whom suspicion swirls has not involved himself in our debates. What say you, Lucius Catiline? If you are not involved, please tell us what is your stand?" Marcus Marcellus draws a spiteful look from Catiline, who changes his demeanor.

"I agree with Caesar and Cato. We should allow Manlius time to see if he changes his mind and send envoys to him. If he does not recant, let him be dragged as the law says for any traitor."

"That is an interesting stand coming from someone who had Manlius as a guest at his home on numerous occasions and who has so many rumors swirling around him!" Cato bitterly adds, gaining applause.

"This body is still yet to offer concrete evidence that I have any connections to what is taking place! It is a shame that the Senate of Rome would be so judgmental without a cause! The last time I checked, what I do with my time and who I spend it with is personal!" Catiline shouts back.

"That's only because we did not have enough time!" Quintus Caecilius Metellus Pius Scipio adds, as Cicero quietly watches his opponent.

"When I last confronted you, you assured this body that anyone who attacks you would be met with total destruction," Cato stands.

"I have had enough of this. I do not have to take this abuse," Catiline remarks as he walks out of the house, once again stirring further debate between the two parties. Shoving the slaves at the doors out of the way, Catiline rushes from the house, infuriated. Driven mad by true accusations yet still trying to fight discovery, he mumbles incoherently to himself that when the time comes he will kill them all.

As he enters his home, Catiline sends out every slave that dares approach him, He slams the door of his office, as he is the only one of the conspirators in his home and he throws off his toga as a garment representing hate and oppression. He opens a small cabinet and kneels before it on the floor. From the tiny space, he pulls a red cloth that he places on the floor, a small saucer containing a candle, and a decayed human skull. Pulling his dagger, he slices his palm, allowing the blood to flow into the saucer and over the candle. He then lifts the bloody hand to his mouth, tasting it himself and covering his lips in his blood. As he lights the candle, he begins to quietly mumble and laugh as he lifts the skull, with pieces of flesh still clinging to it, in the air before him.

"Dis, great god of the underworld, I, Lucius Catiline, call upon you to avenge my enemies who have so viciously attacked me! Let their blood flow through the streets of Rome. I pledge myself to you, and offer my body as a sacrifice," he continues, placing the skull on the floor as he lowers his face to the ground in front of it. The ground begins to gently shake under his home and the Forum. "You have heard me! Let my enemies be vanquished!" he shouts, covered in his own blood.

For the next five days, his office door once more stays locked. Sura and Cethegus both try to enter, only to be turned away by Catiline's shouts and vulgar mutterings. Without eating or sleeping, Catiline spends his days and nights alone with the windows open to the cold winter climate to achieve a higher level of endurance. He spends his time scrawling out notes to himself and others—nonsensical ideas and opinions as well as orders that no man could possibly follow. These he slips under the office door, calling Sura or Cethegus to make his deliveries, but quickly returns to his angry tirades that make no sense whatsoever. "Sura!" he shouts on the evening of November 6. Startled by the sudden shout, Sura rushes to the door.

"Yes, Lucius, what is it? What do you need?" he asks frantically, as the voice sounds desperate.

"Do you hear that sound?" he asks from behind the door.

"No, Lucius, I don't. What is it?" Sura replies but hears nothing. After a moment, the door opens to reveal a haggard Catiline with bloodshot eyes and a sunken face from days of starvation.

"Why, it is the sound of a million Romans having their blood spilled in the streets," he mumbles as he wraps his cloak around himself and walks toward the front door. "Are you coming or not?" he asks, stopping to look back at a puzzled Sura.

"Yes, of course," Sura replies, sprinting to Catiline. The two men leave the house headed for the home of Marcus Porcius Laeca. Upon arriving at midnight, the two men enter the small house on what is known as the 'scythe maker's street', finding it crowded with conspirators who cover their faces, all awaiting their leader, who has just arrived.

"Greetings, my friends. I am glad that you could make our final meeting," Catiline remarks, pulling off his cloak and revealing the signs of his self abuse from the past few days.

"Lucius, perhaps we should postpone our plans until this business with the Senate blows over. We can always raise more troops if something happens to Manlius," the young senator's son Appius Fulvius states, drawing disgust from Catiline. He quickly backs away, anticipating action from Catiline.

"You are a coward. You partook of the oath, and now you want out like the child you are. Why don't you run to your father and tell him what you have been up to and see if you get any sympathy from him, because you will get none from us!" Catiline coldly remarks causing the young man to hang his head before him.

"I'm sorry, Master Lucius. I am afraid. I've never done anything like this before."

"Take courage like a man, my young friend, and when it is all over you will have your own province with a rich future in the new Rome ahead," Catiline replies, softening his tone as he continues his speech. "Tomorrow morning Gaius Cethegus and Lucius Vargunteius will convey morning greetings on Marcus Cicero. When he comes to receive them, they will spill his guts right there in his own home," Catiline says with a smile as the two men appointed for the task smile and nod.

"The last time I was at his home, he insulted and abused me. Now it will be my turn," Cethegus mumbles amid cheers of encouragement from the others.

"Quintus Curius, you will then go to the home of Quintus Lutatius Catulus and do likewise, catching the Senate off balance. After a day or so, while mourning is taking place, we will storm the city at night. Cethegus, your men will set the city on fire in several areas, and, Sura, you will direct your men to begin a massacre of the Senate, leaving their bodies in the streets for all to see the next morning. Is everyone clear on these orders?" Catiline asks, looking about the room for any questions.

"What about the one who is feeding the Senate and Cicero information? What is to be done with them?" Lucius Statilius asks, causing each member present to look at the others.

"Honestly, Lucius, I do not care. By the time Cicero finds out, he will be bathing in his own blood. You have your orders. Watch your deadlines, and may the gods be with you." The men quickly don their cloaks, and all leave the home in different directions. Making his way through the streets, Quintus Curius rushes home and finds Fulvia asleep on the couch. He wakes her in a panic.

"We've got to get word to Cicero. Cethegus and Lucius Vargunteius are going to kill him tomorrow morning!" he utters, as a single tear begins to stream down her cheek. "My dear Fulvia, what's the matter?" he asks as a movement from the shadows startles him. Appius Fulvius, the young senator's son, emerges, brandishing his blade.

"I'm sorry, Quintus. He arrived a few minutes before you did and knocked me out. I'm sorry," she replies.

"Sura was right. It was you! It was worth almost getting attacked by Catiline tonight for what I said, just so I could catch you off guard and earn even greater rewards from him!" the young man replies, walking toward the couple with his dagger. "Let the proscriptions begin now. I will take both your heads as an offering to Catiline!"

"Not so fast, my young man," a voice utters, and Gaius Antonius Hybrida and five lictors enter the room, surrounding the two informers.

The lictors bind the young man.

"You only saved them tonight, Consul. When Catiline finds out I have been arrested here, he will know they are the informers, and he will kill them himself!" he shouts. As he struggles, he is finally struck down by one of the lictors.

"Not if Cicero and I have anything to say about it. After all, I think we arrested him trying to attack me in the Forum, didn't we, Quintus?" Consul Antonius asks as Quintus replies with a nod. Rushing to Cicero's home, Antonius relays all of the information, including what had happened with the senator's son and the attempt that is to be made on his life in the early morning.

"If that's the way they want it, then so be it. We will watch for them, and when they arrive we will dispatch our lictors to surround the house," Cicero remarks as the two men retire for the night, anxious for the next day's activity. All night long, Cethegus and Vargunteius sit up drinking, building up their courage. They know Cicero's reputation and that killing a consul is not to be taken lightly. As Catiline's poison fills their minds, they plan their actions, even debating which one will ravage the consul's wife as he lay there bleeding. Donning their togas, the two men rise with the sun after an hour's worth of sleep. They proceed to the consul's home to deliver their "gift."

Confidence builds within them. When they finally reach Cicero's home, no one is visibly stirring except the slave at the front door. "Please tell the consul that Gaius Cethegus and Lucius Vargunteius have come to pay their respects to the illustrious Consul Marcus Cicero!" Cethegus announces as the slaves runs into the home, leaving the two men waiting. A moment later the lictors march from around the rear of the home with swords drawn, and Cicero comes to the door.

"I see you have taken up a new trade now that you are no longer in real estate, Cethegus," Cicero remarks as the two men slowly back away. "Tell Catiline that you are too late. He will have to wait to kill me," he continues as the two men run down the street toward Catiline's home. Cicero walks to the street and follows them with his eyes as long as he can. "Send a message to the Senate that we shall be meeting tomorrow for a special unscheduled session in the Temple of Jupiter Stator and that no one needs to miss, would you please?" he states as he heads into his home "Until then, keep all visitors out. I have a speech I need to prepare."

With the events of November 7, the houses of Catiline and Cicero take their opposite sides and prepare for battle. The two sworn enemies prepare to deal the fatal blow and win the victory. Notes are copied and trashed as Cicero prepares for a legal battle unlike anything he has ever seen, and Catiline sharpens his wit and his knives, ready to deal the death blow that he has pined for for so long. Each combatant stays behind closed doors into the late hours of the night, concentrating on one goal: absolute victory and annihilation of the enemy.

Dawn breaks on the morning of November 8 as Cicero awakens the household slaves, who are accustomed to rising before their master. After eating a simple breakfast of toast and a small cup of cold water, the determined orator gathers his papers, readies his lictors, and heads out the door, endeavoring to clear his mind of unnecessary thoughts that might distract him from his purpose. Catiline surprisingly receives a good night's sleep and is anticipating another day of violent attacks, as he was informed that Cethegus and Vargunteius failed in their attempt and that the consul was waiting for them. Girding his toga, he takes a deep breath and heads out the door, surrounded by his Sullan bodyguard, and parades confidently through the streets, no longer receiving greetings but looks of disgust from those too sickened by his sight to face him. "Gentlemen, I believe our plans have been laid bare by the attitudes of the people that we are receiving today," he quietly states to his bodyguard as they march along.

"It won't matter, Master Lucius. In a few hours, they will all be dead anyway," the leader of the bodyguard states as they near the curia. Recognizing him from a distance, the senators who make it their usual custom to stand outside before the meeting hurriedly rush into the temple. This catches Catiline's watchful eye, along with the vast number of Roman knights surrounding the meeting place of the Senate, armed and seemingly ready for a fight.

"Now I am certain our plans are known. Stay vigilant outside, as I will still attend the meeting and do my best to uphold our honor," Catiline remarks, leaving his men outside. Greeting the knights and doorkeepers, he merely receives scowls in return. Upon entering the house, those nearby scatter like frightened children before him. He finds a seat purposely away from his secret companions. All conversation goes silent, and as one elder senator clears his throat all those near him stand up and shift to the opposite side of the room. He is left in isolation, with the whole of the body staring at him.

Beginning to perform his usual custom, Catulus is motioned to remain seated by Cicero, who takes the incense from his hand and offers it before the Altar of

Jupiter Stator. Taking in the fragrance, he sighs and turns to face the crowd as the doors of the temple slam shut. Cicero shuffles across the silent room. All that can be heard is an occasional cough and the sound of the notes in Cicero's hand being shuffled. Laying his papers aside, the consul lowers his head and closes his eyes, visibly whispering a few short words, and then raises his head and looks directly at Catiline, causing him to slouch in his seat.

"Senators of the people of Rome, there is one among us today who has flaunted his arrogance, abused each of us in his mind, and furthermore has resolved to lay this city and even this house to waste," Cicero declares, making his way around the speaker's area. "Catiline!" he shouts, startling several and enraging Catiline as he points his finger at him. "You sit here among us as one of Rome's senators, but you mock us with your madness and thoughts of murder. Will you ever find an end to the haughtiness that shines on your face? We have guards posted all over the city, the walls are guarded, and all citizens are on alert. Doesn't this bother you? I know what you are doing, Catiline. We can smell murder in our nostrils when you walk by, and let me assure you that there is a stench about you that cannot be disguised! The Senate knows what you have been up to Catiline. We know where you have been, the company that you have kept, and the secret musings that have been going on inside that lecherous place you call a home."

"Senators, I have seen through this man, and I have even presented the evidence before you, and yet he still lives. How is that so? As we debate the issues of the people and the republic, he watches in silence, marking us for death and dividing our property among his thugs." Turning to Catiline, he remarks, "We should have ordered you to die a long time ago and saved ourselves the trouble of meeting today. The ultimate decree has been passed against you, Lucius, and it is only a matter of time before you receive the punishment that you so richly deserve.

"Our ancestors have passed the Decree in times of danger to the republic, and not so much as one day would pass before the offending person was led to die. So why do we wait and allow this miscreant to sit here wallowing in his thoughts of bloodshed? It has been days, Conscript Fathers, since the Decree has been passed, and not a thing has been done to this man or his followers. The Senate's authority has been mocked and made null and void for all to see! This man should be led to the Tullanium and strangled this instant!"

Catiline interrupts Cicero, shouting, "Insults! Insults without a base! How dare you preach to me, consul. My family has served this—" Catiline is soon shouted back to his seat by various senators across the room.

"Then please tell me why there is an army stationed on the border of Etruria? An army, my fellow senators, that has not been sanctioned by this body but rather by the private ravings of a madman! You can sit here as long as you like and ponder how long it will be before I order the lictors to carry you to your death, Lucius, but rest assured that I have my reasons for not doing so as of yet. You disgust me. You have taken what is great about Rome and dashed it to the ground. You have perverted her glory to secure a place of so called honor for yourself; honor built on the blood of your fellow citizens," Cicero continues after a brief pause, allowing the Senate to participate in this open rebuke.

"Believe it or not, there are actually people among us who would defend this wretch and try to absolve him of his errors. We are marked by this radical who, along with his confidants, has begun to line us up for the Tullanium, or worse yet to be sacrificed on the edge of his sword. Catiline, as one citizen to another, I beg you to abandon what you are thinking. Prove me wrong in my accusations. Tell this body that there is nothing going on and prove it by your actions!"

Cicero continues, "Fathers, on October 21, I stated that an army would take the field, did I not? I stand here today, proven right. That army, headed by Gaius Manlius, a friend of Catiline's, has begun its march to Rome, where it will join with its leader and try to usurp control." Turning to Catiline, he says, "There is not a thing that you have done, said, or a place you have went that I do not know about. I know about your night meeting at Marcus Laeca's home. My informant has told me all about what was said there by you and by men sitting with us right now. Yes, Fathers, men who were in that meeting sit here right now, and as I look over and my eyes meet with theirs, they know that they are caught. Fathers, at that meeting it was even decided that I, the consul of Rome, was to be murdered in the morning. Who did I find at my door when I awoke, but friends of this monster seated before me.

"What you did not know, Catiline, was that I had already been informed. I doubled the guard around my home and alerted my lictors. Now what is left for you but to leave us and never come back? I am offering you the right of exile here and now, Lucius. Leave this body and join Manlius on the field of battle. The men he leads are waiting for you, as I am sure you are well aware. The gods have enlightened me to what has been taking place, and, even as we meet here in the Temple of Jupiter the Stayer, the god himself has stayed the hand of murder and revealed the murderer. For a time, Catiline, you plotted only against me, making me the target of your hate. Now that you have failed in your plot, you have made this body and the whole body of citizens your targets. I tell you here and now,

Lucius Catiline, leave the city and take your dregs with you. Draw your battle lines if you must, but leave our city.

"You sit there without a word, Catiline. I wonder why? You have been plotting to leave and return with your army, so why not do it? I have given you leave to do so," Cicero comments.

"You're trying to banish me! How dare a new man attempt to force exile on a member of an aristocratic family!" Catiline shouts, amid boos and hisses from the crowd.

"Lucius, I am trying to help you out of a situation you should have never become involved in. Everyone who is not on your side in this city either hates you or fears you. Your plans are so bare the whole city sees them. Now is the time for you to go, Catiline, and to stop polluting our city with your hate, murder, lies, and treason. Take my offer and leave of your own free will, and don't look back when you do. Look around you, Lucius. You had so many "friends," but how many stayed by your side today? What more do you need?"

Cicero continues to hammer relentlessly at his opponent, who becomes more enraged with every word. Turing from Catiline for an instant, Cicero raises his hands and pleads with the rest of the Senate to banish his opponent. "We have sat here idly by, senators, but once this man is gone from our city that danger will pass. Once he leaves and takes his men with him, we shall be free once more to live and to enjoy our lives. The fullness of time has come for his wickedness. It is time that we cast out the trash and remove the plague that is among us."

Amid hisses and calls for silence, Catiline stands and shouts, "I cannot believe that this Senate, if it should rightly be called that, would allow a man who was not even born a true Roman to address another senator in such a manner! I am disgusted by the practices within these walls! Hear me out! I have served in the uniform of Rome, both in the Forum and on the field, as my family has done since the founding of the city. And this body will sit by and allow me to be accused and embarrassed by such a one as this?"

"Catiline, you are guilty, and this body knows it! Accept the clemency of the consul and flee!" Cato shouts to a fierce Catiline, who is clenching his fists.

"Away with the traitor!" another senator shouts.

"Let him be dragged with a hook! Drag him to the Tiber!" another cry comes from the rear of the temple.

As he slowly rises and bows the Senate, Catiline states, "Very well. If it is deemed by the Senate to be good for Rome, then I will consider going into exile. But let it be known by everyone here that I have done nothing wrong. The Senate

is in error to believe the rumors of a power-hungry consul over one of its own."
Catiline slowly makes his way out, smiling with his head held high.

"Traitor," a knight mumbles as the door of the temple closes. Stopping in his tracks, Catiline turns and faces the knight, allowing his madness to strike fear in the offending man.

"You will be among the first to die. I hope you are ready," he mumbles. He walks down the steps to meet his bodyguard and heads home. "I have been denounced in the Senate, men, so we will postpone tonight's events. I have something much better in store."

"What could be better, Master Lucius, then catching them on the very night that they shamed you and getting revenge?" the lead soldier asks as they make their way through the Forum with citizens fearfully stepping out of their way.

"Joining with Manlius and his two legions, sacking this cursed place, destroying every temple, killing every senator, and raiding the treasury, that's what," Catiline replies.

Later that night, Catiline summons his friends to his home for one last meeting until he returns in triumph to a Rome destroyed from the inside out by Publius Cornelius Lentullus Sura, who has been placed in charge in his stead, assumes his rightful place as consul, and begins a list of proscriptions unlike any Rome ever has or will see. Pulling the paneling back from a secret chamber in the wall of his office, he removes a silver eagle mounted on a pole with the name Gaius Marius inscribed on it. Hoisting it high for his men to see, he drapes his cloak over him and proceeds to leave the city with a force of three hundred strong. He makes his way to Gaius Manlius, and his destiny.

# 10

## *The Gift of Murder*

### November–December 63 BC

---

Lucius Sergius Catiline to Quintus Lutatius Catulus, greetings,

Most honorable and worthy Catulus, I send you this letter in a time of the greatest despair my life has ever experienced. Not satisfied with my losses as consul, my opponents have constructed rumors to degrade and humiliate me all the more. You defended me once in the matter of Fabia the Vestal; now I call upon you to do so once more.

I cannot hope to explain all of my reasoning behind the things I have done of late, but trust me when I say my hand has been forced to the action that I have taken. My soul is sick at seeing men most unworthy being promoted in our city, when I have fought and strived for everything I have, only to end up branded a revolutionary. As I write this I am walking out the door with those who are loyal to me, and I am leaving the city in exile once and for all. Aurelia is a frail child without someone to watch over her. I sent her to Naples when all of this started, but she will be returning to Rome to watch over our home. Don't let Cicero make a mockery or an example of her. On you I hang my trust, old friend. Farewell.

L. Sergius Catiline

"Quintus, what are you reading, dear?" a soft female voice calls out as Catulus makes his way through the atrium of his home, deeply engrossed in the letter.

"A letter that I just received, dear, nothing more," he mumbles as he wads the letter up and throws it in the fire.

"Well then, you need to hurry or you will be late for the Senate meeting this morning," she replies, motioning a waiting slave to dress him in his toga.

"We are not meeting today, my love. It is merely a public assembly in the Forum. Cicero is going to inform the commons of what has taken place in the Senate with Catiline and requested that I be there," he states, kissing her on the cheek and walking out the door. When he arrives at the Forum, he notices Cicero standing atop the Rostra. He sees Catulus and motions him forward to join him and Consul Antonius.

"It's good to see you, Catulus. I am just sorry that it is under these conditions," Cicero states.

"Nonsense, Marcus. You have done a splendid job and have saved many lives with your actions," Catulus replies, bringing a smile to Cicero's face. "I received a letter from Catiline. He begged me to defend him as I did during Fabia's trial and to protect his wife. I could perform the former but not the latter. There is too much evidence against him, unlike at the first trial."

"You are a noble man, Catulus, and Rome needs more men like you to lead her; men who still believe that even the guilty deserve a fair trial" Cicero replies, bringing a smile to the aged statesman's face. As the crowd gathers, Cicero addresses the commons of Rome. "It is my privilege to address you, my fellow citizens. What has made Rome great is that its people can gather here and be involved in its government. Recently a conspiracy by a very notable citizen has filled the city with plots of murder and treason, but I stand here today to inform the citizens that the threat is passed. He no longer plagues us," he continues, scanning the crowd as he speaks.

"In the middle of the night, I received word from those I posted to guard the city that Lucius Sergius Catiline left the city under voluntary exile, along with many men, taking a military standard with him as he went. Know, my fellow citizens, that this man stood here and touted his promises, but all the while he plotted to kill any who did not agree with his philosophy. Plans where revealed in the Senate that fires were to be set, senators murdered in their homes, and total chaos was to ensue once his army marched through the city gates. Citizens, you have been spared a most miserable death and existence under this monster, but now it will take an even greater resolve to cement our victory over him, as informants have told me that he is heading this way even as our consular army prepares to meet him"

"My friends, Catiline has spread word around this city that riches, power, and prestige will be given to those who follow him. His way is devoid of the hard work that has made Rome great. By the name of great Jupiter, I adjure you not to consider joining his cause. His is the cause of the whores, the drunken, the bankrupt, the hopeless, the assassins, and the dregs of this city. Rally to the cause that

I champion: liberty, freedom, and strength in the Roman Republic!" Cicero states amid cheers from the populace. His eye catches groups of Catiline's men who had gathered around the assembly to hear his speech, but then made their way off. As he dismounts the Rostra, several of his friends surround him, cheering his name and his accomplishments as they escort him home.

Meanwhile, making his way across the plains of Italy, Catiline and a portion of his followers slowly make their way outside of Faesulae, where Gaius Manlius is waiting with two full legions of soldiers, numbering over twelve thousand men. Marching night and day, his men are weary, but he presses on regardless of the conditions, knowing that each step brings him closer to his return to Rome as a conqueror. On November 11, the exiles arrive at the camp of Manlius, bearing standards with Catiline's family seal that wave in the wind. Emerging from behind the rampart, Manlius rushes out to meet Catiline and bows before him, urging those with him to do the same.

"My fellow laborers, rise and do not bow before me! We are equals wishing to attain a common goal!" he shouts. "Bow to the gods if you must, and beg them to grant us victory over our oppressors!" he continues, bringing shouts from the camp. As he enters, he courteously greets each soldier who comes near. He pauses for a moment as a group of soldiers catches his eye in the distance; a small group begins making their way through the crowd holding high the bundle of rods with an axe in the center, known as the fasces, which is the lawful mark of a consul. "My friends, you honor me today. Never before has anyone so richly blessed Lucius Catiline. I swear to you by my household gods that I will do all that I can to bring you riches and glory!" he shouts, holding his arms high in the air, amid cheers and soldiers shouting his name.

After a week of preparation, the army, at the orders of Catiline himself, begins making its way toward Rome, stopping at every town and endeavoring to recruit new faces for a glorious mission.

At a meeting of the Senate, however, business as usual takes place. Thoughts of Catiline have been placed on the shelf, and matters of finance have taken precedence. During a speech by Marcus Crassus, the foremost authority on money matters in Rome, a messenger rushes through the door and to Cicero, handing him a message. After carefully reading it he reclines in his seat and sighs. As Crassus takes his seat, Cicero steps forward. "Fathers of the Senate, I have just received word that as of yesterday, November 17, Lucius Catiline has indeed joined with Manlius. They are moving from town to town in this direction."

"He is an outlaw!" one old man shouts from where the former consuls are seated.

"Let them both be branded outlaws, and let the consular armies wipe them out!" Gaius Calpurnius Piso shouts from his seat, drawing cheers and nods of agreement.

"It is reported that he has men numbering two legions strong. This force needs to be engaged before he gets too close to Rome." Cicero adds more facts to the debate.

"I recommend sending Consul Gaius Antonius with his army to stop the traitors and keeping Marcus Cicero in the city to protect against those who remain of Catiline's brood," Cato offers as many in the house nod in agreement, while those of the opposing party shout for envoys to be sent and to avoid hasty engagements. "I would ask those in favor of envoys, will you also send envoys when Catiline arrives to kill you and take your homes? Need I remind you that only a handful of men received letters warning of a massacre. If your names were not included, where do you think that leaves you?" Cato continues, drawing silence from the opposing party.

As the Senate verbally shows its approval, Catalus states, "Let it be so ordered. Gaius Antonius, you are to raise a consular army and engage Catiline's forces, should they come any nearer to the city. Until then, Quintus Marcius Rex, Quintus Metellus Creticus, Quintus Pompeius Rufus, and Quintus Metellus Celer are to sally against them, avoiding all out conflict if possible." Catiline's men make notes during the meeting, carefully watching the emotions of all present. Silently they sit, waiting for the opportunity to seize their weapons and lunge on their unsuspecting fellow senators.

With the field of operations at Sura's home, the late night meetings resume as the new leader in Rome attempts to solidify his place and press for action. Every night since Catiline left, meetings take place by candlelight, with the treacherous senators and knights offering their opinions on what had been said in the Senate, how each had reacted to it, and the emotional level that each man had exhibited when anything was mentioned concerning Catiline. Checklists are made containing the names of senators marked for death, as plans are laid to wipe Rome clean of all opposition—starting with Cicero.

Every night for two weeks Sura has hosted meetings at his home where the proscription lists are added to and never taken from, as more people find their name, regardless of age or sex, added to it. Every other day Catiline sends an update to Rome, giving further details and accomplishments; in return, he seeks fresh information on the progress being made in the city by Sura and his men.

Sura hoists his cup high in the room. "My dear friends, as Catiline himself would say, in one hour the kalends of December will be upon us, and with that the festival of the Saturnalia. I can think of no better gift than the gift of murder, what say you all?" Sura states as others, obviously drunk and suffering from Catiline's mad delusion, cheer in agreement. "On the very night that the festival begins, all the slaves will be free to do as they like and citizens will give gifts to their patrons, who are expecting greetings and presents. At the height of the revelry, each of you will simultaneously rush into the homes, and in a few minutes' time we will have cleared Rome of four hundred useless senators!"

"I say we attack tonight. Rome is asleep except for the handful of guards that Cicero has placed on the walls watching for Catiline. There could be no more perfect time to strike, while Catiline's abuse is still fresh in their minds!" Cethegus raves, getting five or six others to agree with him.

"None of us is to lord over the other, but Catiline left me in charge. We would have a better cover if we attacked on the sixteenth when the Saturnalia begins," Sura states. Cethegus turns away, upset at being overruled. "Just think about it: citizens everywhere will be anxiously awaiting adoration. What would make the greatest impression but the entire Senate being wiped out in a single night! Besides, you know as well as I do that there is no way you could get to Cicero tonight, or any night for that matter. But even he will not shut his door to the festival."

"When do you want Statilius and me to order all of the fires started?" Publius Gabinius Capito asks as he lies on the floor, spilling his drink on himself.

"On the fifteenth Bestia will perform his duty as a tribune and denounce Cicero from the Rostra. When and if he does this, it will be the sign that all plans are in order. Start the fires ten minutes after the senators are killed at sunset. Once the city is ablaze, we are to join Lucius with Manlius outside the city," Sura states, looking about the room for any questions. "Cethegus, I need you to communicate with your men about the weapons caches so that everyone knows where to find them. Until the fifteenth disappear. Be seen or heard by no one, and remember the gods are behind us. We cannot fail," he continues as the men stagger to their feet and disperse.

The very next day on the kalends of December, the Senate gathers to meet once more, as it always does at the beginning of the month. Standing guard outside of the building, Publius Gabinius Capito notices a group of six men who appear to be Gauls by their dress coming toward the Senate. "What is your business with the Senate of Rome? Who are you, and where are you from?" he asks roughly, and in turn receives a rough reply.

"We are envoys from the Allobroges tribe in Narbonese Gaul, and we have come to file grievances against the Roman government for the abuse of power they are allowing in our cities and towns!" the leader replies to Capito as he carefully looks behind him.

"How would you and your people like to be free and rewarded at the same time?" he whispers, moving closer to them. "I am part of a revolutionary group who is tired of the same things here in Rome, and we are going to change it. Meet me and my friend at his home at the base of the Palatine Hill. His is the house with the statue of Apollo in the front atrium," he continues as they nod and then return the way they came, avoiding the Senate altogether. Once the Senate meeting is over, Capito rushes to Sura's home and finds him napping in the atrium. His unexpected entry startles Sura, causing him to jump from his couch, drawing a dagger.

"Don't ever rush into my home! With the way things are, I am disturbed by the slightest sound!" Sura shouts.

"We'll, I'm sure you will be able to look past all of that when you hear what I have for you. Umbrenus was successful on his trip to Narbonese Gaul," Capito states as Sura smiles. "A large group of them came to the Senate today. I directed them to come here and meet you. I told them that you had a proposal for them."

"Excellent," Sura replies, reclining on his couch once more. "Once they arrive, we will dine and share our plans. Hopefully we can entice them to join us."

"And if they decide not to?"

"What do think? We kill them, throw their bodies on the side of the road outside of Rome, and make it look like they were robbed," Sura continues as he closes his eyes to rest. "Send word to Cethegus and Volturcius that the four of us will dine with our Gaulic friends in my home and not to be late."

"Understood," Capito answers as he quickly makes his way out of the house to spread the news. After making his rounds, he finds himself back at Sura's home just in time to see the envoys from Gaul arriving.

"I am glad you decided to make it tonight. I assure you that what we have to offer will not disappoint you."

"Yes, another man by the name of Volturcius told us that this is where we can finally find freedom from misrule," one of the tribesmen states as they enters the home.

"Publius Cornelius Lentullus, at your service, gentlemen. Please make yourselves at home and allow my slaves to get for you anything that you desire." He bows before the men as the other conspirators try to overwhelm the envoys with friendship. "I believe you already know Titus Volturcius and Publius Gabinius

Capito, but these are other friends of mine, Gaius Cornelius Cethegus, as well as Lucius Cassius Longinus. Now please, let's enjoy the meal that my servants have prepared in your honor."

"I have never known a Roman to be so compassionate to a Gaul. I am interested to hear your offer," an elder among the envoys states as Sura clears his throat.

"Very well then, right to business. I prefer to get the details out of the way so that we can better enjoy the evening. How would you like to be free from Roman domination? There would be no more greedy governors, no more legions on your land, and no more trips to Rome to file grievances you shouldn't have to make."

"This sounds far too good to be true," another of the envoys states.

"Well, being that you are obviously interested, I will continue. Our leader, whose name is Lucius Catiline, was driven from the city by the same group that enables your governor and his taxes. He has joined another man by the name of Gaius Manlius and is raising legions to bring them to Rome. Once they arrive, we are going to revolt against the government," Sura states, drawing in his friends, who eagerly listen to every word.

"And what is the part of the Allobroges?"

"Take word back to your leaders that on December 16 during the festival known as the Saturnalia we will start our revolution. If the Allobroges wish to be free from Roman rule, have them send as many troops as they can to join Catiline on his march here and help us sack the city. Once Catiline is in control, he has promised to free your nation from Roman authority. You can be our own tribe with your own laws and magistrates once more."

As they hear Sura's final offer, the group huddles together and whispering their thoughts to one another. Sura and the rest allow the men to talk and make their decision, not knowing that their hosts stand ready to kill them should the answer be no.

"We will join you. For too long our people have longed to be free," the leader of the group states as they all nod in agreement. "However, we need to make one request of you that our elders will expect; we will need letters detailing the plan."

"It is the least we can do for you. I will also send Volturcius to escort you to Catiline on your way back to Gaul so you can see the power of the leader that we have," Sura states as Longinus pulls him close.

He whispers, "The rest of you can, but I will not. I don't trust them."

"Well, my friends, Longinus prefers not to be involved, but the rest of will be more than happy to do anything you like."

"We have an early meeting with the Senate in regard to our business, and we feel it would be good to go ahead with it and not cause any suspicion. Once we are finished, we will come back here, receive the letters, and make our way to our elders with your proposal," the leader states as they rise from a quick dinner. "We look forward to seeing you again tomorrow, Lentullus. Thank you for the meal, but we must be on our way," they continue as they make their way out of the house.

"Should we send someone to follow them?" Cethegus asks as Sura eats.

"No. These men are looking for a way out. I feel we have nothing to fear from them."

"I wish I shared your optimism, Sura," Longinus states.

"Why, my dear Longinus, have faith. The Sibylline Books state that I am to be the next Cornelius to rule in Rome, so the gods are on our side!" he states. Longinus continuing to fell uneasy about the alliance that was just made.

On their way home, the envoys continue their discussion, weighing the offer with the consequences and vice versa. Pausing in the Forum, they debate a proper course of action.

"Honestly, I don't know what to do. Part of me says join them and inflict damage on Rome, but my conscience says we need to report them," one of them men states as the other sit by, seemingly lost in thought.

"We need to report them as soon as possible. It would be most dishonorable if we went along with their ideas of murder," the leader states.

"Then why did you want letters of proposal?" the youngest of the group asks, thoroughly confused.

"Because we will have evidence to give the consuls and whoever else will listen—that it truly happened like we say."

"We need to inform Quintus Fabius Sanga tonight of what has taken place and let him approach the consuls, as they would never grant us an audience as foreigners," the eldest states. They nod in agreement and head for Sanga's home. Inquiring as they go, they finally find their patron's home after an hour. Knocking on the door, the household slave assumes by their dress and their long hair and mustaches that these men are from Gaul and are here on business with their patron. After welcoming them in, the slave leads them to Sanga, who rushes to greet them, sending the slave for refreshments.

"We don't have much time, Quintus Sanga, as we have some very grave information that we felt you should pass to your consul immediately," the leader states as t the group take seats at Sanga's offer. "We just came from dinner at the house of a man named Publius Cornelius Lentullus. He and Gaius Cethegus, Publius Capito, and Lucius Cassius Longinus told us of a plot to burn the city, cut the aqueducts, murder senators and citizens, and then leave the city to join a Lucius Catiline, who was coming with an army and a man named Gaius Manlius," he continues.

"How did this all come about? Surely this was not by chance," Sanga states urgently.

"We met a man in Gaul who called himself Umbrenus. He claimed to notice our plight with Roman oppression and encouraged us to come to Rome. Once we arrived another man by the name of Volturcius, who must have been waiting for us, asked us who we were and then sent us to the Senate house. We met Capito on guard duty, and he told us of Lentullus. We went to his home for dinner, and they laid it all out before us. They are supposed to give us letters detailing everything for us to take back home to our leaders, who will in turn send troops," the leader states as Sanga rises and paces about the room.

"Let me talk to the consul and find out what he thinks. We have been dealing with rumors of this for some time but have had no evidence until now."

"Yes. He said that this Catiline had been exiled from Rome due to this."

"I think the best course of action is to go to Marcus Cicero, the consul, right now. If you want to send the rest of your men to where you are staying, and you and I will go see the consul," Sanga states, wrapping his cloak around himself as they all file out the door. In the street in front of Sanga's home, the group parts company. Sanga and the leader of the envoys make their way to Cicero. After a short walk, the two men arrive at Cicero's home. "Quintus Fabius Sanga and an envoy of the Allobroges of Gaul to see the consul on matters concerning Lucius Catiline," Sanga states as the guards recognize Sanga but watch the Gaul. "Consul, we bring you greetings. We sincerely apologize for disturbing you at this late hour."

"Nonsense, Sanga. Anyone who has information on Catiline can wake me if necessary. I heard you as you came in," Cicero states, rising to greet the two men.

"This man is the leader of a group of envoys from a tribe in Gaul, over which I am the patron. He was contacted today by Capito and then offered a part in the plot, which was laid out over dinner at Sura's home," Sanga states as Cicero listens intently to his words.

"What proof do we have other than a testimony? The Senate is tired of testimony. They want hard facts!" Cicero states, taking his seat in frustration as the envoy steps forward to speak.

"We are going back tomorrow night, where we will receive letters spelling out the plans and asking for any available troops to be sent to join with Catiline in the handwriting of Cethegus, Lentullus, and Capito to take to our leaders, and Volturcius will take us to meet Catiline" the envoy states as Cicero leans forward in his seat and casually smiles. "Consul, they are planning to cut aqueducts, burn the city, and kill as many senators and citizens as they can during the Saturnalia."

"You have no idea how valuable this is. Follow everything just as you have planned, and I will post men to intercept you somewhere between here and Catiline," Cicero continues as he ushers the men out of the house. "Don't tell your men what we decided here tonight. No one should know that we are going to intercept you; they need to be surprised."

The next day all goes as planned. The envoys from the Allobroges depart from their meeting of the Senate, where they are purposely dealt roughly with by Cicero, who knows the unknown followers of Catiline will take the report back to Sura, thus cementing their role even further. As they leave the Senate house and head for their place of lodging to rest before meeting Sura and the others later that night, the envoys share a private laugh.

Patiently waiting for the evening's events, Sura begins to write his progress report to Catiline, detailing what has taken place, along with the news of the envoys joining their cause and the even better news of Cicero's abuse for all the Senate to see.

"What are you doing, Sura?" Cethegus asks walking up slowly so as not to alarm his comrade.

"Writing a progress report to Catiline, letting him know about the envoys and everything else," Sura replies, continuing to write.

"Are you going to ask him about arming slaves?"

"Yes. I'm going to send the letter with Volturcius and the envoys tonight," he shortly replies, obviously tired of being interrupted. "He wrote me in his last letter that slaves and gladiators alike were running away from their masters and seeing him as a modern Spartacus who would save them and give them arms."

"What were his ideas toward it?"

"He doesn't think we should arm them," Sura remarks, motioning a slave over. "I told him he must, but he can't get past the Roman way of not resorting to arming slaves, although it would increase his number considerably."

"Perhaps now he will be ready for it. We could use all of the help we can get."

Meanwhile, miles from Faesulae in the camp of Manlius, Catiline goes without sleep, planning and drawing battle plans and enduring the cold to temper himself for victory. As he sits in his tent, a letter arrives. After opening it, he finds another progress report written by Sura informing him that the envoys from Gaul had arrived and were considering the offer. As he finishes the letter, Manlius walks in. "What news from Rome, Lucius?"

"Manlius, we will be victorious," he states. "Sura tells me that the envoys from Gaul have arrived in Rome and are considering joining us; that would mean they could contribute another two legions, if not more," Catiline continues. "The Senate will be more than surprised when we arrive in Rome with this army!"

"But, Lucius, some of these men don't even have weapons yet. How are they supposed to fight without a sword?" Manlius asks, irritating Catiline.

"Honestly, Manlius, one would think you had changed your mind with all of your complaints and ill omens your mouth has been spewing the past few days," he replies once more settling himself and, closing his eyes. "Cethegus has more than enough arms to satisfy our needs once we get to Rome. When I send the message that we are a day away from attacking, that will be the signal to set the place ablaze. Our contacts in Rome will join us with the weapons, and we will sack the city."

"I just hope this is the proper course of action. No one except Sulla has ever marched on Rome and been successful," Manlius comments.

"I am not Sulla!" Catiline shouts, startling Manlius. "Sulla was an old fool. The cretin died while giving an order to strangle a man! How cowardly is that? He should have done it himself. Mark my words, I will kill you myself if you leave. You will either be rewarded when I win or will feel my wrath as a traitor." Catiline comes face to face with Manlius, their noses and foreheads touching.

"I understand, Lucius. I have been receiving letters from my family, but I haven't responded. The news of being declared a public enemy and all—" he searches for the right words away from Catiline's piercing look. "I will follow you to victory, Master Lucius, and crown you as consul myself," he continues, standing to attention as a foot soldier to his general.

"Excellent. May Dis give you the strength you need as we complete our unworldly task of destroying Rome and remaking it in our image," Catiline states as a malicious smile creeps over his worn face.

As evening falls in Rome, the envoys make their way through the streets to Sura's home with bags packed for their journey, first to meet Catiline and then home. Upon arriving at Sura's house, they receive the same grand welcome they had the first time they had entered.

"You have decided to join us then?" Sura asks, as the men reply with a serious nod, confirming their answer. "Very good!"

"We were insulted in the Senate today, Lentullus. It is obvious that we made the wrong decision in coming to Rome to handle this properly, but we have made the right decision in coming here yesterday," the lead envoy steps up, playing his part most excellently.

"Yes Cethegus and some of our other followers who are members of the Senate told us how Cicero treated you in front everyone; that is what master Lucius had to endure so you can see that his leaving was more than justified as is our plans."

"We will have as many troops as we can join with Catiline and march to Rome with them," the leader continues, drawing Sura and the others in as Cassius Longinus continues to be wary of the envoys. "We are ready to depart whenever you are. We will also need letters to deliver to our elders of the tribe."

"I have them right here, and they are sealed by each of these three men with their family symbols," Volturcius states as he holds the three letters out. Sura, Cethegus, and Capito extend their hands, revealing their signet rings, which they had used to seal the letters. "I am ready if you are, gentlemen. We will betaking a small bodyguard of fifteen slaves with us, and now that it is night fall we can easily slip out of the city unnoticed," Volturcius states as the slaves walk out of the room to prepare the horses for the journey.

"The gods will richly bless you. You are brave men who have honored us with your aid, in helping to liberate Rome," Sura states, bowing his head to the men as they turn to leave.

"And may they also bless Catiline with great victory and Cicero with horrible death," the leader states as they follow Volturcius, mounting their horses and proceeding to leave the city. As quietly as possible, the men make their way through the streets and, noticing a disturbance ahead, take a detour, which, unbeknownst to Volturcius, takes them past Cicero's home where the consul watches as they go by, unaware that their whole plot is about to fall apart before their very eyes. Not a word is spoken as they sit silently in the dark. The leader of the envoys watches Volturcius out of the corner of his eye and casually but cautiously looks around for the ambush that is certain to come.

They are now thirty minutes outside of the city and crossing the Mulvian Bridge. With every noise, the leader becomes more anxious, when suddenly soldiers rush out and block off the paths of escape. Volturcius's slaves draw their swords and try to fight their way out.

"We have been set up! Cut them down slaves, cut all of them to pieces!" Volturcius shouts, but all but seven of the slaves lay dead.

"I am Gaius Pomptinus, the praetor of Rome. What is your business here?" Pomptinus declares as Volturcius looks about in every direction like a frightened animal.

"Merely trying to escort these envoys back to their home in Narbonese Gaul. Is that a crime, Praetor?"

"No, but those letters that you are carrying are. Hand them over so that we can return to the consul," Lucius Valerius Flaccus, the other praetor, replies as Volturcius pulls the three signed and one unsigned letter out. They begin their journey back to Rome, escorted by Flaccus and Pomptinus and their soldiers. Just as quietly as they left, the group makes their way back through the city gates and down the streets of Rome, as the praetors lead them to the door of Marcus Cicero, who is waiting patiently in his office. With the lictors watching, only the praetors, the envoys, and Volturcius enter Cicero's home and are forced into seats across from the consul.

"You are aware that the penalty for treason is death, are you not, Volturcius?" Cicero asks the frightened man who hesitantly nods his head. "Tell me what you know. I am well aware of your simplemindedness and the fact that you were more than likely forced into this little plot. If you comply with me, I will see to it that you are not charged with any crime."

Shaking and whimpering, Volturcius answers, "I was to escort these envoys to meet Catiline outside of Faesulae and to carry to him a letter from Sura, which is unsigned, as well as letters in the handwriting of Cethegus, Sura, and Capito, to be given to the envoys for their elders. The praetors have the letters that you will need to prove the plot," he continues as Flaccus steps forward, handing the sealed documents to Cicero.

"How can I be sure that these say what you claim they do? How do I know you are not trying to make a fool of me?" Cicero shouts at Volturcius, unnerving him.

"Consul, I swear it! I watched Sura write the unsigned letter, as well as the one that he sealed. I promise you that it is true honest!" Crying out, he hits his knees and grabs Cicero's feet.

"Flaccus, you and Pomptinus go to Lentullus's home and arrest everyone you find and bring them here. I will need to speak with them," Cicero states as he steps back and Philologus lifts Volturcius off the floor. "Lictors, we need to get word to the senators that there will be a special session in the morning at the Temple of Concord under guard," he continues as five of the twelve lictors leave the room to notify the senators.

"What shall we do with Volturcius, Consul?" one of the lictors asks, as Cicero turns his gaze on the pitiful but penitent man seated before him.

"He looks hungry. Let's get him something to eat, a warm bath, and a place to sleep for the night. This man is evidence of how Catiline can suck the life out of someone," Cicero replies as he leaves the room, motioning the envoys to follow him with a smile on his face.

Across town at Sura's home, a small number of conspirators gather for their nightly planning session, which has devolved into a drinking bout where revelry takes over. As they carouse, Flaccus and Pomptinus burst through the door, followed by thirty soldiers, quickly sobering the partygoers.

"What is the meaning of this, Flaccus? This is a private home. You have no right to burst in unannounced!" Sura shouts as he pushes away the sword tip pointed at his chest.

"Well, my fellow praetor, Marcus Cicero wishes to see you in regard to your letter writing skills," Flaccus states as the conspirators' demeanor changes.

"Lead on, Flaccus. We will go as you direct us," Sura replies, motioning to the rest of his fellows to submit to the praetor's orders as they all follow the troops out and are escorted to Cicero's home. They are seated in the same room as Volturcius had been, under the watchful eye of the lictors and the two praetors.

"Good evening, my friends. I am so glad that you chose to join us here tonight without any trouble. They weren't any trouble, were they, Flaccus?" Cicero asks as he enters the room.

"None whatsoever, Consul. They came very peacefully once the letters were mentioned."

"I want to know what this is all about. What letters are everyone talking about?" Sura asks, bringing a smile to Cicero's face.

"Excellent show, Sura, but I am afraid I know more than you think I do," Cicero comments as the conspirators seemingly regain their confidence. "The envoys met at your home yesterday, went back tonight, and left to meet Catiline with Volturcius, who incidentally had four letters on him. One is unsigned. The other three are sealed by you, Cethegus, and Capito."

"Prove it," Cethegus states as Cicero cuts his eyes in his direction.

"If you insist. This could have been easy, but you have chosen to make it hard on yourselves," Cicero replies as he takes the letters from a nearby lictor. "Are these or are these not your individual seals? Perhaps we need to check them with the signets that you are wearing, although I am quite certain they will match," he continues as he holds the letters out for the men to see.

"The seal is mine," Sura states, refusing to even look at the letter. The other two men nod, confirming the consul's accusation. "I also wrote the fourth letter, which is addressed to Catiline, but I did not sign it, as he would know it was from me."

"Lictors, I want two of you with each man. Take them to three separate senators' houses to keep them until the meeting in the morning. But first I want the names of every knight and senator who is apart of your little game," Cicero states.

"Publius Autronius Paetus, Quintus Curius, Cassius Longinus, Servius Sulla, Lucius Vargunteius, Quintus Annius, Marcus Porcius Laeca, and Lucius Bestia, all of the senatorial order, along with young Appius Fulvius and Marcus Fulvius Nobilitor, and Lucius Statilius of the equestrian order," Sura mumbles as the trio are shoved out the door to their place of imprisonment; Philologus writes the name down.

"Lentullus," Cicero calls. "Why would you ever have done such a thing? If a sense of right and wrong could not change your mind, then surely the face of your most noble ancestor on this seal should have," the consul remarks as Sura hangs his head and is taken out of the consul's home. "Lictor Gaius," Cicero calls to another of the twelve who has remained behind to protect the consul. The man steps forward, acknowledging his name. "We need to assemble several bands of armed men loyal to the Senate to stand guard around the homes where these men are going. They each have numerous slaves, and, unless they are totally oblivious, they probably gave orders to attack if captured."

"We'll take care of it at once, Consul," the lictor states as he bows to leave, taking two others with him. Three lictors stay with Cicero. For the first night in a long time, Cicero rests, knowing that the body of the conspirators have been arrested during the night, Catiline is far from the city, and a slave uprising intending to rescue the arrested men has been stopped, according to a message he had received in the early hours of the morning. Laying awake before the sunrise, he looks at his wife as she sleeps, soaking up her beauty that a madman could have taken from him. He gazes at her lovingly one last time, as he will not see her for a couple days.

As the sun rises, Cicero also rises before the rest of household and prepares for the meeting of the Senate at the Temple of Concord, where the final nail is to seal Catiline's fate. Followed by his lictors, he slips out the door.

The streets of Rome are uncharacteristically deserted at such an early hour of the morning, but Cicero knows that havoc has overcome the minds of the dregs;

their heroes have been discovered, and the streets are no longer safe for their kind. A few senators are out for a morning stroll after breakfast and salute the consul. Some call out to him, wanting to know the latest news; others simply want to know why they must meet again so soon, to which the consul merely smiles and waves and continues on his journey. The doors of the temple creak open as the lictors make way for Cicero to enter before even the priests have arrived to perform their duties.

Upon entering, a single priest lights the torches and sprinkles the incense on the altar, while several slaves finish setting up chairs for the Senate's meeting, which is to start in a short time. While the lictors stand at the door and the army of knights gather outside, a few senators start to make their way into the temple. Among them is Marcus Cato, Cicero's confidant. "You've got them, don't you, Marcus? You caught every last one of them, didn't you?"

"We certainly did. We ambushed a group of them at the Mulvian Bridge, then captured the leaders at Sura's home, and then took the rest that Sura named in the middle of the night."

"Then what is on the agenda today?"

"We will bring them in for testimony, show the evidence to the Senate, and then debate their punishment, which will hopefully be quick and severe."

"You know Gaius Caesar will be opposed to that, don't you?"

"Yes. If he does, we will stay here all night. But by the time we leave, these men will be punished for the crimes they have committed against the people of Rome."

"Consul," Gaius Calpurnius Piso calls out, walking up as a larger group of senators begin to take their seats. "Forgive me for interrupting, but I couldn't help but overhear your conversation. Caesar is going to try to hold up punishment for the conspirators because he knew of it and is friends with them. You have those letters in your possession. Why don't you sign his name to one of them? We can be rid of him before he starts any real trouble in Rome if we produce hard evidence that he knew of the conspiracy."

"I cannot do that, and I wish you would not ask me to. I care nothing for Caesar and his politics, but, if the facts do not point to him, I cannot bend them so that they do," Cicero responds as Piso becomes perturbed at the response.

"But you know that he and Crassus were friends with Catiline and—"

"What if Caesar came to me first and asked to get your name on the letters?" Cicero asks, interrupting Piso.

"Point taken, Consul. Thank you for your time." Piso walks to his seat. The temple is now full, and Catulus is in place to begin. After offering his usual greeting and calling the Senate to order, Catulus steps aside as Cicero makes his way to the speaker's area, holding four rolls in his hand, which he lays on the altar of the temple. As he turns to face the senators, all is quiet. He nods to his lictors at the door, who return ushering in the group of senators, knights, and freemen, along with the envoys from the Allobroges tribe, seating them on the front row under guard. Mumbling is heard throughout the Senate as the familiar faces of their colleagues are seen among the conspirators. The young son of Appius Fulvius hangs his head as the eyes of his father pierce him through.

"Consul," Fulvius cries out, trying to hold back his emotions, "was my son involved with Catiline? What did he do?" the old man asks, quivering in shock, knowing that he is about to lose his son if he is proven guilty.

"Senator, your son was present at the meetings of Catiline, tried to murder my informant, Quintus Curius, and furthermore was head of those who were to lead the youth in killing their fathers," Cicero solemnly responds as both father and son hang their heads.

"Then let him be dragged with a hook to the Tiber river as a traitor, Consul," he states. The young man tightens his jaw, choking back his tears at the condemnation of his father.

"For those of you who do not know the facts, Conscript Fathers, I will lay them out plainly for you. I will also leave the Senate chambers and allow this body to debate without pressure from the consul." He pulls his notes and begins to read. "On the kalends of December, these envoys entered the city, bound to take their grievances to the Senate, and upon arriving were met by Publius Capito, a knight who was standing guard outside of the Senate house. After a brief discussion, Capito told them of Publius Cornelius Lentullus, also known as Sura, and that if they were interested in plans to shake off the 'Roman oppression,' as he called it, to meet at Sura's home that night. Upon arriving, the whole plot was laid out for them, concerning burning the city, massacring citizens and senators, cutting aqueducts, and finally leaving to join Catiline, who would be outside of the city.

"After hearing the proposal, the envoys talked among themselves briefly and chose to accept. They asked for letters in the hands of those present, namely Publius Capito, Sura, Cassius Longinus, and Gaius Cethegus, with only Longinus refusing to comply. Excusing themselves from the meeting under the pretence of resting for their meeting in the Senate, the men left the home of Sura and went to their patron's home, Quintus Fabius Sanga. After retelling their story to him, he then came to me and, along with the leader of the envoys, once more retold the story, along with the fact that they were supposed to meet at Sura's after their meeting in the Senate. I abused them in the meeting to fuel the conspiracy in the sight of those hidden among us.

"After leaving their meeting, they headed straight to Sura's home, who had already received word of their rough treatment and had three sealed letters, which lay here before you, along with one other letter which by Sura's own word he had written to Catiline but did not sign. With Volturcius as their guide and the letters in his hand, the envoys set out for Catiline's camp but were ambushed by Praetors Flaccus and Pomptinus, who then brought them back to my home, where Volturcius turned in exchange for immunity. Once this was accomplished, I ordered the arrest of all those at Sura's home, namely Capito, Cethegus, and Sura, who were then brought to my home, confessed on seeing the letters, and were taken to various homes under guard to be held until today. Sura also gave me the names of those you see sitting here before you that were once part of our ranks, and they were also arrested during the night. A slave uprising was also crushed, which attempted to free all of those you see here. A large cache of weapons was recovered from Gaius Cethegus's home, and others just like it were recovered at several other sites throughout the city."

As he looks toward the body of conspirators, Catulus asks, "Is the consul speaking the truth, or has he misled this body?"

Sura rises and takes off his toga. "It is as the consul has said. The three letters were written by us and bear our seals. I confess openly to writing the fourth and not signing it. Consul, if you will permit me one last favor. Will you allow someone to bring me a toga more fitting to my condition, as I can no longer wear the toga of praetor?"

"Consider it done," Cicero states as he takes the toga from Sura and lays it on the altar next to the letters. "Fathers of the Senate, you have heard the evidence. Not one of these men have tried to refute it. I leave you to debate their punishment as I go to inform the commons of what has taken place from the Rostra. However, I want it to be known by all here that I recommend as consul that these traitors be put to death as soon as possible so that a message may be sent throughout our generations that Rome will not suffer a traitor to live," he continues as he walks out of the meeting. Several senators stand as he passes, and many begin to applaud him as he walks out.

No sooner than he leaves, the Popular party erupts with accusations of cruelty and abuse of power, before Catulus himself rises and calms the room, bringing the meeting to order once again. "Fathers, please, this is not how the Senate works! We are to have an orderly debate. We have all heard the evidence, and none of these men have refuted it. As the rules of order apply, I call on the consul-elect, Decimus Junius Silanus, to bring his opinion first of all," Catulus continues as he takes his seat.

Silanus rises to address the body. "Conscript Fathers, it is my privilege to stand here. I only wish that it was not under these conditions," he states, facing the body. "It is my opinion that these men, whom evidence has proven guilty, deserve the utmost punishment, to be put to death immediately and without hesitation," he continues. He takes his seat, and Catulus motions to Gaius Caesar, also an elected official for the new year.

"Senate of the people of Rome, it is of no secret that I have declared myself on the liberal end of the debates in this house. Once more I stand to reaffirm my stance," Caesar offers, drawing his audience in as he parades about on the Senate floor. "I am a lover of this country that our ancestors helped to procure for our people. It is with that love that I say we cannot justly put these men to death on such trivial evidence," he continues as the body of conservatives call for him to sit.

"I fail to see how we can sit here as an advising body and decide the fate of a handful of our own who even sat beside us on these benches, engaged in the same debates that we did." A deep sigh goes up from the Optimate's side, with several conservative senators continuing hissing at him as he speaks. "Hiss all that you wish, but as a senator it is my right to state my opinion, whether the Optimates like it or not. These men should have their property confiscated and should be driven into exile in separate areas of the country, even separated by oceans and seas if necessary." He straightens his toga and takes his seat, content with the firestorm of rhetoric that he has begun.

"Caesar is calling for amnesty and mercy for the traitors!" Piso shouts as Caesar stares him down.

"Marcus Porcius Cato, the Senate now calls for your opinion in this matter," Catulus states as the staunch conservative rises from his seat, preparing to pronounce his denunciation not only of the conspirators but of Caesar himself. Confident as ever, Caesar and Crassus both watch the stoic senator make his way to the floor, certain that they are going hear a long drawn-out speech.

"I am disgusted by the tripe that has come from the mouth of the young senator who has spoken before me. I too am a lover of my country, but not at the peril of sacrificing her and putting her back in the hands of the madmen seated before us. In a time when our city and our country is facing a murderous take-over, Caesar would rather throw the gates open and allow Catiline's hordes to freely take the place, starting with the Senate! I wouldn't be surprised if Caesar himself wasn't connected with Catiline as well!" he shouts, turning Caesar's smile to a look of disgust.

"You have no right—" Caesar starts to interrupt but is cut down once more.

"You had your chance to spew your venom, you viperous letch. Now give me my turn to deliver my opinion on the murders before us," Cato continues as Caesar and his ilk become more sullen. Cato continues, and the conspirators become more restless at the harsh atmosphere that the orator is creating for them. "The great Caesar wishes to extend a hand of mercy and grace to those who would stand over our bodies and look us in the eye as they removed our heads to be taken to Catiline. Perhaps he feels that he owes it to them, due to the fact that he received a letter warning of the attack?" Cato continues, offering a questioning look.

"But enough about Caesar. His designs will eventually bring his own destruction. Today we are debating the current state of the republic and that some of our own seated here wished to destroy everything that has been put in place. Normally, I am a most reserved person. But I am most definitely unreserved in the feeling that these men must be executed under the ultimate decree, that even Catiline himself voted for in an endeavor to hide his own guilt.

"I am well aware that we are dealing with matters of life and death, and these matters are most important to the gods as they are to me. But on the same token I remind you that these men have also been dealing in matters of life and death. The only difference between our parties is that we are dealing with the life and death of a handful of criminals; they were dealing with the life and death of the Senate, the city, and the whole of Italy and it didn't matter to them what the gods thought or anyone else for that matter," the statesman continues, solemnly appealing to the body of elders. "In their minds, the blood of our wives, children, and ourselves was already spilt, and they had begun to spend our fortunes before we were even dead. We must combat this assault with the utmost severity, just as the senator replied in the matter of his own son being a participant. Conscript Fathers, I vote that we send these men to the Tullanium and let them feel the hand of punishment that our laws have decreed," Cato calmly states as he takes his seat amid a solemn atmosphere.

Lucius Volcacius Tullus stands. "Senators, I speak for the ex-consuls seated next to me and say that we are in favor of the consuls' recommendations, as well as that of Cato. Let the conspirators be put to death under the ultimate decree."

Meanwhile, outside the building while the senators continue to debate, Cicero makes his way to the Rostra to report to the people the actions of the Senate and the recent news of Catiline. Lictors cry, "Make way for the consul!" as they move through the crowd. Slowly the consul ascends the stairs and, clearing his voice, begins to speak. The whole crowd watches his every move in anticipation of what he is going to say.

"People of Rome, never before have I been so privileged to be a citizen, let alone your consul," Cicero states, endeavoring to bring the swarming masses together to hear his speech. "I wish to update you on the workings of your consul and make myself accountable to you. At this very moment, the Senate has before them members of its own, as well as knights and a senators' son, who were all captured last night, thanks to information that stopped a general massacre of each and every one of you. Catiline made it clear in his speeches to you on election day that he was for the poor and downtrodden, but I assure you today that it was merely his ploy to get you vote. Once he had gained control, those of you who did not match up to his idea of Rome would have been systematically murdered and never allowed to enjoy his idea of prosperity.

"It is a sad day when we must rely on tribesmen from outside of our city to save our city from our own citizens, but that is exactly what happened. Tribesmen from the Allobroges in Gaul came to my home a few nights ago detailing the whole plot of Publius Sura as it was told to them in his own home, and, after receiving letters in the handwriting of the conspirators, they all set out on a midnight journey to meet Catiline but were intercepted by the praetors. They were questioned and subsequently found themselves before the Senate. Their punishment is being debated as we speak," he continues as the populace listens intently.

"It is my intention that justice should be done to those who would harm the people and the city that I love and was elected to protect. I now return to the halls of the Senate with a promise: I have done my best within the laws of our republic to save you and preserve justice within the walls of this city and the borders of our country," Cicero states as he finishes his address to the commons of Rome, who are either overcome with patriotism, rage against the conspirators, or tears of joy over the consul's actions.

The crowd remains silent as Cicero leaves the Rostra and makes his way toward the Senate house. "The gods bless you, Consul!" a man shouts out from somewhere in the crowd, and the whole populace erupts in praises for the consul who, wiping away a tear and smiling, enters for the Senate's decision. "What is the Senate's decision?" he asks as he stands on the Senate floor, surrounded by lictors.

"It is decreed that Consul Marcus Tullius Cicero will be awarded the Civic Crown for delivering the city from conflagrations, the citizens from massacre, and Italy from war," Catulus remarks, bringing a smile to the consul's face. "It is further decreed that a period of thanksgiving is to be held in your honor for all of the good that you have done and for your vigilance."

"But what of the conspirators?" Cicero questions, feeling as though the action is being dodged.

"The Senate decrees a sentence of death by strangulation in the Tullanium to be carried out immediately," Catulus replies, as a few conspirators sob while Sura and Cethegus sit stone faced, accepting the consequences of their failed plans.

"This is an outrage and a reckless abuse of power by this Senate!" Caesar shouts as he rushes towards the door. "I may have failed within these walls, but the people will hear me from the Rostra, and these proceedings will be stopped!" Just then a group of conservative senators blocked Caesar's access to the door. Shaking his head, Cicero motions the senators to move away, as Caesar tries to recover what pride he can from his encounter. "The Senate will pay for this insult and for its reckless abuse of power!" he shouts, as he storms out, shoving a senator out of his way.

"Come, Lentullus," Cicero remarks, turning to the seated conspirator and offering his hand. "You made a bet with your life and lost. It is time to pay for your crimes." Slowly Lentullus takes Cicero's hand as the consul leads him out of the Senate house to the Tullanium. One by one, they are turned over to the keeper of the jail and are lowered into the dark subterranean chamber of the two-storied prison, with some of the men helping the keeper while others fight, knowing this is their last journey. "Any last words before the sentence is carried out?" Cicero asks Lentullus as the ex-praetor climbs down to the chamber without any help from the keeper.

"Thank you for your courtesy in allowing me to change my toga, Consul," he utters as his head disappears into the hole. Silence is heard as the keeper lowers the rope into the hole, which is used to strangle the prisoners, and the men fit the knot around their necks and are hoisted up, sometimes breaking their necks or simply dying by strangulation, as the decree stated. When death is determined, the bodies are removed and another man is called forward to place the knot around his neck and accept his punishment. One after another, the criminals meet their fate, some slowly and some quickly, until lastly Lentullus's name is called. The rope begins to move until a firm tug is given as the signal, and with a hoist his body is lifted off of the chamber floor. His gasps for breath and coughs are heard for a few moments as his hand reaches up through the hole until the rope once more becomes motionless. His hand goes limp, and his body is pulled from the chamber. He is pronounced dead at the feet of the consul and several senators.

With a sigh of frustration, Cicero and the senators, satisfied that the sentence was carried out, emerge from the Tullanium, only to be greeted by an assembled group of citizens anxious at what the latest outcome is. "The conspirators are—" Cicero starts but pauses and gathers his thoughts. He merely nods his head, as a mixed atmosphere of joy at victory and sadness in death overcomes the crowd.

"Consul Marcus Tullius Cicero, father of his country!" Cato shouts from the group of senators gathered nearby, at which the whole populace begins to chant his praises and ring his name to the heavens. A smile makes its way over Cicero's face, pushing aside the grim details of his elected position and reminding him of what makes Rome great: it is not the armies or the politics, but the people gathered around him. Crowds of well wishers and senators alike escort Cicero to the home at which he is staying while the Bona Dea, a sacred and secret ceremony hosted by the consul's wife for women only, is taking place at his home. Marcus Cato leads the troop shouting, "Father of his country!" as lit torches burn all night long in his honor.

# 11

## *Pistoria*

### December 15–January 2, 62 BC

After leaving the city with only three hundred men, Catiline now finds himself at the head of more than two legions of men, recruited both by himself as well as Gaius Manlius. The plains northeast of Faesulae, where Manlius had been sent, have been their home since Catiline's exile in early November, but on word from Lentullus Sura of the Allobroges participation, Catiline eagerly encourages his men day to look forward to when they get to march on Rome and further entices them with promises of homes that consuls have lived in. As each day goes by, slaves who have heard of his revolution escape from their masters and flock to Catiline, hoping to find freedom, arms, and even retribution for years of slavery under Roman masters. But abiding by the Roman tradition of never arming slaves, Catiline continues to ignore the suggestions of Sura, which could ultimately add another legion of armed men to his number.

After a month in exile, Catiline sits in his tent, contemplating the condition of his men and his makeshift army, which is forced to steal food to survive and is barely equipped to drill in the field, let alone to take on an army that Catiline is certain the consuls will send after him. Biding his time, he hopes to stay out of harm's way until word comes that it is safe to march toward Rome; if only he can dodge the armies Rome is sure to dispatch. As he sits in his tent, the sounds of an army camp fill the afternoon, but lost in thought he hears nothing, not even Gaius Manlius. He has entered his tent and has called his name twice as Catiline sits staring at the silver eagle that once belonged to Gaius Marius.

"Lucius!" Manlius shouts, startling Catiline from his thoughts. "Lucius, I have been calling you, and you haven't answered me. I've got a letter from Rome," Manlius continues, visibly disgusted at being ignored.

"My apologies. I have too many thoughts," he answers, taking hold of the letter and opening it. "Who is it from? Sura, or did the messenger say?"

"The writing on the front didn't look like Sura's."

"Cicero!" Catiline shouts. "The letter is from Cicero of all people!"

"How did he know where to find you?" Manlius remarks as Catiline nervously paces the tent and reads the letter, his lips moving with every word. He crumbles the letter and slowly sits.

"Sura, Cethegus, Capito, Longinus, and the others are all dead. They were strangled in the Tullanium," he states. "Curius was the informant we were looking for, and the Allobroges as well, and Volturcius turned states evidence. The weapons Cethegus stored have been discovered, and the plot is out for all to see," he continues, nervously begins running his fingers through his hair until in frustration he grabs his hair by the handful.

"Then all is lost, Lucius. There is nothing more for us to do."

"No, you are incorrect. We will march the army into Gaul and side with them. They hate Rome and will gladly take us as exiles" he remarks still hanging his head grabbing his hair.

"If Cicero knows where we are, then he is certain to send an army after us. They are probably not far behind this letter. What if we don't make it to Gaul?" Manlius asks as Catiline sits motionless on his cot not answering Manlius who begins to grow impatient. "Lucius, what are we going to do?" he finally asks, desperate for an answer.

"We will wait for them to come to us," Catiline mumbles, nervously rocking back and forth and laughing like a madman. "We will attack their pitiful army with all of the fury of the underworld when it arrives," he utters, looking up at Manlius with tears of madness running down his face, enhancing the bloodshot appearance of his eyes from lack of sleep. "We will slaughter as many of these fools as we can, and, if we die, then so be it. Lucius Catiline will kill his enemies and allow Rome to know my fury for generations to come!" he shouts, causing Manlius to have even more reservation than before. "Give the order that unless we see signs of an army by December 20, the men are to pack their things and prepare to march to the mountains. We will cross over into Gaul, where we can live in peace far from consuls and Rome," he remarks as he sits at his desk to gather his things while Manlius walks out. "Come, Cicero, and bring Cato with you. I promised you that if attacked I would respond with utter destruction. Now is the time," he mumbles to himself.

On December 18, in another part of Italy, Quintus Metellus Celer and his army have received a letter from Cicero detailing the location of Catiline's hidden army, and, on the consul's recommendation, the order is given to intercept the army and to destroy the conspiracy at its source. As the army makes its way across Italy, the order is given to prepare for attack, as a party of men are spotted in the distance. But as they get closer, Celer realizes they are fugitives and has them brought to his tent, which is hastily set up. Frail and weak, the men are merely able to whimper for mercy as they struggle for breath. "Who are you, and where are you from?" he asks, puzzled by the men.

"Followers of Catiline, sir. We heard that his plot had failed and tried to escape, but we were beaten and by feigning death we managed to get away," one of the men states.

"Catiline and all of those with him are declared enemies of the state. Why should I grant you mercy when it is in my power to execute you as the law states?" he remarks as, at Celer's motion, a lictor removes his axe from the bundle of rods he carries.

"We were deluded by Manlius that one of the consuls had set himself as perpetual dictator and that Catiline was leading a force to combat him and restore the republic. When we found out the truth, we were beaten. There are others in the camp just like us, but who are not willing to risk death to flee from him. His mind is gone. He is planning to take his army to Gaul in exile, or the armies of Rome to the underworld if he is stopped," another man speaks up, and Celer motions for a slave to bring food and drink to the men.

"How far is Catiline from here?"

"If you continue marching in the same direction, you will come to Arretium. Once there, you will cross the Arno River. Catiline's army is about a half day's march northeast of Faesulae. You should reach them by the twentieth. Slaves are even flocking to him, but he won't arm them, either because he doesn't want to or because he barely has enough weapons for his followers who are free men."

Once more facing the men in front of him, Celer states, "Lictor, compose a letter to Consul Hybrida requesting that he bring his army. Let him know that I will attempt to move past Catiline and cut him off from the mountains, as he is planning on reaching Gaul. We need to get these men good clean clothes and a place to stay. They will be honored as heroes in Faesulae when this is over. However, the small matter of your arming yourselves against Rome is of great concern to me, so your price will be that you fight for Rome and Faesulae with us. If you survive the battle, then you will be honored. If you do not, then the gods and Rome will accept your sacrifice as payment for your treason," he states.

Within hours after Celer's army resumes their march, a letter is received from Quintus Marcius Rex confirming that Catiline's army was indeed about two hours from the city in a secluded place. On the consul's orders, he continues to monitor Catiline's movements and pick up deserters from the rogue army attempting to escape certain death. Taking a moment to post a brief reply, Celer catches his friend up on events in his area and his goal of cutting the army off and destroying it soon. For the next two days, Celer marches his army through the Italian peninsula headed for the Alps, until the standing orders from the consul at Rome state that Catiline is not to be engaged until Hybrida can arrive with a consular army and formally declare hostilities. Frustrated, Celer slowly moves his army around Catiline, and Marcius Rex keeps his men quietly stationed west of Faesulae prepared for anything but waiting on Consul Hybrida to arrive.

From a distance, Catiline and his men spot the fires of Celer's camp as night begins to fall on December 21 while they break camp and head for the Alps. "What did I tell you, Manlius? The gods have allowed the darkness of night to reveal our enemies to us at an opportune moment. We will march this army past them and if we can gain the upper hand by position then so be it," Catiline utters. After briefly gathering their things, the men try in vain to march through the darkness without arousing suspicion. But even with Catiline's ranting and raving, the army is once more forced to camp for the night not half a mile from where they originally were. Yet another sleepless night is had by Catiline, as his insomnia plays tricks on him and he sees visions of the gods, the dead, and sometimes the future dancing before his eyes. He sits in a drunken stupor, unable to shake himself from the grim reality that his end is certainly near.

As dawn rises on the Italian countryside, a grim wake up call comes to Celer's camp. One after another, his men confirm the same awful tale: Catiline has spotted their arrival and has escaped during the night. Frantic, Celer orders searches, demanding that Catiline be found. Under no circumstances is Catiline's position to remain unknown. Not long after his men are dispatched, word arrives that the small army is merely half a mile from its previous location. Accepting the consul's orders, Celer makes camp and prepares to hear from Consul Hybrida outside of a small town called Pistoria.

"A letter has arrived for you, Consul," a young boy states as he enters the tent of Consul Antonius Hybrida, who sits reclined with his lieutenants just outside of Arretium, a small town just south and east of Faesulae. "With it, Quintus Metellus Celer sends his greetings, Consul," he continues as Hybrida opens the letter and reads it to himself.

"It appears as though Catiline has been surrounded outside of Pistoria," he remarks, taking a drink from his cup as if nothing had happened.

Struck by his apathy, Marcus Petreius, one of his lieutenants, clears his throat to hopefully rouse the consul to action. "When do we begin our march to intercept him, Consul?" he asks, drawing a resentful look from Hybrida. "We are going to intercept him, aren't we?"

"When I see fit, we will march on Catiline's army. Until then we will keep this news and await orders from the senior consul at Rome."

"Did we not have our orders when we left Rome, Consul?" he continues irritating Hybrida.

"We will await further orders. Lieutenant," he coldly comments as the infuriated lieutenant storms out of the tent.

"You can't walk out on a consul, Marcus!" another young man comments as he races to catch up to him. "If you're not careful, he'll send his lictors after you!"

"Let him, but the one they should arrest is the consul for disobeying the orders of the senior consul. The only reason he is doing so is because he was once allied with Catiline," Petreius remarks, stopping just briefly to make the comment then continuing on his way.

"Write a letter to Cicero then to do something to force Hybrida's hand. Just don't endanger your own life by insulting a consul."

"What do you think I'm doing?" Petreius replies as the two men arrive at his tent. Upon entering, he hands the young man a sealed roll. "Take this to Rome as quickly as you can. It details how Hybrida is disobeying Cicero's orders to seek out Catiline," he continues as the young man takes the roll with hesitation and rides off to Rome. For seven days, the armies of Catiline, Celer, Marcius Rex, and Hybrida sit motionless as the young rider arrives at Rome to deliver his message and leaves again.

Becoming restless in his camp, the order goes out from Catiline that they are to begin their march to the mountains regardless of whether Celer follows. If at all possible, they will leave Italy and forever turn their back to Rome.

As they begin to mobilize, however, Celer receives word of the activity, and the two armies move about the plain without attacking—one searching for an avenue of escape and the other moving to prevent it. Darkness sets on December 29 as Manlius sits alone in his tent and begins penning a letter, all the while looking over his shoulder to make sure he is not surprised. Hurrying to seal it, he once more checks to make sure no one is watching as he hands it to a slave with ten gold coins to keep him quiet and to hurry his journey and reply. As the slave rushes out of Manlius's presence, Manlius makes his way to Catiline's tent to check on his leader. "How goes the night, Lucius?" he calmly asks as he enters Catiline's tent, finding him working.

"How do you think, Manlius? We are surrounded by armies and no matter where we go we are fenced in on all sides. Men are deserting every day, and my second-in-command is thinking of leaving too," he states, not even looking up from his desk.

"What did I do to make you think that?" Manlius asks nervously while Catiline faces him, haggard and weary.

"Do you think I don't know what you have done?" he states starring Manlius down as he tries to hold his composure in front of his mad leader. "You are thinking of leaving me too, aren't you, Gaius? I can see it in your eyes. You cannot hide your soul from Catiline." He slowly rises from his chair and walks toward Manlius, who has begun to step back. With the candle on the desk behind him, Catiline's face is shadowed as he approaches. Manlius looks in horror as Catiline's eyes begin to glow, as if he were solely driven by an unworldly power. "What are you thinking, Manlius? Tell me what is on your mind," he growls as he steps into the light, revealing his unshaven face and tired eyes.

"Lucius, I swore to you years ago that I would follow you, and I took a solemn oath that I would fight for you. I will not betray that now," he states as Catiline's look softens and he halfway smiles turning and sitting on his cot. "If we die in battle, then we die as true Romans do: with our faces to the enemy and our swords in front of us."

"I counted forty-three deserters today, Gaius. If this keeps up, we will have no army." Catiline hangs his head as he sits.

"We don't need them, Lucius. They do not share our desire to succeed. If we do fight, they would be the first to die," he states. He begins to leave Catiline's tent to await his messenger's return at his own.

"Antonius Hybrida's army is on the move. I have determined that, once it arrives, we will attack him. Now go to your tent and await your response from Celer," he states, as he raises his head with a look of madness and begins to laugh as Manlius walks backward out of the tent, trying to figure out how Catiline knew about his letter. As he walks away, he hears Catiline's laugh become more audible. Then he begins to run to his tent. Panting and with his heart pounding in fear, Manlius falls onto the floor of his tent, only to find the slave he sent off looking at him curiously.

"What did Celer say?" he asks, still panting.

"Celer was pleased to hear that you wish to lay down your arms. But he has no power to absolve you of your crimes. If that is what you seek, you must petition the Senate yourself."

"There is no time for that. It appears that I am caught where I am. I must play the game that the gods have set before me," he states as he lies on his cot, not removing his armor and holding his sword close, not knowing what the night will bring. Throughout the night, Manlius stares at the roof of his tent; even the wind blowing seems to carry the fear of Catiline in it. He passes the night with a sleepless fear, unwilling to close his eyes, but eventually human senses lose control and nature takes over.

"Death to traitors," Catiline whispers in his ear as Manlius awakens, turning suddenly, expecting to find his crazed leader kneeling at his bed. When he finds nothing, something else catches his attention. He looks toward the door of his tent, seeing the young slave standing there in the moonlight, who then falls forward, landing on top of him with his tongue cut out and Manlius's sword in his back. Pushing the slave's body onto the ground, he rushes to the door of his tent, only to hear the low wild laughter of Catiline.

For the next two days, Catiline and Celer continue to square off and trade positions, each one trying to outmaneuver the other while Antonius begins to advance after receiving a scolding order from Cicero. The kalends of January arrive as Antonius arrives on the outskirts of Faesulae and sends messengers to Celer and Marcius Rex, notifying them of his arrival. He takes position just south of Catiline's camp in the conspirator's plain view, with the standard of a consular army waving high. Catiline's camp stirs at the sight of a consul's banner; each man tries to get the best view of the armies opposing them, though Antonius has tried to hide the true size of his force with the trees and hills surrounding them.

Eventually Catiline emerges from his tent and walks to the perimeter of the camp. Laughing slightly as he faces the army across the plain, he spits in its direction and turns to walk off, amid a growing cheer. "Master Lucius," a soldier comments, drawing his attention. "Someone's coming," he continues as Catiline turns to see two men on horseback slowly galloping toward the camp.

"Bring me my horse, and get Manlius to ride with me," he remarks, focusing on the pair.

"It is already here, master," a slave comments as he begins to mount the horse without taking his eyes off of those coming toward them. As Catiline and Manlius ride out of the camp, the other two men stop midway, allowing Catiline to meet them in the middle of the field.

"What is it you want?" Manlius remarks as the four men come together. They study each other intently.

"Consul Hybrida extends an offer of peace to you if you will lay down your weapons and return peacefully to Rome," one of the men states, as Catiline stares at the other.

"And if we refuse?" Manlius replies.

"Then you die in this field."

"Now I remember you," Catiline suddenly comments, taking Manlius and the other two men off guard by changing the subject. "Marcus Petreius, correct?"

"I am," the other man remarks.

"I remember you when you were nothing more than a messenger boy arriving on Pompey's ship. You've come a long way, boy," Catiline remarks with a smile.

"So have you, Lucius: praetor, governor, consular candidate, murderer, conspirator, and traitor," Petreius comments, wiping the smile from Catiline's face.

"You will be the first to die tomorrow," Catiline remarks as he turns to ride off. "Tell the consul I won't forget his oath or his friendship," he continues as Manlius and Catiline return to camp and pass the night away planning for the next day. As night falls, an eerie darkness creeps over the camps as the moon lies hidden from the world. And just like every night before, Catiline sits alone in his tent: deluded and mad.

Morning comes somewhat quickly as each army arranges for battle, but Consul Hybrida is still absent from his post, causing Petreius to return to the consul's tent where he finds the lictors still outside. Once granted entrance, he finds Hybrida drinking. "Consul, the men are ready for war. Are you coming?" Petreius asks as the consul stares into space.

"I am placing you in command of the army today, Marcus," he replies much to Marcus's surprise and disgust. "I have come down with a bad case of gout, as you can see by my swollen foot, and I will be unable to take the field. You are in command. Begin when you are ready."

"Consul, does this have anything to do with what Catiline said to you yesterday?" he remarks, irritated with the consul.

"Begin when you are ready, Lieutenant," Hybrida replies, refusing to look his lieutenant in the eye.

"If your foot is that bad, perhaps you should consider elevating it, Consul. That's what a doctor would prescribe for gout," Petreius replies as he storms out of his tent as Hybrida rises and walks across the tent to refill his cup with ease. With the consular army now in battle formation, Catiline and Manlius send all their horses to the rear, even Catiline's, as he begins to address the men who are barely armed.

"Today is the day that we have longed for, my friends. Today is the day that Rome and the consuls find out where we stand." He paces back and forth among his men, as banners bearing his crest wave in the wind and men tremble in fear, knowing that loss is most certain. "I have tried my best to lead you to victory, and you have given me your support even in the face of this hateful army!" he shouts as a cheer rings from his men. "We will most likely die on this field today, as our enemy has superior numbers. If we die, it does not mean failure. It means merely that we have done what no other man has done, and that is single-handedly challenge the might of Rome.

"They may conquer our bodies, but fight as never before. Do not let them take your spirit but fight to the last drop of your blood. We will drag as many as we can to the underworld with us!" he shouts as he gives the signal for the trumpets to blow. In a rush his men storm the field of battle to meet the opposing force. Seeing the sudden rush of Catiline's men, Petreius sounds the trumpet to engage as the two armies clash in the plains outside of Pistoria. Driving their spears into the ground to mark their battle line, Catiline's men pull their swords and mercilessly hack away at the enemy line, cutting holes in the consular army and wounding centurion and cavalry alike, much to Catiline's approval as he watches from the rear, standing beside the silver eagle of Gaius Marius.

Manlius begins to push the consular armies back until another signal is given by the opposing side and reserves rush over the hill, while Catiline looks on in horror as his army begins to be swept up and systematically eliminated. He watches as Gaius Manlius meets his fate at the end of a spear. Looking up toward the sky, Catiline turns, signaling a slave who is holding his horse to bring it near. "The gods are calling for me, young man. I must not keep them waiting," he states, and he leaps onto the horse and receives the silver eagle standard from the slave. Slowly he begins to ride toward the field of battle as he releases the reigns and looks toward the sky, closing his eyes and reciting a prayer, consecrating himself and those he kills to the underworld. Pausing on the field, he grits his teeth and, spurring his horse, rides full gallop into the midst of the fighting. Drawing his sword, he leaps from his horse, cutting down as many as are within his reach. Pushing his way through the bloody hordes, he winces in pain as swords are swung in his direction hitting their target and daggers are thrust into his side but failing to stop him. Blood covers his face until he is finally swallowed up by his enemy and is seen no more.

As the fighting begins to die down, the men of the consular army look for Catiline's force, but seeing none a sense of shame comes over them. They realize that for the first time since Sulla Romans have killed their fellow Romans. A line of Catiline's men lay facing the enemy in the spot where they first planted their spears, not giving ground but merely holding what they had with every last drop of blood. Petreius solemnly makes his way through the field of dead soldiers.

"Marcus," a faint voice grumbles amid coughs and wheezing as the young lieutenant turns around and sees movement in a pile of bodies. He pushes some aside, revealing Catiline, his face drenched in blood and with a spear in his chest, still trying to find the strength to swing his sword at his adversary. "I almost won.

You tell Cicero I gained ground," he states as he closes his eyes and breathes his last breath, but not before flashing the characteristic smile that won (and cost) the hearts of so many.

◆    ◆    ◆

After recent archaeological research done in the Roman Forum near the Lake of Curtius, three bodies where found at the bottom of the hole. Among them was a little girl.

## The end

# Bibliography

Although not cited word for word, I give full credit to the following authors and publishers for the historical facts and dates appearing in this manuscript. I am greatly indebted to the works posted here. A special thank you to the Loeb Classical Library, from which the timeline of Catiline's conspiracy was laid out. Thank you also to Amada Claridge, for helping to better identify places existing in the Forum of Rome during the time of this conspiracy.

Appian, *The Civil Wars Book II*. Loeb Classical Library. www.penelope.uchicago.edu/Thayer/E/Roman/Texts/Appian/Civil_Wars/2 *.html.

Cassius, Dio. *Roman History Book XXVII*. Loeb Classical Library. http://penelope.uchicago.edu/Thayer/E/Roman/Texts/Cassius_Dio/37 *.html.

Cicero, Marcus Tullius. *In Catilinam I–IV*. Translated by C. MacDonald. Loeb. Classical Library # 324. Harvard University: Cambridge, Ma., 1996.

Cicero, Marcus Tullius. *Pro Murena*. Translated by C. MacDonald. Loeb Classical Library # 324. Harvard University: Cambridge, Ma., 1996.

Cicero, Marcus Tullius. *Pro Sulla*. Translated by C. MacDonald. Loeb Classical Library # 324. Harvard University: Cambridge, Ma., 1996.

Claridge, Amanda. *Oxford Archaeological Guide to Rome*. Oxford University Press Inc.: New York, 1998.

Crispus, Gaius Sallustius. *Bellum Catilinae*. Translated by J. C. Wolfe. Loeb Classical Library #116. Harvard University: Cambridge, Ma., 1980.

Crispus, Gaius Sallustius. *War with Jugurtha*. Translated by J. C. Wolfe. Loeb Classical Library #116. Harvard University: Cambridge, Ma., 1980.

Everitt, Anthony. *Cicero: Life and Times of Rome's Greatest Politician*. Random House: New York, 2001.

Livius, Titus. *The War with Hannibal Book XXX.* Translated by Aubrey De Selincourt. Penguin Classics: New York, 1972.

Livius, Titus. *The Early History of Rome Book IV.* Translated by Aubrey De Selincourt. Penguin Classics: New York, 1971.

Plutarch. Lives of Marius, Sulla, Cicero, Caesar, and Crassus from *Fall of the Roman Republic.* Translated by Rex Warner. Notes by Robin Seager. Penguin Group: 1972.

Van Deman, Ralph. *A Study of the Topography and Municipal History of Praeneste.* Magoffin Release: June 29, 2004 [E-Book #12770]. Produced by Juliet Sutherland, Wilelmina Mallière, and the Online Distributed Proofreading Team. COPYRIGHT 1908.

Wikipedia Online Encyclopedia, Articles on Gaius Julius Caesar, Lucius Sergius Catiline, Gaius Calpurnius Piso, Publius Cornelius Sulla Felix, Marcus Licinius Crassus Dives, Marcus Porcius Cato, Gaius Marius, Gaius Antonius Hybrida, Roman Triumph, and Events of 70–62 BC. www.wikipedia.com.

Yonge, C. D. *The Orations of Marcus Tullius Cicero: In Verrem.* Translated by C. D. Yonge, B. A. London, and Henry G. Bohn. York Street, Covent Garden,1856.

Yonge, C. D. *The Orations of Marcus Tullius Cicero: In Catilinam.* Translated by C.D.Yonge, B. A. London, and Henry G. Bohn. York Street, Covent Garden, 1856.

Yonge, C.D. *The Orations of Marcus Tullius Cicero: Pro Rabirio.* Translated by C.D.Yonge, B. A. London, and Henry G. Bohn. York Street, Covent Garden, 1856.

# About the Author

Brandon Winningham was born and raised in Michigan, where he graduated high school in 1995, and moved to Tennessee in 1996. His love for classical literature was inspired by his high school English teacher and cultivated over time, centering on republican Rome; he even taught himself the basics of the Latin language. He currently resides in Tennessee with his wife and daughter and is employed in the grocery industry.

978-0-595-67996-6
0-595-67996-X

Printed in the United Kingdom
by Lightning Source UK Ltd.
131248UK00002B/16/A